THE DEAN'S LIST

KELLY COLLINS

BOOK NOOK PRESS

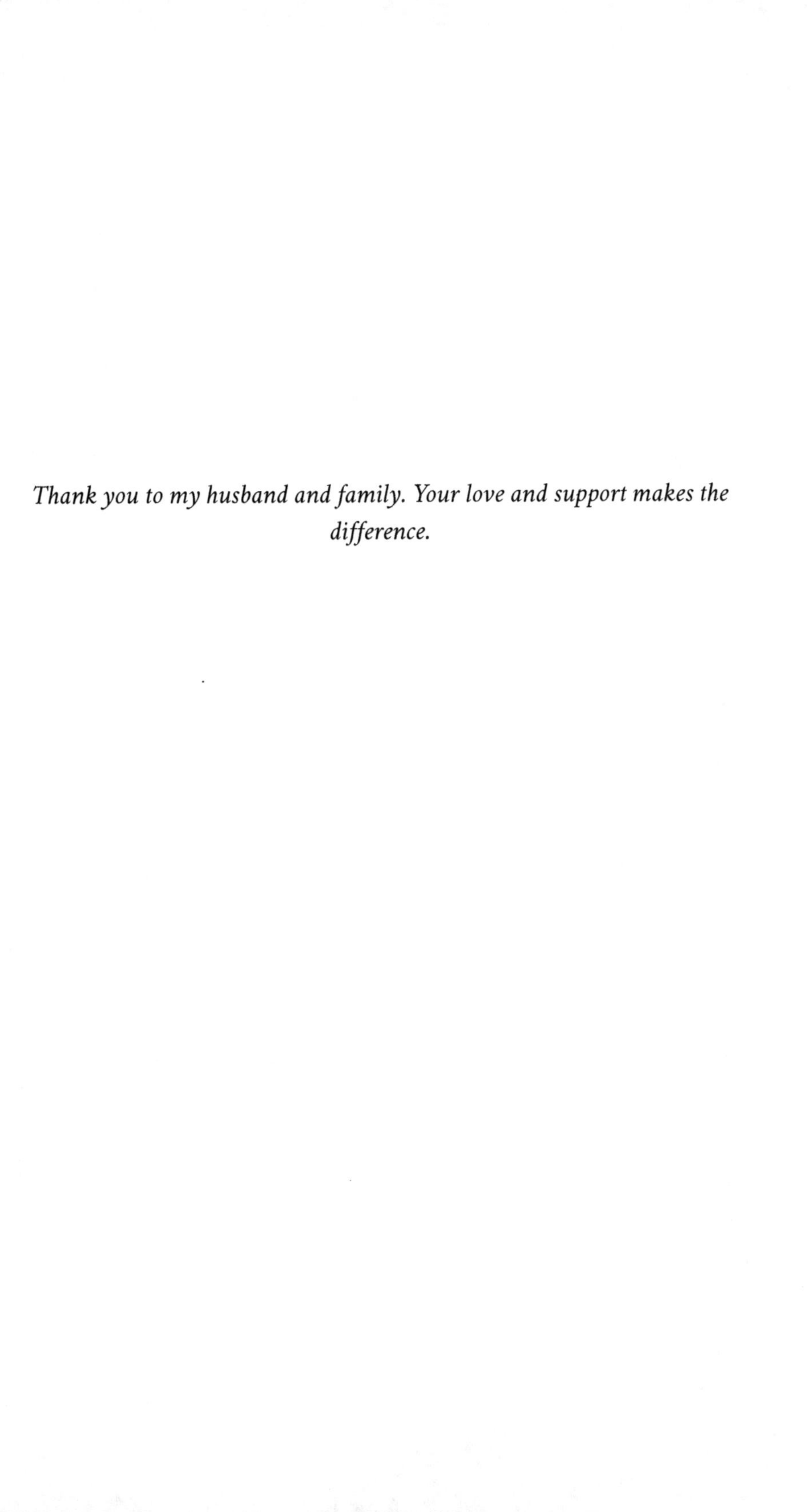

Thank you to my husband and family. Your love and support makes the difference.

Chapter 1

I'm told that sex sells. Tell that to the cheap bastards who come to The Grind and gawk at the bikini baristas. While I froth their coffees and warm their cinnamon buns, they stare.

I dumped the jar that contained way more quarters than dollars on the table. The change clattered across the worn Formica and plopped onto the pleather bench of my favorite booth. It was here that I tallied my tip totals while the afternoon sunlight slanted in the window.

Today was a bear market day. Forty dollars would hardly pay my weekly transportation costs. How was I supposed to make my rent and eat?

Pride had kept me from asking for help, but I was going to have to call Jade. From the little I'd seen of her lately, she appeared to be weathering the economic downslope better than I. She'd have a plan; she always did. I dropped my head to the table with a thunk, closed my eyes, and silently asked the universe for a solution.

"River, are you trying to knock yourself out?"

Jade's appearance startled me. I'd been asking for a solution, and here she was, standing in the center of the dead coffee shop with the smell of stale coffee and burned toast filling the air.

Without effort, she slid in beside me and dragged me into her thirty-eight double Ds. The way she stayed upright defied everything I'd learned in physics.

"Oh, Jade, I'm so glad you're here." Catlike eyes the color of moss peeked from behind the curtain of her raw, honey-colored hair. "I'm running out of options. I need a real job, and I need it now. I need one that pays a shitload of cash and lets me off when I have to study. Classes start next week. I need a miracle."

Desperation accented every syllable. I wasn't one to exaggerate, and Jade knew it. For me to say things were bad, they had to be beyond dismal.

"Girl, there aren't any miracles; only solutions. How bad is it?"

"This month, I have to decide if I want to eat or ride the bus. It's a conundrum because if I walk, I get hungry; if I ride the bus, I get hungry. I'm just so tired of being hungry." I hardly recognized my voice. The whine sounded more like a sulky teen than the independent woman I was. "My student loan is due. My phone is close to being silenced. How in the hell do you survive?"

Jade leaned back, gaining distance. Her expression was guarded. Her eyes skimmed my body. Today was career day at The Grind, and I'd dressed up as a naughty nurse. My stethoscope hung from my neck all the way to my bare belly. My white bra was embellished with two red crosses, one on each breast. My panties had a matching cross that covered my crotch. We pushed the line when it came to city code, but a girl had to eat.

Jade eyed the girl behind the counter who was busy studying her recent manicure. On the counter sat her empty tip jar.

"You look better than anyone who works here, and you're obviously making more money."

"This outfit used to make me bank, but with the stupid stock market falling, gourmet coffee isn't a must-have for a lot of brokers. I'm hoping tomorrow will be better. It's pasty day."

Maybe if I wore the tassels and gave demos on how they spun, I could make enough to buy a used textbook for my International Business class, as well as a bus pass. Big dreamer. At this point, I couldn't afford the lead in my mechanical pencil.

It hadn't always been this bad. I'd lost the Sunday shift from last semester, and with fewer tips, which had previously been an added bonus, my situation had become dire.

She gave me a warm, sisterly look—the kind that said, *I could take care of this.* And I was desperate enough to want to climb inside Jade's world and take shelter. *She had it together.* Somehow.

"What if I could help you get a job where you wore more clothes, most of the time, and made more money in a week than you do in a month?" Jade spoke in one long sentence, her pitch rising to the finish. When she reached the end, she held her breath and waited.

"I'd tell you to sign me up. It would have to be a step up from working here. The average customer at The Grind is middle-aged, white collar, and horny. Nice enough, but they don't come for the coffee." Yep, the brew was just a bonus.

Jade looked out the window, seemingly absorbed by the rush of Wall Street traders racing back from lunch. She let out her breath and then inhaled until I thought her lungs might burst. She was sucking in more than oxygen. Courage?

"Let's talk white collar and horny. What I'm about to tell you can't be repeated. I swear if it gets out, the FBI, CIA, and Homeland Security will come to arrest you. They'll fight over you and tear you from your top to your toes."

"If you're trying to scare me, you're failing. You don't have the fear factor. You wear Hello Kitty pajamas and drink caramel lattes, for God's sake. Who could be afraid of someone who likes cats and caramel?"

"Don't underestimate the strength and power of a caramel macchiato. Show me a double, and I'll show you fear. The caffeine alone is deadly."

From the deep recesses of her purse, she pulled out two energy drinks and handed me one. They were the kind of drink you bought for purpose rather than pleasure, and I wondered why I would need three hundred milligrams of caffeine after my shift had ended.

"Are you an assassin? Is that how you keep so damn fit?" I popped the top on the can of Bang and thought it ironic.

"No, I'm not killing anyone, but if you don't pay attention, I might begin with you. Remember when I told you I was working in hospitality?" Her voice softened to a purr. "Well, that's the truth. I'm very hospitable." The words brushed past her lips like a lover's kiss.

"What the hell are you talking about? Aren't you the concierge at that fancy place on Fifth Avenue?"

I swore she said she was the concierge. Maybe she'd said something about customer satisfaction. Hell, with the clothes she wore, she had to be raking in the tips.

"I never told you I was the concierge. I told you I was in charge of making sure clients' needs are met. I tried to get a job when I graduated, but you know a bachelor's degree doesn't cut it anymore. That's why you're here." She slipped from the booth and sat across from me. Something big was going down, and she was distancing herself. "Have you ever heard of The Dean's List?"

The high-octane drink was beginning to thrum in my veins. "Um, yeah…I made the list in my sophomore, junior, and senior year. As a freshman, I was still figuring things out." What did that have to do with making moola?

Jade scooched and settled into the far corner of the booth. I moved so I sat directly in her line of sight.

"No, think about rumors. I'm talking about 'The Dean's List.'" She emphasized the word *Dean's*. "Think in terms of secret societies, like the Illuminati or the Freemasons."

"Are you trying to recruit me for a religious sect? Count me out. Religion and I don't see eye to eye."

Jade knew I was the poster child for what *not* to do as the daughter of a pastor. When I was caught blowing the mayor's son behind Dad's pulpit, I was told I was going to hell. But I gave that boy a boner-fied religious experience.

"Shut up and let me explain." Her black look silenced me. "The Dean's List is an exclusive group of people who meet to propel the university and its students toward success."

"Perfect, what can they do for me?" Her guarded look told me she intended to dance around the truth. In fact, I knew Jade well enough to know she'd create an overpass to avoid it completely. "Get to the point." I didn't have time to dawdle. I needed to decide whether to ride the bus home or jump in front of it.

She tapped her fingers across the tabletop like she was typing an overdue thesis. "The Dean's List is about students seeking 'sponsorship' from members in their field of study. These members can be very 'accommodating.'" Her use of finger quotes around the word 'sponsorship' and 'accommodating' had me tilting my head.

"You're still speaking a different language. Plain English. Now. If I didn't know better, I'd think you were asking me to prostitute myself."

"Let me explain." Her shocked expression told me I'd hit a bull's eye.

My heart pitched forward, then tumbled swiftly into the hollow pit of my stomach. I kept my voice low. "Shit. You *are* asking me to become a hooker. There's no way you've been dishing yourself up for dollars. No. Damn. Way."

Prostitution wasn't a gig I could see Jade participating in. She was always so...so above board. I'd have been less shocked if she'd told me she was a man.

Her eyes shifted to every corner of the shop. Her body relaxed when we appeared to be alone. There was no one close enough to hear her secrets. Hell, The Grind would be like a morgue for the remainder of the day.

"Shhh, 'prostitution' is such an ugly word." Her voice became uncharacteristically small. "I have a couple of advisors, also known as mentors or sponsors. They're successful members of their community. They work in hospitality management—my specialty. They donate obscene amounts of money to the university—my program. They take care of their own—me. And in exchange, I take care of them." She pulled the high throttle drink to her lips and drank like a marathon runner who'd just crossed the finish line.

"You screw men for money? How many men? Does the school support this?" I leaned forward and mouthed the words. "Do you screw them on the regular?"

How did I miss her pimpin' her kitty for cash? We hadn't hung out as much over the last few months. I had missed her, but we were both busy with studies and our part-time jobs. Or so I'd thought. *This* is not what I'd expected.

She slapped the table and glared at me. I hadn't seen that look since the day we graduated from high school, when she told me we were moving to New York.

"River. Listen." Her voice demanded compliance, and I'd listen because whenever Jade had a plan, my life inevitably got better. "I know this is sounding weird to you, but it's important this doesn't go anywhere. Got it?"

"It's a little late to get my sworn affidavit, don't you think? I never told your mom you spent Fourth of July being a groupie for that grunge band. I never told Mr. Esly your grandma didn't really die when you skipped finals week. You know me."

She reached over and held my hand just a little too firmly. Hand-holding could only mean some serious shit was going down.

"Okay, well...The Dean's List only takes graduate students. Educated men and women. No giddy juveniles. Like you, I was broke. An opportunity came along, and I took it."

"You. This. How long?" I would consider myself the worst of friends if she told me years.

Jade made no excuses. It wasn't her way. "Several months." She released my hand and leaned back in the booth. With her fingers laced, she turned them inside out and pressed them forward.

Pop.

Pop.

Pop.

The disgusting sound of knuckles cracking made me cringe. My discomfort gave her the edge, and she knew it. She had my full attention.

"Get on with it." She was going to try to sell me on the possibility of selling myself. *Had my life come to this?*

"Three positions are open, and interviews are happening now, but there are only two positions you qualify for since you don't have a penis." Her tone was matter of fact.

"I have to interview to be a prostitute?" My heart pounded so loudly, I was certain Jade could hear it across the booth. *A prostitute? Really?*

She gave me a slow, disbelieving head shake. "How many times have you had a one-night stand and received nothing but a hangover and dirty snatch?" She lifted her perfectly plucked brows in question.

"You make it sound like I'm already a whore," I swear she flinched at my reply. "I'm not loose. I'm experimental." I tried to lessen the tension I was feeling with witty commentary. "Hell, the average woman has had six sexual partners by the time she's thirty. At twenty-five, I've had eight. So…I'm an overachiever."

"I never said you were a whore. I'm only telling you that you can earn a lot of money being an overachiever." A sly smile lit up her features. "Your number, when divided, doesn't add up to one a year. That's so far below ho—we can't count it. You're treading on virgin territory, and we can change that." Her eyes danced with delight.

"I don't get it, Jade. How did I not know?" I let my head fall forward in shame. I had no idea what my best friend had been up to.

"I had to keep the secret in order to participate. I had to participate in order to survive." Her strong voice had lost its power. "Right now, you're where I was several months ago."

"And you want me where you are now?" Could I consider it? Could I afford not to? Elbows on the table, I laced my hands and rested my chin on the flat of my knuckles. The busy sounds of New York dimmed as my mind raced and raged and rallied.

Could I?

"I'm listening, tell me the rest."

"My boss asked me yesterday if I had any pretty friends who could fill the empty positions. I thought of you, but I wasn't sure. With your dad being a man of God, I didn't know if you'd risk his wrath. I know your relationship with them isn't perfect or pretty, but…"

"'Isn't pretty' is like saying herpes is a form of chapped lips. Seeing them twice a year doesn't keep me connected or establish a relationship. Go on."

Jade was the star debater in high school. She could sell a purple cape to Superman. I was curious to see how she'd sell this.

"You'd be set up with people who have influence in your field. Being an MBA, you have a broad reach, and with your looks, you'll have a big audience. We're talking about lots of men with boatloads of money."

"Lots of men? Okay. Great. But are you forgetting this whole thing is illegal?" I looked at her with wild-eyed shock.

"It's not illegal. Who doesn't barter for goods and services? It's muddy at best. You might barter for clothes, jewelry, vacations, cars, and of course, there's also cash. They're gifts, and the mentors can be very generous. We're talking Prada and Gucci, Channel and Dior. Sleeping with a date is not illegal."

Gifts of that magnitude weren't given to girls like me. I was thrift store and Goodwill—the hand-me-down princess.

"Why would a man pay that much for one night?"

"We give them something they can't get anywhere else. It's like going to the on-campus shop and buying a monogrammed sweatshirt. You know what you're getting when you shop there. It's high quality, not cheap, and it behaves the way you expect it to. Think of yourself as a luxury purchase."

"I'm not a sweatshirt, Jade. One size doesn't fit all." Of all the things to compare me to, couldn't she have come up with something more alluring than a sweatshirt?

"That's where you're wrong. You're adaptable. You can fit in anywhere." Jade pulled her ringing phone from her purse, looked at the screen, ignored the call, and tossed it back into her purse. "Don't let your parents destroy your self-respect."

My parents? They annihilated my self-esteem long ago.

"I'm intrigued. What do I have to do?"

"You get to eat at Michelin Star restaurants, stay in five-star hotels, and come all the time. Who wouldn't love that?"

So, the mentors were good lovers. Her argument had merit. But could it be that simple? Could I do casual sex for cash?

"How many men do I have to entertain?" What else would I call it? Escort? Date? Lay? It all came down to money for sex.

"You can do as many, or as few as you wish. I started out with several and then worked my way to two. I'm engaged in 'school activities' four nights a week. On occasion, my mentors have me travel with them."

"Oh my God, so when you said the school was sending you to that conference in California, you were with your mentors?" She was gone for a week and came back with a sun-kissed glow and a new wardrobe. Shortly after that trip, she moved into a new apartment. One I'd yet to see. "The apartment you're in…is it…oh, you little lying slut. You told me you had to move closer to work. You moved *into* work." She's my best friend. How had she so easily been lying to me about all of this?

"I struggled to keep things under wraps when you and I lived together. They wanted more time, and I couldn't give more without you getting suspicious." Her hands darted all over the place while she talked about her situation. "I was given an ultimatum. I had to give them more time or give them up. We bartered, and I ended up with the best possible outcome." It was funny to watch her get riled. She was usually so unflappable.

"You could have told me." I felt…betrayed.

I didn't think we had any secrets from each other.

"I couldn't. That was against the rules." Her voice was tinged with sadness and regret.

"Wow, okay. So, what happens to the apartment if they dump

you?" I didn't want to bring up the possibility, but it was something to consider. She'd only been in her new place for a few months. A few months, and I'd been clueless.

"My mentors signed a one-year contract with me, regardless of whether they use the service or not. They don't live with me. They visit four nights a week. Sometimes it's more, sometimes it's less. I'm good for a year."

"I don't know what to say."

There was too much information to process. Jade. A prostitute. Wow. She looked happy. Was *I* happy for her? Hell, I think I was.

"You don't have to say anything. I know what you're going through." She looked around the coffee shop. "Dead-end job, no prospects, and dreams bigger than you can afford."

We had both been struggling, but then things had changed for her. Only moments before, I'd wanted to climb into her world. Well, perhaps I could.

"Tell me about these mentors. Are they old and decrepit?"

The word *mentor* brought all kinds of images to mind. Dirty old men shaking with Parkinson's and leering at my naked body topped the list. I looked around the café and realized that exact scenario happened here all the time, and I rarely got more than a fiver. I certainly never got an apartment.

"No, one of my mentors is forty-five. The other is fifty-two. I'm not saying the mentors can't be old. I've seen men as old as eighty and as young as thirty-five. On average, they're between forty and sixty."

I've always liked older men. Not grandpa old, but ten to twenty years older is perfect for me. I'm attracted to the confidence found in mature men.

"Sixty. Damn." My nervous laughter drew the attention of several patrons who had recently arrived.

She leaned in toward me and whispered, "Early on, my bits hardly saw action. Many of them only want to come on your face or between your tits." She raised her brows and gave me a coy look that probably melted the resolve of every man she'd ever been with.

"You're shitting me. You made money letting men—" How could I chide her? I'd done worse for less.

"Shhh. That's part of the negotiation. You fill out a form, very much like an employment application. It has several sections on limits. If you hate anal, then you check the *no* box. If you don't like sex toys or screwing in a Jell-O bath, then you can write that in. Generally speaking, the more open you are to trying things, the more popular you'll be."

"Jell-O baths? Really?" Nothing that a little soap and water couldn't remove, I suppose.

"It could happen. Some of them just want to go to dinner and talk."

"They paid you to talk?"

"Yes."

"Unbelievable. I would want the talkers." Would it be possible to get only the talkers?

"It's not that simple. After a couple of months of trying out several mentors, I was asked for exclusivity from one of mine. Basically, I see only him and his partner." She gave me a look I recognized as her *don't judge me* look. "Yes, I do both of them. It works out well for all of us." Who was this woman, and what had she done with my best friend?

"Partners? As in plural? Who are these men? I've never heard you mention anyone's name." These secrets had robbed me of my friend.

"That's part of the deal. They remain anonymous, and I get through my grad program debt-free, well-fed, and housed. It's my goal to build good relationships with these people. They're in my industry, and they have the connections I need to succeed."

"Do you ever get attached to them? Aren't you afraid of falling in love?" Would it be possible to be in an intimate relationship and keep it superficial? Doesn't intimacy lead to love?

"Don't fall in love. I went into this knowing it wasn't a real relationship. It's a job. I give them what they want. They give me what I need. The only way to survive is to keep that in the forefront of your mind." Her tone seemed to fade as the words slipped hesitantly from her mouth.

"Are they married?"

How would I feel about being the other woman?

I may have had sex with more than a few men, but I'd never cheated on anyone, and I was never the girl anyone cheated with.

"The men I see are single, as far as their profile states. I know it's a lot to absorb, but the call I got was from my boss. She wants me to bring you to her office for an interview and to size you up if you're interested. What do you think?"

What do I think? How does one get sized up for a job peddling sex?

I turned in the booth and looked around the mostly empty coffee shop, spotting my co-worker. She rolled her eyes at some possibly cheesy comment the man in front of her at the counter said. No more shitty comments and equally shitty tips.

What did I have to lose?

"Let's go. Can I at least go home and change? I'm not sure wearing my nursing uniform is appropriate." I looked down and considered my voluptuousness. Despite the placement of the red crosses, these suckers had only made me forty today.

Was I *really* considering this? This wasn't how I was raised, but given my parents' opinion of me, it wouldn't have been too far outside their expectations.

Chapter 2

We raced straight to her apartment, where I shopped her closet. Thankfully, she had a few "when I lose ten pounds" dresses hanging about. We were about the same size, with the exception of our boobs. Where hers resembled airbags, mine were more like balloons. Jade handed me a dress the color of Pepto-Bismol. I wasn't a fan of pastels, but I figured if things didn't go well, I could lick the dress and hope for some kind of relief.

A pair of nude heels landed at my feet. When I picked them up and turned them over, I became breathless at the site of the red bottoms. Girls raised in churches didn't wear shoes with red soles.

I bounced on bare feet. "These are Louboutins. How many pairs do you have?" She walked into her closet and pulled out three more pairs. One black, one blue, one red. "I'm keeping these." I slipped my feet into the shoes and walked the beige carpet.

"One of my perks is having a personal shopper and an expense account at Bloomie's. A care package containing anything I might need arrives every two weeks."

She dragged me into the bathroom—the enormous, hotel-like bathroom. Marble counters. Marble floors. There were more jets in the shower than body parts to spray. The tub was so big, it could fit three comfortably. Given her new lifestyle, it would have to fit three.

To say I was shocked would have been an understatement. A few months ago, my best friend was living with me in a rent-controlled apartment, now she was living large on Fifth Avenue.

"You must be covered in come to get all of this. Damn girl, let me feel your skin." I ran my fingers across the exposed skin on her chest. "It must be soft and supple with all the moisture it gets." She slapped my hand away from her chest and pushed me toward the counter.

"Stop. You're making me regret inviting you to the club. Sandra is waiting, so let's get you ready. You have to look like a model and behave like a saint while in public—no cussing. When you're alone with your mentor, you can be anything he wants you to be."

The gravity of her statement hit me. This wasn't a game of dress up. "I got it. What about my schedule?" I searched through her makeup bag and pulled out her blush. Even her makeup was top of the line.

"It's a negotiation. Listen, if you have classes on Monday, Wednesday, and Friday, then you're available on the other days. If you can't work on a certain day, you call Sandra and tell her to black out your schedule. My situation is different. My mentors own all my minutes, and I make myself accessible for their needs."

"What about dating?" I never realized she wasn't seeing anyone. She always seemed so busy, and I thought there were dates. "How do you have a personal life when all your minutes are taken?" Jade had always been a serial dater, but more recently I hadn't met a single one, and now it made sense.

"I don't. My education and future are more important. I decided four months ago that if I gave up dating now, I could have everything later. I lucked out. My mentors are both handsome and amazing men." She grabbed the pink-tinted lip-gloss and coated my cupid's bow. When she was finished, she whipped me around in front of her and stared into my eyes. "River Roberts, what do you want your future to look like? You and I know a bachelor's degree is, sadly, like a high school diploma. You need a master's degree just to enter the game." She dabbed at the corners of my mouth, making sure my lips were perfect.

"How sad. All those years of school, and I'm qualified for nothing." Maybe my parents were right. Maybe education was simply a waste for everyone. Not wanting to dwell on the value of an education, I probed for more immediate information. "Tell me, what happens if someone gets violent? With such a secret society, how is it policed?"

"I've never had a problem. Some men are into dominance, but that's part of the negotiation. Because each department has their own set of mentors and students, they seem to be self-monitoring. No one wants their reputation to be tarnished, so everyone behaves by a code of conduct that's acceptable to the group."

She twirled me around and pointed me toward the full-length mirror. I stared at myself and wondered if I could do this. I didn't have much choice. My options were seriously limited, and there was no way I was heading back home.

I smoothed the dress across my fluttering stomach. Analyzing the girl in the mirror, I turned left, then right, and then toward Jade.

"What do you think?"

"I think you look like an expensive ho." She pushed on my shoulder, almost knocking me off her four-inch heels. "Let's go."

WE STOOD in front of an unassuming building, tucked between two law firms. *Concierge Services* was etched into the glass door. I took Latin in my sophomore year and knew 'concierge' meant 'fellow slave'. How funny I would remember that word. I turned to Jade and gave her my best *you have to be kidding me* look.

Standing in front of the building made the situation real. I was plunging into water I'd never tested before. I'd never been this nervous in my life.

"Oh, I didn't want to tell you this before, but you're going to have to strip down to nothing so she can look at your body. She may take photos, she may not." Her tone was relaxed, like stripping in front of strangers was an everyday occurrence. Hell, it might have been for her, but not for me.

The acidic sting of bile burned my throat. I stopped dead in my tracks. My heart dropped, taking up residence next to my spleen. "What do you mean I have to strip naked?"

Several passers-by looked at us with interest. Jade pulled me in front of the door, out of earshot, out of sight and out of the way.

"Don't freak out. It's not like you won't be stripping naked for your mentors." Her hand ran across my back. Was she trying to comfort me or push me forward? I wasn't sure.

I swallowed the walnut-sized lump in my throat. "Some advance notice might have been nice. I could have prepped myself. Now you expect me to walk in knowing within minutes I'm going to have to show some stranger my parts? I could have at least trimmed." I took a fortifying breath and pulled my shoulders back. I had Louboutins on, for goodness sake. They should be worth at least an ounce of courage. "All right, it's all in a day's work, right? Let's get this shit over with." I listened to the strength in my voice and wondered where it had come from. My insides were trembling.

High ceilings, pale walls, contrasting dark wood flooring, and elegant finishes…I didn't expect the place to be so nice inside. The receptionist recognized Jade and picked up the phone to presumably alert Sandra of our arrival. I took a moment and walked the perimeter of the room. Original art decorated the walls. An espresso bar sat in the corner, and I felt like I should don an apron and offer drinks.

Jade walked toward me and whispered, "Nice, huh?" There was no one around, but it felt like the kind of place where a whisper was required.

"Does the school operate this?"

My business brain had been thinking of how the school got away with pimping their students. Now it appeared they had a buffer. They hid behind a service. The whole setup was ingenious.

A young man walked in the door and approached the pretty blonde sitting behind the desk. "I'm here to pick up theater tickets. The name is Abbot."

The pleasant blonde checked her books and confirmed the order. "Two tickets for The Lion King. Sign here." The man signed the log, took his tickets, and headed out the door.

The wall to our right opened up. A secret doorway into a life full of mystery and intrigue. I wondered if I were falling down the rabbit hole.

From the moment the doors opened, I felt the silent appraisal of the petite brunette gracing a Chanel suit.

And it began.

I stood taller and put on a smile in much the same way I did lipstick. I applied it and hoped it was the perfect hue for the moment.

If she was going to size me up, I wanted her to see all five feet, six inches of me. With Jade's shoes, I was rocking four additional inches. I looked at Jade and tried to convey a *thank you* with my eyes. I hoped she saw my gratitude for dressing me. Her clothes boosted the confidence that fear was trying to trample.

Jade squeezed my shoulder and walked me to her boss. "Sandra, this is River Roberts. River, this is Sandra Tierney."

The woman offered me her perfectly manicured hand. Her grip was strong. It was in stark contrast to the small woman who stood before me. Maybe her firm shake was her way of telling people she shouldn't be underestimated.

"Ladies, come in." She stepped aside and let Jade escort me into the room. I heard her tell the receptionist she wasn't to be bothered.

In the center of the room, I turned in a circle and took in my surroundings. With a deep brown, burled desk, decadent ivory sofas, and beautiful flower displays adorning several surfaces, the room screamed opulence. Graceful simplicity. Control.

"She is beautiful, Jade." Sandra walked around me like I was up for auction and she was considering a bid. "Do you have any body piercings or tattoos?" Her hand ran the length of my hair. She came close and inspected the ends. Thank God I'd recently had a trim.

"No, I don't have anything marring my skin." She smiled. My answer seemed to please her.

"Sit, ladies. Let's get comfortable so we can talk candidly."

She led us toward the sofa. I waited for her to take her place first. She held the position of power, and I didn't want to overstep my boundaries. She sat at the edge of the upholstered chair and folded her legs to the side. I sat on the sofa directly to her right, while Jade took the seat across from me.

She analyzed everything I did. The way I adjusted my skirt. The way I flipped my hair. She watched me mimic her body position when I folded my legs to the left. I didn't lean back or settle in, I sat at attention and waited for her to give me direction. I'd played this game before. As a pastor's daughter, I was an expert in etiquette.

I sat in silence as she observed me. My eyes glanced toward Jade. She appeared to be the epitome of calm, while every cell in my body was ready to bolt.

"River is an interesting name." Her voice had an air of sophistication. "Is there a story behind it? I find the stories of people's names fascinating." She pulled a notepad from the table next to her and began to jot something down. Her movements were fluid but measured.

"My name is River Jordan Roberts." The name question was usually one of the first ones asked. I found it easier to be honest than juggle lies. "I'm the only daughter of a Protestant pastor. As you're most likely aware, the Jordan River has significant meaning to Christians. It's where John baptized Jesus. It's also where the Israelites crossed into the Promised Land. I'm not sure my parents would say I've been the promised land for them, but that's the long and short of my name."

"I love it. You say your father is a pastor?" Her regal posture never faltered. She sat primly in her seat. "Will that be a problem with the line of work you're seeking?" It was like we were talking about a librarian's position instead of a job selling my body for tuition.

"I don't see myself calling my father and asking for his blessing or permission. However, my upbringing should be an asset to you. My manners are impeccable when they need to be. I've been exposed to people from all walks of life, and I've never had legal problems."

Sandra released her ankles and leaned back in the chair. She scribbled a few more notes and looked up.

I glanced in Jade's direction. If her glow was any indication, I suppose I'd made it past the first impression.

"Tell me, River, do you like sex? And if so, what do you like the most?" She straightened her skirt and stared at me. There was more to this question than the question. She watched me intently.

"Yes. I like sex. I think an orgasm is the biggest ego boost. I love how sated I feel afterward. How the release can liberate my soul." Every word I said was the truth. I'd always loved sex. I wasn't sure if I'd been blessed with talented partners or if I had a receptive body, but I couldn't remember a time I didn't enjoy it.

"I'm sure Jade has explained what it is we do here. I want to emphasize the fact that we're dealing with important people who have a lot to lose should their 'philanthropic' work get out." She leaned forward as if she might tell me a secret. I leaned toward her, not wanting to miss a word.

Silence.

She appeared to be waiting for me to acknowledge her statement.

"I assure you I can keep a secret. I've been privy to people's darkest secrets living in a home attached to a church. I've never uttered a word. Secrets are like vampires—they can suck the life out of you, but they can only survive in darkness. I will never lie, Sandra, but I won't tell someone else's story either. It's not my job to bring people's secrets into the light."

I think I may have surprised her. I looked at Jade and saw her biting her lip. Had I said something wrong?

"I like you, River. I like your intelligence and your candor. If you're anything like Jade, you know when to be a lady and when to be a…I don't have to finish that sentence, do I?"

She stood up in front of me, held out her hand, and helped me up. She inspected my hands and tsked. Her mouth pinched. It was a look I never wanted to see again. Disgust covered her face like bad foundation. Unfortunately, I was sure my toes would disappoint her further.

Something had changed in that moment. I wanted to please this woman. I wanted her to choose me. "I apologize for the condition of my manicure, or lack thereof. My hands are in water all day. I can remedy this immediately." I couldn't afford a manicure, but I would figure out how to get one.

"We have resources for that." She turned me around and pulled the zipper of my dress down. My heart plummeted at the same time. "I'll need you to remove your clothes so I can see what I'm working with." She gently nudged me forward, giving me the impression that I should stand several feet from her, as if on display. "Leave the heels on, they'll make your legs look fabulous." I'd never stripped for a woman. When I'd stripped for a man, it was always a joint effort. We would race to see who was the first to get naked.

Was it weird that I was excited about making the cut as a whore? No. I was excited about being able to eat, I told myself. I was also relieved she was allowing me to keep a piece of my self-esteem intact by permitting me to keep my shoes on.

Most days I would have tossed the dress to the floor and kicked it to the side, but this was an interview, so I walked away from her, letting one side of the dress fall off my shoulder. How would I strip for a client? *Seductively.* With a sway to my hips, I took three steps and looked over my shoulder. Jade was barely containing her laughter. As I turned slowly to face them, the dress fell to a soft puddle at my feet. One foot stepped to the right, and the other to the left. I straddled the pink material.

My lace undergarments hugged my body. Tightness gripped my nipples as they puckered under the lace demi bra. I wasn't aroused. I was simply cold standing in the middle of an air-conditioned room in next to nothing. Thankfully, I had always rewarded myself with nice undergarments. Feeling pretty started with the basics.

"Turn around." Sandra's voice was calm but commanding.

A shift of my feet had me rotating three hundred sixty degrees in front of her shrewd hawk-like eyes. I wondered if she could see my knees quake.

"Do you exercise, River?" Her eyes traveled down my body. "You are in fine shape, but I wonder about stamina. Some girls are blessed with good genes. Are you one of those?"

Blessed with an athlete's body and a pretty face, I'd never had to work hard to stay in shape, but I did walk a lot, and I took care of myself by eating healthily when I could afford to eat.

"Yes, I have good genes, but I exercise and eat right. I try to sit in on a yoga class a couple times a week to stretch and maintain flexibility."

She didn't actually smile, but there was a hint of something pleasant in the upturn of her lip. "Yoga is an excellent way to stay in shape. I recommend you keep that up."

Yoga classes could put me in the poor farm if I quit The Grind. I traded coffee for classes. However, I would imagine I'd make enough to pay for classes if I were working for Concierge Services. Sandra was the boss, and if she said yoga was a good idea, then I'd do my best to participate.

"Can I ask you some questions, Sandra?"

"I would hope you would. Get dressed and come back to the sitting area. We'll discuss the details there."

She walked over to the wall and pressed the panel, and another hidden door opened. This one concealed a built-in bar and beverage center. There were lots of secrets in this building. This was a woman whose lifestyle depended on hiding the obvious.

Jade helped me back into the dress and gave me a hug. "Are you doing okay?" Her voice was barely above a whisper.

"Yes, but I don't know if I'm more excited or nervous. I think nervous. Who gets excited about something like this?"

This was overwhelming, but it was good to have her near. I now knew why she had been distant during the last few months. She'd been living a life she couldn't share. It must have been a relief for her when I agreed to the interview. At least now she would have someone who could share her secrets.

Sandra had placed a tray of beverages and snacks on the table and then took her original position.

I sat on the edge of the sofa and waited for her to begin the conversation.

"It may be easier for me to explain who our clients are and what they expect. If you have additional questions, I'll be happy to answer everything, but first I'll need you to sign a confidentiality agreement acknowledging anything you hear or talk about can't be discussed outside this room."

So much for the candid conversations with Jade. She handed me a clipboard and the agreement. I scrawled my name across the bottom of the page and looked at her with anticipation. It felt like the day I'd found a Penthouse Forum under one of the pews. I hid it under my shirt and snuck it into my room. All night, I'd read the titillating articles. They were naughty and forbidden, and that made reading them so alluring. Was that how the mentors would see me? Naughty? Forbidden? Alluring, even?

I'd always been attracted to living on the edge, but on my terms. It was why I had such a tough time embracing religion. The rules were too confining. Too rigid.

Sandra picked up the phone and told her receptionist she needed some paperwork processed. She took the clipboard and my courage when she exited the room. Jade and I sat in silence as Sandra disappeared into the foyer.

Chapter 3

A manila envelope was pressed against Sandra's chest when she entered the room. Like a scarlet letter displayed against her bosom. My eyes followed the parcel while she sat down and placed it on the table. Not knowing what it contained was torture.

"River, we will always refer to our clientele as mentors, sponsors, advisors, or friends. After today, we will never discuss money, and you will never discuss money with your mentor. When our clients come to Concierge Services, they are looking for a wide variety of services." She gave me a glance as if to make sure I was following her line of thinking. I nodded my head. "Most of them are looking for companionship—a girlfriend experience. These men run Fortune 500 corporations. That should be of great interest to you since you are a business major with an emphasis in finance."

She reached toward the tray and picked up a bottle of sparkling water. Once she poured it into the small crystal glass, she brought it to her lips. Jade and I were offered a drink with a silent push of the tray. Diet soda was my choice, Jade selected apple juice—her favorite.

Sandra waited for us to pour our drinks. "Many students are

excited to spend their time with men who are at the top of their fields. It's a very stimulating experience to be with such talented peers." She readjusted her position and leaned in toward me. "This is how it works. We are an exclusive club. I would liken us to a country club. We have rules, we have dues, and we have an exclusive client list. We offer a range of services. Most importantly, we guarantee anonymity if desired. Not all of our clients seek that. Many are happy to flaunt what they purchase around town. Honestly, River, who doesn't like to show off their fancy new acquisition?"

It was odd to think of myself as a purchase, but when it came down to it, wasn't I already selling a peek of myself at the coffee shop? Here, I would offer an expanded menu.

"I understand."

Jade leaned back into the cushions. She was readying herself for a long conversation. I followed her lead and sat back gracefully, letting the sofa support my body.

"Most of the mentors are single. They never made time for relationships. Work took precedence, and still does, but they have needs that must be met. That's where you come in. You would be a companion to help your mentor fill those needs. In return, they will help you meet yours. Sometimes, it's merely a dinner. Sometimes, it's more."

Was I supposed to respond in some way?

After an uncomfortable silence, she pressed on. "Some of the mentors are married. Is that a problem for you?"

I answered honestly. "I don't know. I've never been the other woman. How does a person handle that situation?"

She sipped her water and placed it on the table. Shifting her knees, she looked directly at me and answered in a tone much like my professors used when they were trying to steer me to a neutral position.

"If a married man came to your place of employment, would you deny him service?" I processed the information under her watchful eye.

"No, I make coffee for a living. If he wanted a coffee, I would serve him."

"Exactly. Once you know you're selling a commodity, whether it's time, coffee, or something else, it's easier to blur the lines. However, if that's a hard limit for you, then you can remove that from the list. Think about it. I have to say the married clients require less and are often more grateful. That is something to keep in mind."

I wasn't sure I could live with being the other woman. If I were married, I wouldn't mind if my husband bought coffee at a coffee shop, but I would mind if he bought a female, especially if he had sex with her. That *would* break the very essence of our marriage. It would break the vow of fidelity. Jade said she didn't ask, but I would always wonder.

"How would I know what my client is looking for as far as services go?" Did they pick you up with a prepaid invoice in their hand? One blowjob paid in full.

"First of all, our process is streamlined. It's very much like going out with someone for the first time. Both parties are on even footing. If one party doesn't feel comfortable or the meeting isn't mutually beneficial, you go your separate ways. What we do differently is set up every first encounter as a dining experience. That meeting lasts a maximum of two hours and is free to the client. If it turns into something more, then it's up to both of you to take it further. I'm not selling sex here. If that's where the date takes you, then that's your call." She sipped her sparkling water. "The women who are open-minded tend to get more dates. Most importantly, our clients are looking for an authentic experience. They want to have dinner with a woman who is smart, articulate, and has something in common with them. They expect to be entertained."

Sandra was a master at mincing words. She would never come out and say I received money for sex, but that was exactly what she was selling.

"How exactly do I get the help I need?" I was trying to find a nice way to ask how I would get paid.

"We pay our student interns through PayPal. You do have an account, right? You log on and submit your hours, along with the client's name, and we issue payment every Friday. Of course, the client also fills out a form. We charge them for consulting fees. We rarely have a discrepancy in reporting, but if there is one, we almost always side with the client. We would hate to lose a mentor haggling over fifteen minutes."

"Tell me about the wages an intern can make." I was curious if this would be worth my time. Jade mentioned something about making in a day or week the amount I would make in a month at The Grind. That was hard to believe.

"We have a flat rate. It's three hundred fifty an hour, or fourteen hundred a night. It's actually a bit on the low end of the scale, but our interns are getting more than money. They are often getting a foot in the door of a prestigious company. Most of you girls, and a few men we have on contract, have more opportunities than they know what to do with. We feel the benefits package makes up for the cut in wages." There was a smugness to her answer, like she was telling me *you're one lucky lady.*

Did she just say three hundred fifty dollars an hour? That was what I averaged working five days a week between tips and my salary.

I tried to remain calm. I didn't want to sound overly eager, but my financial brain began to do the math. If I could book six hours a week, I would make over eight thousand dollars a month. I could be debt free in eighteen months and still live ten times better than I did now. I felt a twitch between my legs. It was telling me to get on board fast.

"You mentioned a benefits package. Does that include more than connections?" God, if she told me I would get full medical and dental, I was going to come right here, right now.

"We don't have a traditional medical or dental package."

Damn it, too good to be true.

"What do you offer?" How weird was it to be negotiating benefits for the sale of sexual favors?

"We take care of all your medical needs. We have an exclusive agreement with an MD who sees to our interns. We understand how busy your schedules can be, so he makes house calls. We don't offer dental. We do offer weekly spa maintenance, which you are in sore need of. You need a good manicure, pedicure, and a waxing. We don't shave our nether regions. We wax—every four weeks—on schedule. No excuses. You will also have access to the Athletic Club to keep in shape. No one wants to rent a Lamborghini and have a Kia show up."

The Athletic Club was a state-of-the-art facility that catered to the rich and famous. It offered any service you would expect a health spa to provide. Just a membership to the Athletic Club alone would be worth signing on for.

"I'm impressed. So, if the client is not paying for the first encounter, is the intern required to donate that time?" How many first dates would I have to endure before I saw a dime?

"That's an excellent question. As I mentioned earlier, our clients pay a hefty sum to belong. The first two hours are paid by Concierge Services. You are paid as a consultant. You will always be paid. Without you, we have no service."

It was nice she recognized that fact. In all honesty, she was just a pimp in a designer suit. I wondered what her cut was.

"How do you get money from me?"

She eyed me as if I'd just broken a rule. Maybe I shouldn't be talking about payment, but honestly, money was the only consideration when taking on this kind of job. She said after today she wouldn't discuss money, so this was my only shot at clearing up my questions.

"Concierge Services makes their money from the client in dues. We never pass on costs to our interns. Our clients also send us lots of business in other ventures, like hotel and dinner reservations and entertainment packages. We are a full concierge service provider. It's what we do. This," she pointed between the three of us, "is a small portion of our business, but it's probably one of the most important aspects of our services. It's all about making our clients happy. Happy clients are return clients."

"How does the school benefit?" Her scowl made it obvious she wasn't keen on my questions, but I did sign a non-disclosure agreement, and I needed information to make an educated decision.

"The university has one of the highest placement records of any school its size. Charitable donations are at an all-time high. The more successful the school is, the more valuable your degree. Our mentors are alumni of the university. They are part of what we refer to as The Dean's List. It's a group of men and women who are loyal to their Alma Mater. In exchange for their loyalty, they're rewarded with certain benefits. We are not dealing with small wealth here, River. We're dealing with more money than you know what to do with. A two-hour block of time is a rounding error for these people. A fourteen-hundred-dollar evening is a normal night out."

Jade started laughing as my mouth nearly hit the floor. I looked down at her Louboutins and said, "I'm definitely keeping these." I'd have every color in her closet if she continued to have fun at my expense.

"Well, River, it looks like I've given you enough to think about for a night. I have another interviewee arriving in a few minutes." By her move-along tone, I believed we'd just been dismissed.

The mention of another interview made me nervous. It was that damn competitive edge I had. If someone were holding a contest, I wanted to win. I didn't care if it were a wet T-shirt or a pie-eating contest, I would do my best to come out on top.

Sandra pulled the manila envelope from the table and handed it to me.

"In here you'll find a contract of sorts. It's really just a list of things you're willing to do. There is also the address of a spa. Merilee, my assistant, has scheduled you an appointment for ten o'clock tomorrow morning. If you don't show, we understand you've opted to not accept the position. Should you decide to come on board, call me at this number tomorrow morning. There are other details that need to be addressed, such as current employment and wardrobe." She handed me a business card that simply said *Sandra*, and a phone number was written under the name. "This isn't for everyone. Take the night to think it over. You have my permission to ask Jade anything. She can help you understand the details better than I. I'm simply the coordinator."

Out of habit, I began to clear the table. She pressed her hand on top of mine and shook her head.

"River, your days of cleaning up other people's messes are over. We hire out for that. You and Jade should go out to eat. In fact, I'll have Merilee make you reservations at Smith and Wollensky's. They have the best steaks around. They also have an amazing raw bar. Dinner is on me."

Never in my wildest dreams had I thought my day would look anything like this. Jade, an escort. Sandra, my potential boss. The possibility of eight thousand dollars a month, and now, dinner at Smith and Wollensky's. I felt like I was being pranked.

She escorted us through the secret door to Merilee's desk and instructed her to call a car and make the necessary arrangements for dinner. Sandra was sleek and sophisticated, confident, and completely capable of taking on the world. I'd just met my idol. I wanted to be her.

The chairs by the window offered the perfect position to watch for our car and the next interviewee. Like a hawk, I watched the door, wondering who would enter. Would she be beautiful and charming? I hoped she would come before our car arrived so I could appraise my competition. Would she be able to hijack my offer?

The door swung open, and the hottest guy I'd ever seen walked in. Dressed in a tailored black suit, he could have walked off the pages of the financial times. He was a cross between a sexy day trader and a Dolce and Gabbana model. He walked up to Merilee and in a deep timbre said, "I'm Luca Gregorio, here to see Sandra." His eyes skirted the room, taking it all in. He looked our way and nodded his head. I could swear he stripped me of my clothes in a glance. Oh, his eyes could melt the panties off a girl or maybe the trousers off a man.

There was no way I could compete with him. It was a good thing he was servicing a whole different clientele than I was. At least I assumed he was servicing women. Lucky Sandra, getting to strip him down.

All I knew was when I finally made it, I was signing up for The Dean's List and I was getting me a Luca.

Chapter 4

Jade leaned over and whispered, "Wipe the drool off your chin. He's not for you. He's for rent, and you can't afford him yet."

Yet. That was the keyword—*yet.* Jade stood up and straightened her dress. In all the excitement, I hardly noticed what she was wearing. Beautiful geometric shapes decorated the silk shift that came just above her perfect knees. Black pumps made her three inches taller than her five-foot-six-inch frame. A cashmere sweater hung over her shoulders. She looked like she walked out of the country club. Why had I not noticed the changes taking place in her?

Maybe it was because I could barely keep my head above water. Jade and I had shared so much of our lives together. There was so little we didn't know about one another. Except, up until today, this.

How had she managed to keep the secret? In my self-absorbed state, was I not paying attention to anything? Had I disappointed Jade in not even noticing the changes in her?

I took one last look at Luca and sighed. If ever a man made my heart swoon, it would be him. He was there, right next to Ian Somerhalder and Alexander Skarsgård. Jade walked past me to the front door. Over her shoulder, she said goodbye to Merilee and led me out into the bustling streets of New York City.

The driver was standing next to the town car, holding the door open for us.

"Hi, Tony." Jade breezed past the man and climbed into the back seat.

I mimicked her greeting and slid in next to her. "How do you know him? Don't tell me he's a perk as well?"

"No, but he's been known to drive clients occasionally. He mostly takes care of out-of-towners."

I reached into my purse to check my phone for messages. Nothing. I didn't know why I looked. My phone was always idle. My life was boring. I could use a little excitement. By the time we got to the restaurant, it was nearly five o'clock. We arrived for an early dinner by New Yorkers' standards. Tony opened the door like a personal chauffeur. I could get used to that.

Jade approached the hostess with confidence. The utterance of Sandra's name had us ushered quickly to a private booth. I wondered if Sandra requested this particular booth since it provided privacy for a more intimate conversation. The manila envelope felt heavy in my hand.

The waiter approached and took our drink order. We decided on a nice bottle of Merlot. It was not a choice I could have made on my budget, but Jade assured me we could have whatever we wanted.

Her eyes glanced to the envelope I placed on the table. Like a strobe light in a dark room, it demanded attention.

"So, how do you think I did?" Would she tell me the truth, or would she buttercream-icing it because that was what friends did?

"She basically offered you the job right there. I think you did well. If she didn't like you, she would have dismissed you. It's not like she's desperate. Do you have any idea how many girls would kill to be in your position?" She placed the neatly folded napkin across her lap.

"No, I have no idea. I've never sold my body before. Tell me, what makes this deal any better than the rest? What separates it from a pimp on the corner?"

"For a smart girl, you're so dumb. Sandra is a facilitator, not a Madame. This is a referral-only job. I referred you because I thought you might like the job, as well as the money. You are intelligent, sexy, and funny as all get out. It's a good combination. That's what's good for them. What's good for you starts with the clientele. All the men are vetted. No records. Business leaders. Lots of disposable income. You don't have to worry about your safety. Hell, I might even go as far as saying you wouldn't have to worry about diseases, but there is never a guarantee with that. I wouldn't ever go without a condom, no matter what, no matter whom. You certainly won't have to worry about getting stiffed."

Her use of the word *stiffed* was hilarious. Wasn't that what we were talking about? "I imagine I'm guaranteed to get stiffed." A giggle bubbled up from my stomach. I couldn't help myself. The whole situation was laced with humor.

"I mean money. You'll be paid more than you can imagine. The rate is a pittance compared to the perks."

The waiter approached and poured a splash of wine into Jade's glass. She swirled and sniffed and nodded as if she'd been doing it for years.

When did she become a connoisseur?

Burgundy liquid shimmered in my glass as the waiter finished pouring and disappeared. "It all sounds too good to be true. Tell me what the downside is." I sipped my wine and thrummed my fingers over the envelope.

"It can be lonely." Her words were direct and succinct. No emotion. Just facts. "Your time is paid for, there is no risk of an emotionally intimate relationship. You have to turn that part of you off. You'll see people in love and feel envious. Keep your eye on the prize, and you'll be fine."

"The prize meaning an advanced degree with a possible job and no debt? I think I could be lonely for a while. What else?" I pulled my napkin from the table and laid it across my lap.

"The hardest thing for me was to wrap my head around the idea that I was selling sex. In essence, you're a prostitute. I finally came to terms by referring to it as transactional sex. Everybody does something for money. I go on dates and enjoy men. Most jobs screw you; my job is just a bit more literal." As much as I was now seeing these colossal changes in Jade's confidence and poise, there was the feisty girl I knew and loved.

"All right, so if I open the envelope, is there going to be something in there that will scare me?" I rubbed my hand over the brown paper. It was funny how a brown envelope had the ability to change my life.

"Yes. If it doesn't, then you probably shouldn't take the job. No fear makes you dangerous. You're not that girl. You're smart and can weigh the pros and cons. What's important is to know when you open the envelope, you have choices. It's imperative that you take a stand on certain issues. Open the envelope, River. I'll try to clarify everything I can for you."

Just as I pushed my finger under the flap, the waiter approached to take our order. I scrambled to look at the menu while Jade ordered by memory. She rattled off her selections and returned her unopened menu to the waiter.

The waiter turned his attention to me. Oysters on the half shell were one of my favorites. After placing an order for a half-dozen oysters and a steak, I opened the envelope and pulled out the papers.

The first paper was a leaflet about Chris Chang MD. He offered all facets of family medicine from pap smears to throat cultures, all of which a working girl might need. My eyes bugged out at the next page. I fisted up, ready to slap the laughter out of her. She knew exactly what I was looking at, and she thought it was funny. I was so glad she could find humor in my shock.

"Are you scared yet?" She scooted around the horseshoe booth. The papers I gripped were now placed in front of her. A pat on the leather seat had me moving toward her without question.

"Holy shit. What the hell is blood play?" I quickly cupped my mouth, realizing I had said the words too loudly. Thankfully, no one noticed. Jade pulled a pen from her purse and set it near my hand. She placed the stack of papers in front of me and gave me a minute to adjust.

I took a sip of my wine but thought better of it and tossed the remainder back, swallowing hard. This shit just got real.

I don't think I've ever been shocked into silence until that very moment. On the top of the sheet in big, bold letters were the words **SEXUAL CONTRACT.**

The page contained rows of descriptive sexual play. Lesser-known fetishes like Knives and Blood Play, Urination, Fecal Play, Breath Control and Electrical Current followed nipple Play, Role Play, Masturbation, and Cunnilingus. The list ended with Bondage Ropes and Tapes, Handcuffs and Restraints, Spanking, Whipping, Clamps and Other. To say I was stunned would have been an understatement. I was paralyzed with fear.

"Take a deep breath. This is like a menu—very much like the one you just ordered from. You like the oysters, I don't. I didn't order oysters. I chose shrimp cocktail. I will never choose oysters. It's a limit for me. Let's go through the list one by one, and you can choose what you're willing to offer or try. One word of caution: it's yes or no. Never write maybe. It's basically perceived as a yes until proven otherwise." She picked up the pen and began to go through the page like it was a shopping list. Mine. See aisle four for spanking and whipping, aisle two for oral pumps and electrical currents.

What the hell?

"What if I say yes to something and hate it?" My mind went straight to anal. I'd always wanted to try it, but if I hated it, I didn't want to be stuck taking it up the ass for the next couple of years.

"You amend your contract. This is really that simple." She started at the top of the page, which began with nipple play. I said yes. In fact, I said yes to everything until we got to vaginal fisting.

"Exactly who allows that? Oh, my God. Wouldn't you be stretched so wide your next lover would need a two-by-four strapped to his ass so he didn't fall in?" Jade laughed at my description. I could see her mind putting that scenario to work.

"So, I guess that's a no." She wrote *no* and moved on. We progressed several more lines before we got to anal intercourse. She turned to look at me.

"Okay, so tell me the truth. Does it hurt as bad as people say?" I looked at her as I spoke. She had never been able to fool me with those easy-to-read eyes. They widened, softened, and then glimmered with humor.

"No freaking way. You haven't done it?" As she asked this, she dropped the pen and stared at me wide-eyed and open-mouthed. I wanted to reach inside her gaping hole and tweak her tonsils. She had been getting entirely too much enjoyment out of my shock today.

"No, I haven't been with anyone bold enough to ask. I assume that because you're with two guys, they take advantage of all your orifices," I answered. My eyes pinned her in place, looking for the truth. As friends, we had talked about nearly everything. However, I didn't think the subject of certain orifices had come up. It wasn't like you had dinner, asked for the ketchup, and inquired how it felt to take it up the ass last night. Those are subjects reserved for drunken slumber parties. Something we had not done in years.

"Yes, well my mentors are bisexual, so we take advantage of each other's orifices. As far as my ass, I enjoy it. It takes preparation to make it comfortable, but once in, the sensation is incredible. So, is it a yes or a no for you?" She picked up the pen and hovered next to anal intercourse.

I poured us another glass of wine as the waiter brought our appetizers. His eyes scanned the page, but he didn't respond to the top even though it said in large font, Sexual Contract. Hell, in a city like New York, it was probably as common as a prenuptial agreement.

"Definitely yes. I want to try it if it comes up."

Jade wrote in *yes* next to anal intercourse.

"It will definitely come up." She marked fisting as a *no* and continued down the list.

Yes.

Yes.

No.

"What the hell is blood play?"

"It's a no, River. Some sickos like to draw blood and lick it off you. They get hard from it. It's dangerous and gross." She wrote *no* next to it and the next two. We enjoyed our appetizers in-between contract options. She licked the cocktail sauce from her fingers and picked up the pen. "I can't see you pissing or shitting on someone, so let's move past those."

No.

No.

She wrote in the remaining items as I called them. No gags, no electricity, no whipping, no clamps, the rest was fair game.

When we got to *other*, she asked if I had write-ins. I pondered the possibilities for a few minutes and asked her to write in *no married men*. I couldn't bring myself to be a home wrecker. A marriage license implied exclusivity to me. It was a hard limit.

She tucked the papers into the envelope just as our dinner arrived. I was famished.

"How did you get this whole thing past me? Have I been that out of touch? We see each other every week, Jade. I should have noticed the great clothes, the hair, *and* the nails. I should have questioned the move more thoroughly. I'm an awful friend. Now I'm paying attention, I can see you've changed in so many ways. You're put together... refined. You look happy." I placed the first bite in my mouth and groaned. Amazing.

"I didn't let on that anything had changed except for my clothes. There was no way I was wearing Wal-Mart if I had Prada in my closet. We ate at the same places, went to the same clubs. As far as the apartment, I couldn't take you there. It would have been obvious had I done that. Now you know, so now you can visit." There was a look of relief in her eyes. It must have been hard to keep a secret that big. Would that have been another incentive for her to want me to join? To, in some way, take away some of her loneliness?

"We went to crap clubs when you could have taken us to someplace really cool? You cheap bitch." We looked at each other and cracked up. Several tables looked in our direction. We hunkered down and lowered our voices.

"The rest of the papers in the packet contain the legal stuff like confidentiality, etc. It's pretty standard stuff. There are also some additional perks that will come your way if you call Sandra. She will set you up with a personal shopper who will show you how to dress for the lifestyle. You will be ushered off like a movie star to be primped and pampered. Take the night and think about it. Like I said, what happens between your legs is easy; it's what happens between your ears that's hard."

"I'll need the night to consider my options. You have to tell me one thing, though: are all the guys fat, old and wrinkled with quivering, nasty ball sacks?" I put my finger in my mouth and faked a gag. Lord, if I took this job, I was going to have to censure myself. No cussing. No faces. No inappropriate hand gestures. It would be like living at home without the hate.

"No, but I won't lie to you. The majority of men are older. They are wealthy, so they will most likely be well-groomed and well-mannered. That's not to say that once you get behind closed doors, they won't be kinky. Most of them want the girlfriend experience. If they wanted the porn star experience, they could get that by dialing 1-800 I-want-a-whore. They expect more from us. My initial experience was that most of the men wanted a companion. It wasn't always about sex."

"Give me some examples." If it wasn't about sex, then what was it about? If they wanted a companion, they could go to a coffee shop and talk the ear off a waitress. They would be in for less than five bucks if they only ordered coffee.

Jade set her plate aside. "If you decide to come on board, you will be like the shiny new penny. Your line will be ringing off the hook. The cool thing is, the first meeting is always neutral. No expectations. You meet the… let's refer to them as mentors. You meet the mentor, and you sit down over a meal. If there's no chemistry, there's no second date. It's a paid interview." She flagged the waiter over and ordered two coffees and a dessert called Chocolate Sin.

"Jade, it just seems too easy. How does this stay secret?" I glanced at the manila envelope and thought about the contract. There was no way I would want that posted on the Internet.

"Everyone has something to lose. Discretion is paramount. That's why you were unaware of what I was doing. Sure, the mentors have a lot at stake, but so do you. Your entire future is balanced on everyone's ability to keep things on the down low. Many of the men will flaunt you around at meetings, events, etc., but they would never tell their co-workers you're an escort. In most circles, you would be their date or, in a more exclusive agreement, their girlfriend. Although, as you know, you're never really their girlfriend."

What would it be like to stay single for years but "date" all the time? Long-term wasn't on my radar until I graduated, but I wondered if I would miss dating. Time would tell.

The waiter brought the coffee and the piece of chocolate cake Jade ordered. He asked if we needed anything else. When we responded with a no, he left us to our conversation.

"So, it's an unwritten mutual blackmail rule." It was the only way I could wrap my head around it.

"I guess it could be looked at that way, although I would never bring that up in conversation. Blackmail, like prostitution, is a dirty word." Jade put her fork into the cake and picked up a delicate bite. "Try this. If you think sex is good, you're in for a treat." She placed the bite past my lips and watched my eyes float into the back of my head.

The chocolate coated every surface of my mouth. Its richness was indescribable. I hummed with satisfaction as I swallowed the most perfect part of our dinner. The oysters had been wonderful, the steak divine, but the smallest bit of sin was the perfect way to end the night. I reflected on that thought. A dash of sin could round out every experience.

Chapter 5

Jade offered to have a cab take me home, but I needed to think, and the best place for me to do that was the subway. How far would I go to have a life? I had less than a day to decide.

Mindless activity buzzed around me while my head raced through my options. In reality, I had two. I could take the job, or I could continue making it day to day. Option number two looked less and less appealing as I recalled the overdue notices sitting on my table and remembered the discomfort that came from an empty stomach.

I watched impeccably dressed women enter and exit the subway. Professionals. It was what I wanted to be. I wanted to wear a tailored suit to a Wall Street consulting job.

I didn't bury myself in numbers for years to end up a day trader. I studied for my future. I wanted to provide solid advice on securities pricing and strategies for creating shareholder value. I wanted to do economic forecasting and analysis. I had to prove my education wasn't a waste of time and resources.

Since sleep evaded me, I opened the envelope that had been calling to me all night long. Calling me was too subtle. Screaming *Open me up and study me, you idiot* was closer to what I'd been hearing. Subtle. Not. The rest of the documentation was straightforward. One paper asked about my schedule, the other requested I list any medical issues I might have. After moving to my desk, I spread the papers out in front of me and scanned them once more. I carefully looked over the check-marks Jade placed on the contract. I heard her voice tell me, *Just amend the contract, it's that easy.*

"Oh, what the hell," I mumbled to myself.

I searched my desk for a pen and scribbled my name across the bottom of all the pages. What was life without a little risk?

My fingers punched in a text to my boss at The Grind.

Lacey,

Sorry for giving no notice, but I have to quit. I need to focus on finishing school.

Thanks for everything,

River

I felt bad about not giving notice. It was not my norm, but I knew from that point forward my life would be about school and mentors. I didn't have time to appease a coffee shop manager. In all honesty, she would probably be relieved. Business had been slow lately. My hours could be divvied up among the other girls. It was probably a win for everyone.

I pulled Sandra's card from my purse and stared at it for a long time. Now that I had quit my job, I had one option left. I glanced at the clock and wondered if seven o'clock was too early to call. Taking my chances, I punched in the numbers and waited.

"Hello, this is Sandra."

Her voice sounded awake and energetic. I pictured the put-together woman in the Chanel suit I met yesterday and tried to imagine her with her hair mussed up from a hard night's sleep. I couldn't process the thought. I bet she woke up with her hair in a perfect chignon and her silk pajamas wrinkle-free.

"Hello, this is River Roberts." Should I remind her of our meeting yesterday? She didn't seem like the type of person to forget a name, much less a person.

"River, it's lovely to hear from you. I assume you've made a decision with regard to your future." She certainly knew how to get to the point quickly.

"Yes, I hope I haven't called too early."

"Well, the old cliché that says the early bird gets the worm is an accurate one. While others are sleeping, the movers and shakers of the world are moving and shaking." I could hear the life of the city in the background. She was not only up and ready, she was on the move.

"I'm ready to join the ranks of the movers and shakers, Sandra. I've signed the necessary paperwork, and I'm ready to proceed." I thought this call would be harder to make, but everything inside me said it was the right move for me.

"That sounds wonderful. I know you'll be very successful in this endeavor. You have everything it takes. You're witty, charming, and intelligent. You exude sex appeal. You'll be a popular hire."

I wasn't used to people telling me I was acceptable. I'd certainly never heard I was witty, charming, or intelligent. Sandra's opinion was important to me, and her praise validated my decision. Wasn't it time I surrounded myself with people who lifted me up? I wanted to impress her.

"What do I do now?"

"You have a ten o'clock appointment at the spa and Merilee will get the car service set up for you. Bring your signed paperwork with you. I'll send a messenger over to retrieve it. Merilee will then set you up with the doctor this afternoon. You'll need a clean bill of health to start. Tomorrow, you'll have an appointment with a fashion consultant. Your initial wardrobe will be provided as part of your contract. By signing on, you agree to stay for a minimum of one year. We're making an investment in you; staying is your investment in us. Of course, we expect you to stay throughout your graduate program. That is how you'll get the most out of your experience."

She made it sound like I'd just won a scholarship. I suppose in a roundabout way, I had.

I SHOWED up to the spa with five minutes to spare. The waiting area decorated in light blues and browns was serene and soothing. I followed the waxer into a brightly lit, small, windowless room. A sheet-covered table waited for my vagina.

In a sweet voice, the waxer, Michelle, said, "Take your pants off and lie on the table with your head here." She pointed to one end of the table. I turned my head and expected to see a speculum on the counter nearby. This appointment seemed more like a trip to the gynecologist than a spa. Popsicle sticks, a container of steaming goo, and a stack of fabric swatches sat on the table next to the head of the bed.

My heart pounded in my chest. Sweat began to build on my brow. "It's my first time, and I'm a little frightened." Terrified, was more like it. I'd never been waxed. I've always been a fan of trimming, but waxing seemed so severe.

"No need to be scared. We do these all day, every day. I haven't lost a client yet."

Her attempt at humor didn't erase my anxiety. I hopped on the table wearing a bra, shirt and nothing else. The waxer started some friendly conversation.

"Where are you from?" I was instructed to fold my legs Indian style. As I lay flat on the table, I answered her questions. My open vagina was on display for a perfect stranger. I better get used to this— it would be a constant in my new life.

I didn't know what kind of nerve endings were on top of my lady parts, but when she ripped the wax free, I was certain she'd ripped my soul straight out of my little love nub.

I wanted to punch her face as my body lifted off the table. All the while, she was telling me about her favorite Chinese restaurant on

Broadway. She was spreading hot wax all over my sex and talking about wonton soup.

After ripping my pubic hair out of my body, she told me to lift my legs and spread my butt cheeks. The minute the wax was ripped from my ass, I could only take comfort in knowing should that part of my body be desired, it was trimmed and ready to go.

Just when I thought my ordeal was over, she brought out the tweezers. One by one, she plucked the hairs that weren't smart enough to hide.

"Okay. We're done," she said.

I exhaled the scream I kept locked inside. All I could think was that anyone who said this shit didn't hurt was a big, fat liar. The butt part was bearable. After a stranger ripped the first layer off, the butt area felt like a lazy stroll.

Maybe that's why they did that first. Shit.

With my crotch on fire, I dressed and made my way to the front desk. The messenger was waiting for my manila envelope. I handed it to him reluctantly. He walked away with the contract that said I was up for this torture on a regular basis.

The receptionist handed me a card for my next hair-ripping experience. I had four weeks to recover. Four weeks for my soul, and possibly my lady bits, to come out of hiding.

Next, I was guided to another room for a manicure and pedicure. Those, I could handle.

* * *

"Waxing today?"

I lay on the table with my legs spread once again. Dr. Chang sat between my thighs and inspected my bits.

"Yes, please tell me it gets easier." He chuckled as he slid the speculum into me.

"I'm told it does, but electrolysis or laser removal is also an option.

You would be a good candidate because you have dark hair. The laser would be an excellent choice."

Laser. Yes. No waxing with wonton soup-eating Michelle next month. That plan sounded good.

"Even though I'm going to insert an IUD today, I'd recommend you use a barrier method to protect yourself from disease. An IUD doesn't offer protection against HIV, herpes or gonorrhea."

"I'm aware of that, Dr. Chang. The IUD is my backup plan against pregnancy. It's effective and won't cause me to gain weight."

The cramp and pinch of the insertion were nothing compared to my experience at the spa. I gave a vial of blood, dressed, and headed off to my next task—school.

With my new income potential, I visited my advisor and signed up for classes I couldn't afford yesterday. I managed to maintain a Tuesday and Thursday schedule and put myself on track to graduate in less than two years. The thousands I charged at the bookstore didn't freak me out. If everything worked out, I'd have those paid for in a week or two.

When I arrived home, there was a package waiting for me. Inside was the cutest Coach purse, a brand-new cell phone, and a hand-written note.

River,

Welcome aboard.

Erica from Bloomingdales will be waiting for you tomorrow at nine.

This is your work phone. It's intended for work only. All communications from your mentors and me will come through this phone.

A photographer will be at my office tomorrow at two o'clock to take your profile pictures. Don't be late.

An email will go out to the sponsors in your area of study tomorrow. Your profile will be posted on the Alumni Boards tomorrow afternoon. Expect that phone to be ringing as early as tomorrow evening.

I hope you enjoyed your spa day.

Sandra

A person would have to be a masochist to *enjoy* that spa day. The only consolation was it was supposed to get easier every time. The waxer was bold enough to say that sometimes the hair was so scared, it didn't grow back. I was thinking the recipient was so scared, they never went back.

Free for the rest of the day, I texted Jade to see if she wanted to hang out.

I've joined your crazy club. The paperwork is filed and I paid my dues at the spa. Ouch. You could have warned me. Every four weeks? Really? How about dinner and a movie at my place or yours?

River

She didn't respond immediately. In fact, she didn't respond until well after five that evening.

Sorry,

I am booked tonight. I have a meeting with my mentors. They want to discuss the ins and outs of my options. :-) I'm happy to hear that you took the plunge so to say. As for dues, you'll be paying those until you resign from the club. I have to say by the second or third month, the payment isn't nearly as painful. Call me next week and we'll chat. I will probably be tied up for a few days.

Jade

Tied up? I wondered if that was a figure of speech, or was she being literal? My world was upside down, and I wasn't sure of anything.

I found leftover Chinese in the refrigerator—no doubt my roommate's, but fair game if left behind. My chopsticks waded through the Kung Pao Chicken and avoided the peanuts. I'd never been a fan of peanuts. With my feet on the coffee table, I watched reruns of *The Vampire Diaries* and relaxed. It might be the only time I'd get to kick back and be me for a while.

I dragged myself to bed and fell asleep with images of Ian Somerhalder in my mind. He entered my dreams as the mentor I would meet first. He would require all of my time, and I giddily accepted. Just as I began to feel the first flutter of a nocturnal spasm settle between my legs, my alarm shrilled and sent Ian back to dreamland. With a sigh, I turned off my alarm and prepared for my day.

In the shower, I shaved my legs and admired my pretty, red toenail polish. Miraculously, my recently accosted crotch was no worse for wear. It was amazing how quickly my private parts regrouped and recovered.

What did a girl wear to meet a fashion consultant? In the end, I imagined anything I wore would fall short of her approval. I threw on a sundress and sandals since the weather was warm. I would hold on to summer for as long as possible. Before long, the icy cold fingers of winter would be tapping me on my shoulder.

Erica was waiting for me when I arrived at guest services. She led me into a private area where racks of size eight clothes hung patiently waiting to be tried on. By me.

Holy shit.

I wondered how she knew my size, and then I remembered how closely Sandra had analyzed my naked body. That woman was amazing.

"You will need a couple of little black dresses. They are timeless and can be dressed up or down."

Erica handed me a couple of sexy black dresses and a pair of black pumps. They weren't Louboutins, but they were damn cute. I slid the perfectly fitted dresses on and looked at myself in the mirror.

Where had this woman been all my life?

They say that clothes don't make the man, but I disagree. Quality clothes can make just about anyone look and feel better. The next two hours were spent in the back room trying on everything. I never thought I could tire of trying on clothes I could never afford, but by eleven o'clock I was exhausted. Several items had been placed on a rack to the side. I'd assumed it was the purchase rack.

"Is there a specific budget we're supposed to stay under? You have quite a collection on that rack, and I don't want to take advantage." I pulled on my lower lip, dragging it between my teeth. It was a nervous habit since childhood.

"I've been doing this for Sandra for years. Let me assure you that you haven't begun to break the bank." I wondered how much she really knew. "Lunch will be here in a few minutes, then we'll move on to lingerie."

"You're going to feed me and then make me try on lingerie? Somehow, that seems cruel." I laughed at the wrongness of that scenario. It was kind of like sending me to a waxer and then to the gynecologist.

"You're having a salad, and honestly, I have your size. You only need to choose styles and colors. After that, I've been instructed to dress you and send you to the hairdresser. They'll be doing your hair and makeup for the photo shoot."

Wow, she knew a lot more than I thought. I didn't question anything the rest of the day. I dressed in what I was told, and I showed up where expected.

When I left Bloomingdales, I was told my purchases would be delivered to my house that evening. I felt like Julia Roberts in Pretty Woman, except she was leaving prostitution and I was entering it. Irony. Much? Other than that, our stories were quite similar. I walked into the discreet office on Fifth Avenue and greeted Merilee.

"Oh, River, you are stunning."

Her compliment eased some of my tension. The girls at Bloomingdales did a remarkable job. It was funny how a new outfit and makeup could make me stand taller and feel more confident. I was ready to conquer the world. Maybe Jade's confidence had been similarly boosted. The wall opened, and Sandra stepped forward. I wondered if she would be pleased.

Her look of satisfaction made the pruning of my pubes and the plucking of my eyebrows worth the pain. My skin had been cleansed and creamed, my hair had been washed and glossed. I had more makeup on, and yet, I looked natural. There was something so wrong about that. However, when Sandra looked at me, her slight nod told me I'd met her expectations. It was a silent *job well done*, and that made everything right.

"River, the photographer is here to take your pictures. Let's not keep him waiting."

She moved aside and had me enter the room ahead of her. A chair and a black backdrop weren't what I expected. Prepared for a boudoir shot, I half-expected to be laid out on the white velvet sofa with a cocktail in my hand and a feather boa around my neck.

"This is David, and he'll be taking your photos. After, you and I will chat about any lingering questions you may have." She took my beautiful black Coach bag and set it on the table.

David led me to the chair. I sat properly. Head up. Shoulders back. Confident. He pulled my long hair over one shoulder and asked me to tilt my head to the side. The click of the camera sounded again and again as my position was changed and my hair rearranged. David asked me to look sexy. Sandra told him I was sex. That statement made me laugh. The shutter clicked furiously as I continued to let loose. I couldn't contain it. I'd never thought of myself as sex. I'd been called a whore and various other names throughout my life, but sexy was never uttered.

At this point in my life, I was a commodity. I was sex. The contract proved that. The rapid clicks of the shutter ended our session.

It took David minutes to disassemble his equipment and disappear. When Sandra said she had to take pictures, I was thinking nudes. I almost downed a glass of wine to bolster my courage before I came over.

"That wasn't too bad, right?" Sandra pulled two diet sodas from her hidden bar area and walked to the sofa. "Your phone will start ringing in a few hours. Are you prepared for that?"

"Yes. Jade told me I would be a shiny new penny. Is that how it always is? Do all the men want the new girl?"

The reality of being passed around several men never crossed my mind. Somewhere in my fantasy, I imagined a few regulars calling me.

It was too late to have second thoughts, but I should have asked more questions. Questions I *couldn't* think of now.

"There are many men who like something fresh and new. You certainly will find them among your callers. We call them connoisseurs."

Connoisseurs? Aren't they normally experts in their field? I'm not certain I like that thought, being passed from connoisseur to connoisseur. Would I once again feel not good enough?

Unaware of my internal debate, Sandra continued. "However, there are many who simply want a regular companion. The choice will be yours."

"How did you get involved in this? How does a concierge become a facilitator of the flesh?"

She turned her head and in a direct no-nonsense fashion told me, "I created The Dean's List. I saw a need, and I filled it. The Dean's List has been around for over twenty years. I am one of the many alumni of the University. I needed things that only men could provide at the time. You see, the world is getting better, but don't fool yourself, River. It's still a man's world, and you have to learn to play in their sandbox."

The realization that Sandra started as an escort shocked me. The woman was so refined and put together. "Wow." I stared at her. It was as if we now shared a small secret. I felt better knowing that this amazing, successful woman had been just like me twenty years ago. "So, my phone will start ringing. I'll meet these mentors for a meal. How do I know what happens after that?"

"That's the easy part. You log on to your account, check a yes or a no next to their name after the first meeting. *No* means you have no chemistry and it's not a good fit. I recommend seeing several people in the weeks that follow so you can make some good connections. Remember, the first meeting is neutral. It's simply a meal. What you do after that is up to you. As I explained earlier, I am a facilitator, nothing more. I make the introductions, you decide how far they go."

She made it sound like a dating service. I imagined that was how this business flew under the radar. "Thanks for my new wardrobe. I'm shocked at how many items you purchased for me."

She dismissed my thanks with a wave of her hand. "It's a perk—one of many you'll come to appreciate. On the other side of that coin, there are some things you'll have to learn to navigate. Secrecy, loneliness, and guilt to name a few. The good ones always manage to find a balance."

"Is there any advice you want to give me?" I hoped she had a few words of wisdom that would help tame the nervousness in my stomach.

She tilted her head back and forth in contemplation. Her tongue darted out to lick her cherry-red lips. "Be yourself. I'm told you have a wicked sense of humor. Men don't want to be fooled; rather, they want to have an authentic experience. You don't have to act. Some will like you, and some won't. Isn't that the way life is anyway?"

"That's it? Be myself? You buy me a wardrobe fit for a princess and expect me to be authentic?" I wanted to roll my eyes but refrained.

"Did you purchase anything today you wouldn't have if given an unlimited budget?" My mind shouted, *Hell no.* She must have seen the answer in my eyes. "There you go. I just gave you the resources to dress the way you always dreamed you should. You came into contact with your authentic self. Embrace her. My only other bit of advice is to never let anyone take nude pictures of you. They always show up somewhere."

Her warning seemed to come from a place of experience. I logged that bit of information into my personal rulebook. It seemed like common sense, but at this point my life was anything but common.

Chapter 6

Packages from Bloomingdales lined the hallway. Tiffany looked at the parcels and walked away saying something about the lottery and making my rent. Her abrupt demeanor made it difficult to embrace her. She sublet a room to me, and that was the extent of our relationship. In New York, who could afford a place of their own?

My mind immediately screamed *me*. Given my new circumstances, I might just be able to afford something nicer than a sublet room in a substandard neighborhood.

Three hours later, my work phone began to ring non-stop. After several brief conversations, I had my weekend completely booked for breakfast, lunch, and dinner. I certainly wouldn't be hungry now.

My first meeting was tonight with Jonathan Ferris. He offered to send a car that I readily accepted. Until next Friday, when I got paid for the first time, I was living on a shoestring, basically the forty dollars in tips and my last paltry paycheck.

My outfit from today would have been appropriate for dinner at Per Se, but changing clothes was a necessity. I couldn't wear the same outfit my photos were taken in.

When Mr. Ferris told me we'd be dining at the exclusive restaurant, I almost fainted. I'd heard of people waiting months to eat there. He obviously had some clout.

I googled his name to find out that Mr. Ferris owned Integrity Financial Services. His company catered to the top tier of society. They offered wealth management and estate planning services. He was forty-two years old, a widower, and lived on Center Island.

After finding a picture from a recent golf tournament, my heart did a little happy dance when I realized he was *pleasant* looking. His hair was dark like mine, only his was peppered with silver. Having to endure an evening with a man who gave me the creeps was perhaps my biggest fear. No risk of that tonight. Jonathan Ferris seemed to be a dream come true as far as clients went.

Hmmm. What would the handsome Mr. Ferris like? My eyes took in the clothes laid across my bed. More clothes than I'd ever had or could imagine having, and yet, they were mine.

Lucky to have a small waist and abundant chest, the purple sheath dress I chose accentuated my hourglass shape. It hugged my body perfectly, highlighting my curves. I used to be embarrassed by my breasts and hips. I thought men wanted waif-like models who sipped broth and exercised like Olympians. I was so wrong. Men wanted women whose hips were perfect for grabbing and whose breasts spilled over into the palms of their hands.

I embraced my shape and my love of food. To be a waif, I'd never be able to enjoy restaurants like Per Se. To be a waif, I would never rock this dress.

I put on the black stilettos and freshened my makeup. With fifteen minutes to go before my ride arrived, I let my nerves get the best of me. My mind began to race through the evening. Would he be staring at me all night like a predator getting ready for his next meal? Would I feel like the prize turkey in the window of the butcher shop in a Dickens' novel? Would he look at me and dismiss me, causing me to feel inadequate in every way? All that confidence I had surrounding my curves vanished. Maybe he preferred waif-like women.

I scolded myself for allowing my self-esteem to be rocked without reason. The man obviously saw my picture and decided to call. That in and of itself showed he was interested. He was only one of ten men who would fill my calendar over the next few days. As part of my get-through-the-night plan, I poured a glass of last month's chardonnay and gulped it down. One glass was just enough to take the edge off, but not enough to get me drunk.

Hearing the doorbell, I pressed the intercom and said, "Hello?"

"Car for Ms. Roberts."

"I'll be right down."

Showtime. He was early. I grabbed my purse and headed for the elevator. My driver was a kindly, elderly man who opened my door and helped me inside. He knew exactly where we were going, so the thirty-minute drive passed in silence. I watched the city float by, street by street. With Central Park on my left, we were only blocks away from Columbus Circle and the restaurant.

My shaking fingers searched my bag, feeling around in the dark for a mint. The taste of peppermint always seemed to ease a queasy stomach. The strong mint floated in my mouth, drawing moisture to its suddenly dry surface. As the car slowed to a crawl, I pulled out my lipstick and reapplied the soft pink shimmer. I was as ready as I'd ever be.

The driver opened the door in front of the Time Warner building. The restaurant was tucked inside the piece of real estate gold that stood in front of me. I unfolded my legs one at a time and rose to my heel-enhanced, five-foot-ten-inch height. A man approached the driver and handed him a wad of folded bills.

"Thanks, Howard. I'll call when we're finished." The driver nodded and headed for the car.

My eyes took in the man who stood in front of me. Dressed in a tailored blue suit was none other than Jonathan Ferris. This gig was getting better by the minute.

"River, I'm Jonathan." He leaned in and gave me a chaste peck on the cheek. He smelled of cedar and some kind of spice, like sweet basil. "You look absolutely stunning. Your pictures don't do you justice. You're so much… more in person." His warm hand took mine. Placing it in the crook of his arm, he led me to the restaurant.

"It's a pleasure to meet you, Jonathan. I'm at a bit of a disadvantage as far as pictures go. I haven't had the opportunity to see what was chosen for my profile."

He stopped and looked at me with a look of surprise. Pulling out his phone, he began to tap away. "We'll have to remedy that." Dexterous fingers flew over the keyboard until he found what he wanted. "You had three pictures posted by Sandra. This is by far my favorite."

He showed me the picture where I was laughing. I remembered the exact moment it was taken. It was when David told me to be sexy and Sandra told him I was sex. I have to admit, the picture captured my free spirit. It was fun and without pretense. It was authentic.

"It's hard to believe that was only a few hours ago. It seems like a lifetime has passed."

My hand found itself locked around his arm again. We made our way to the front of the restaurant. Jonathan didn't have to say a word. The maître d' intercepted us as we walked through the door. He looked at me in that way people do when they're judging you. I knew the minute I had his approval. The corners of his lips rose, and his eyes lit up, telling me I passed. Is this how it would always be?

We were escorted to an out-of-the-way booth where the din of the restaurant was muted. The candlelit table held a vase of miniature roses. A glance around the room showed this was the only table with such flowers. This table was made special for me. A warm heat suffused my body. I was forced to remind myself this wasn't a date. It was a contract negotiation, and the flowers were merely a sign-on bonus.

Soft, plush fabric caressed my thighs as I scooted around the booth. Jonathan slid in next to me. He wasn't too close, but close enough to exchange intimate conversation. The maître d' waited for Jonathan to acknowledge him.

"Mr. Ferris, should I tell the sommelier to bring the white you selected, or the red?"

Jonathan looked at me and talked in a melted chocolate voice—hot, smooth, and sweet. "River, I've taken the liberty to select two wines that will pair well with tonight's tasting menu. As you are probably aware, Per Se serves a nine-course tasting menu. You can choose between their regular menu and their vegetarian menu. Both have items that will pair beautifully with the wine. We can choose red, white, or both. Your choice."

His eyes searched mine; I wondered what he was searching for? Was it merely my choice in wine, or was it my ability to choose at all? I felt like this was my first test. I looked at the maître d' and asked him what meat would be offered most frequently during the meal. He informed me tonight's tasting menu consisted mostly of fish and shellfish.

"Why don't we start with white? If we feel we need something with more body, we'll let you know." The maître d' nodded, looked to Jonathan for confirmation, then left. "I like a woman who knows what she wants. Confidence is incredibly sexy. What do you want, River?"

He pulled my napkin from the table, snapped it open, and handed it to me. He repeated the action and laid his napkin on his lap. In seconds, the sommelier was at our table, explaining the highlights of the wine chosen. He poured. Jonathan swirled, smelled, tasted, and nodded before our wine was poured and we were left alone.

All the while, I thought about his question. *What do I want?* "I want a lot of things, Jonathan. First and foremost, I want to have an enjoyable evening."

He handed me my glass of wine and raised his own in a toast. "To a wonderful evening."

We tapped glasses. Our eyes met over the rim of our drinks. Neither of us hurried to put our glass down. It was as if looking over the rim provided insights into the other person. I studied his eyes. They were the color of Turkish coffee, with flecks of amber spread throughout. His skin was smooth, with the exception of the shadow on the lower third of his face. I was tempted to reach up and run my hand across his chin to see if the slight growth was rough to the touch or if the shadow only created that illusion. My eyes fell to his lips, which looked soft and succulent.

Lost in my inspection, I didn't realize he had tabled his glass of wine. He sat silently, letting me inspect his features. Blushing, I took another sip and set my glass in front of me.

"Is purple your favorite color?" His hand slid over the shoulder of my amethyst gown.

"No, but I like it. I like bold colors. They're more indicative of my personality. I've never been a fan of pastels. They seem to be boring—uninspired colors. It's almost as if they were trying to be the fully pigmented color but fell short." I paused momentarily. I didn't want to bore him. He smiled gently and tilted his head to the side, and I took that as a gesture to keep going. "I'm not one to fall short. I may fall down, fall over, or fall flat on my face, but I will never fall short. I'll always get back up and move forward. Pastel colors are quitters. That, I'll never be."

He kept his eyes forward, completely focused on me. Sandra told me to be authentic. That I could be. My answer was honest and upfront. He could read into it what he wanted, but it was the essence of who I was. He should know right away. We were forging a relationship of sorts, and those never went well if formed on pretense.

"I like your candor. You would be surprised at how many women are afraid to be themselves. I like that you know who you are. Many women don't, and quite honestly, I don't have the time or inclination to help you find yourself."

I raised my glass and proposed a toast to authenticity. We tapped our glasses and once again studied each other over the rims. The soft wrinkles around his eyes didn't make him look old. They made him look wise. When he smiled, they smiled with him. Those lines reinforced his emotions. The eyes rarely lied. Apparently, wrinkles didn't either.

The waiter brought our first course. It was a mix of pearl tapioca, oysters, and caviar. They called it Oysters and Pearls, and it was amazing. Being a fan of oysters, this little morsel was heaven on Earth.

Jonathan watched me as I savored the pearls of tapioca and let the oysters slide down my throat. Either he was not a fan of oysters or he got more enjoyment from watching me eat than eating himself. His plate of oysters sat untouched.

The next course came right away. It was a bay scallop on polenta. They called it Tsar's Caviar. I took a bite of my scallop and moaned. How they got the outside crisp and kept the inside delicate showed the cook had a skillset that rivaled a Michelin Star chef. I'd never been able to cook scallops. They ended up turning into rubber pucks.

"Are you going to eat or just watch me eat?" I asked.

He sipped his wine and glanced over the rim. He didn't say a word, didn't smile, and didn't frown. He watched, and for some reason having his full attention pleased me.

I scooped a perfect mix of scallop and polenta on my fork and lifted it to his mouth. His eyes grew wide. It dawned on me that my action was something generally shared by two people in an intimate relationship. He opened his mouth, and I slid the bite inside. His lips covered my fork and slipped slowly past the tines. My eyes focused on their ruby color. His tongue darted across them as I stared openly. Talk about chemistry. How lucky was I to feel something for the first man I met? I watched for any sign he felt the same way. He appeared to be intrigued. It was the only reason I could give for his constant staring. A warm flush raced through my body and sat between my legs. I could have sex with this man without a second thought.

"What do you like, River?"

His questions were always so open-ended. I liked a lot of things, like rainbows and daffodils, milk chocolate, and puppies. But again, I felt as if this were some sort of test. Jonathan Ferris wasn't a man of many words, yet he seemed intrigued with me and seemed to want to know more. Not quite knowing how to answer, I decided to again simply be me.

"My tastes are varied, so what do you want to know specifically?" I waited, wondering if the subject of sex would come up. Was this his way of finding out what I was into? I pushed our little plates to the side and twisted to face him. I was all in when it came to this conversation.

"I just wanted to know what makes you tick. Why finance?" Oh, he wanted to know my career aspirations, not whether I liked it rough or from behind.

"I come from a poor family. My father's work required that he gave everything he had. We lived a simple life, and I always felt if my father had managed the money better, he could have provided for us better. Don't get me wrong, we had the necessities, but I always wanted more." There was no shame in wanting more.

"I'm the king of wanting more," he said. I waited for him to elaborate, but he didn't. He watched me and waited. The way he looked at me made me feel like the third course.

"I want control over my life, and smart finances are the way to go about it." I wished I could have said my choices had always been smart, but my sixty-two thousand dollars of debt said differently.

"Your emphasis will be on finance, then?"

The waiter delivered course three, and I was a bit disappointed it wasn't me. I would have happily lain on a plate and let him lick food off my tines.

Focus.

"Yes, I want to do estate planning and financial management." The plate in front of me contained a tiny salad of grapes, kale, and olives drizzled in light pepper vinaigrette. This time, he took his fork and fed me. I had no idea why this thrilled me, but having him place a bite in my mouth felt nourishing on so many levels.

"I can help you attain your goals. I'm in the perfect position to lend support."

And here it was. He would trade his services for my services. This was what it was all about, right? He surprised me when he poured us another glass of wine and changed the subject.

"So, if purple isn't your favorite color, what is?" His index finger swirled across the back of my hand. Goosebumps sprung along the surface of my arms. He would have to be blind not to see them.

"Oh, that's a tough one. My closet is full of red, so I suppose I might lean toward red, but I love bold blues like sapphire and azure. How about you?"

"I'm your basic blue guy, but I also like bold colors. They convey power." He lifted his crimson-colored tie. Silk. Not the kind you got at JC Penney, but the kind you got at Bergdorf Goodman.

"River, is this the first time you've done a job like this?" Direct. I liked that.

"Yes, I was recruited on Monday by a friend, and here I am. Why?"

"You exude sex appeal, which gives you the air of experience, and yet I get the feeling you're trying to figure this all out for the first time."

Bingo. The man was very in tune to everything, from people to his surroundings. I imagined it was those observation skills that helped him achieve his success.

I didn't know if I exuded sex appeal, but since that was the second time I'd heard it today, there must have been some truth to it.

"I have no idea what I'm doing. Right now, I'm having a lovely dinner with a man who intrigues me. Short of that, I'm winging it."

His laugh was full-bodied. The crinkles in the corners of his eyes were fully committed. He looked happily handsome.

"You are fresh and fun, River, I like you. What are you so intrigued by?"

"Your lips." The words spilled out. "I keep wondering if they are as soft and supple as they look."

Leaning in, he pressed his full lips against mine. Soft and pliant, his lips covered my own. He didn't press hard, but he let his lips hover against mine for a languid, soft, nipple-hardening minute.

He leaned back. My hand came to my lips. "Wow." His lips were everything I imagined them to be and more.

"What else intrigues you?" I watched his finger trace the rim of his glass. I listened to see if it would start humming.

"About you, or in general?"

"Anything."

The waiter brought course four.

Duck Foie Gras.

I pondered his question for a moment. "Who do you think decided to cook liver and charge a small fortune for it?"

"A genius. I love this stuff." He slid his fork into the delicate meat and lifted it to his mouth. His audible moan made my insides coil. All I could think about was recreating that sound in bed. I *was* a total whore.

Course five consisted of lobster with leeks, carrots, and watercress sprinkled with bordelaise.

Course six was grilled salmon.

Pork jowls with Yukon gold potatoes in korma curry sauce was served next.

Course eight was a veal medallion with maitake mushrooms and a cabernet reduction.

Our date was coming to an end, and that saddened me. In-between the small parcels of mouthwatering food, Jonathan's appeal grew. He was witty, charming, and enchanting. He didn't seem to mind my humor, and I felt...comfortable. Surprisingly so. How I hoped he would check *yes* on his chemistry sheet.

I wanted to see him again. I was going to log in to complete mine right away. In fact, I would do it on the way home. It was sad that I would have to see other men, as Jonathan was so perfect for me. I reminded myself that this wasn't a traditional date. How many times would I have to think it to believe it?

"What are you so deeply in thought about? I can see the cogs turning in your head." He pushed the empty plates to the edge of the table and poured more wine into our glasses, giving me the largest portion.

"I was just curious about a few things." I sipped the wine while the waiter set a plate of assorted bite-sized desserts in front of us.

"What do you want to know? I am happy to answer anything within reason."

Should I ask the questions that floated in my head? Somehow, they didn't seem like first encounter inquiries. "I'm sitting here thinking about why a nice guy, who has amazing lips, needs a girl like me?"

His facial expression turned from a look of contentment to a mask of indifference.

"I was married and lost my wife to cancer several years ago. She was irreplaceable. I don't want the entanglements of a relationship. I'm not interested in pleasing a woman in every aspect of her life. I'm not interested in experiencing the kind of pain I felt when Claire died in my arms."

Well, if I had any notion this was a relationship, I was just schooled. Whatever this was…it would never be more than a business arrangement.

"I'm sorry to hear about your wife. Being the child of a pastor, I've had a front row seat to grief."

"Pastor's daughter? Holy hell. Wow, I didn't expect that."

Me neither. I didn't expect the details of my life to spill out of my mouth. It just goes to show you that wine loosens lips and hips. In spite of everything, all I wanted was to kiss him again.

"Yep. I'm a real saint." I twirled my finger around my head like a halo.

His suppressed laugh shook his shoulders as it escaped like bursts of steam from a pressure cooker. Once on simmer, he continued. "What was the other thing you were curious about?"

I didn't tell him I was curious as to whether he would choose me. The concept was moot. He either would, or he wouldn't. In the end, it didn't matter; it was a job. The more I repeated that, the more likely I would believe it.

"I was wondering if you'd be kissing me goodnight?"

Chapter 7

His eyes widened, and the intake of a quick breath told me another kiss was something he too craved. He walked me to the car and kissed me senseless. My lips parted, and his tongue dove in to sweep my mouth. It ended much too soon.

He slid me into the back seat of the car and sent me on my way. I pulled out my phone and pressed *yes* next to his profile. In fact, I would have said *hell yes* if it had allowed me. The man made my body vibrate for his touch. The sizzle he created had caused a fire to burn between my legs.

I headed straight home and enjoyed the power and efficiency of a Hitachi Wand and a 110 outlet.

I showered and readied myself for bed. My next encounter would come early. I already didn't like him because he was an early bird. Early birds may get the worm, but who wanted a worm?

I glanced at my work phone to see if Jonathan had filed his review. It was really just a notification that said the client felt positive about the encounter and would like to seek future meetings. My phone remained blank. Maybe I scared him off. Sadly, I could see myself having enjoyable encounters with him.

MARK PLANK MET me at the corner bistro by my house. It wasn't the amazing dinner I'd had with Jonathan, but it was bearable. He was the CEO of Usatrade, a large stock exchange company that oversaw the trading platforms for small investors. His work was interesting, and he loved to talk about it. As an escort, I would have to learn to be an excellent listener. After the first hour of him talking about how stupid small investors could be, I was full. Full of breakfast, full of discussion, and full of Mark Plank's bullshit. It was sad that after an hour, I'd already met my limit. I stared at the man, trying to find one redeeming quality that would allow me to lie with him. When I started counting deductions instead of adding assets, I decided he wasn't a good investment of my time. We parted after an hour, and I immediately filed my time and checked *no* to his profile.

Lunch was with Paul Yoder. Paul was charming and took me to a posh cafe outside of the Rockefeller Center. We chatted for two hours about his job as the Chief Risk Officer for a leading Wall Street trader. Paul was nearly bald, but his blue eyes sparkled with delight when we discussed movies and music. I watched his hands throughout the date. Nicely groomed nails and soft-skinned palms would feel nice exploring my body. He gave me a peck on the lips before telling me he hoped we would have an opportunity to see one another again. I tapped in *yes* on his profile and headed home. A girl could do worse. She could have to listen to Mark Plank bore her to death for hours.

Dinner was a fancier affair. I met Donald Zane at Shun Lee Palace. We feasted on crispy duck and sautéed prawns with vegetables. We discussed his job as the CFO of Globe Tech. Although not a traditional job in Wall Street, his job was interesting and I listened with fascination. I would say he was in his early sixties, but he was in decent shape. He had a pleasant personality and good manners. He gave me a peck on the cheek before he said goodbye. I checked *yes* to his profile and readied myself for the next day.

Sunday morning, Stan Driver and I met for breakfast. We enjoyed omelets at the little cafe in Central Park. His eyes were the color of dark chocolate. They were similar to Jonathan's but lacked the amber chips that gave them softness. I found myself wanting to check my phone all morning. So far, Jonathan had not responded to my profile, and I wondered why. I left the park and checked *no* to Stan. In all fairness, I wasn't engaged in the conversation and felt he didn't get a fair shake, but in the end my interest waned, and I couldn't imagine being with a man who had eyes that reminded me of another.

Lunch was spent with Carl Schaeffer, asshole extraordinaire. He was a man so full of himself, there wasn't room for anyone else. His red, bulbous nose was an indication of a heavy drinker, and his bad temper flared when the waitress spilled water on the table. It took me two seconds to send my *no*.

By Sunday night, I was exhausted and hadn't spread my legs once. The preparation for these dates was taxing.

I was afraid I would sprout hairs, but thankfully none had been brave enough to break through the skin. The thought of my next waxing made me shudder in fear.

Dinner was a laid-back affair at a small steakhouse on 46th Street. Ben Daniels and I ate filets and discussed politics. As the owner of a lucrative financial planning company called Masterplan, he now spent more time golfing and fundraising than he did at the office. He was a pleasant companion and a true gentleman. Although he appeared younger, I would have guessed his age to be somewhere in his seventies. He put me in a taxi after our meeting, and I typed in *yes* to his profile. I didn't know what sex would be like with him, but he had the ability to charm the pants off me.

I checked my phone several times throughout the day. I was happy to find Mark Plank felt the same way about me. His name disappeared from my account, indicating he had removed himself as a candidate. The rest of the men claimed to want to pursue something further.

Requests were coming in for second meetings, but I hadn't confirmed any yet. I was flattered so many men were interested and saddened because Jonathan didn't seem to be. I had hoped he would be my first encounter. It looked like I would have to remove him from my list and consider the remaining options. I wanted my first to be a good experience, as I believed the first encounter would set the precedent for all others.

I finished my last three meetings for the week on Monday. Craig Hagen was a yes, Tom Silian was a no, and Hugh Baxter was a definite no. Anyone who came to a meeting with food in his teeth and smelling like a sweaty prizefighter was not getting up in my goodies.

SCHOOL STARTED TUESDAY. Jade and I met for coffee before class. She looked tired but happy.

"Let me see your wrists." I grabbed her arms and looked for ligature marks.

"What the hell?" She pulled her arms back and laughed. "They never leave marks that *you* can see." A twinkle sparkled in her eyes.

"So, you really were tied up." I tried to call her several times, but her phone went directly to voicemail. I could have used some advice but managed to waffle through it on my own.

"How's it going?"

"Excellent. I've had several meetings, ten to be exact. I have about a fifty percent pass rate, but I haven't scheduled my first sexual encounter. I really liked my first meeting and was hoping he would be the one to bust my cherry, but he hasn't responded to our first meeting. He may not feel like we had chemistry."

"Your cherry was busted by Tommy Baldwin during our junior year. I stole the condoms from my brother's drawer for you." Jade sipped her latte and wiped the foam from her lips.

"You know what I mean."

"Yep, and let go of any notion that these men are after more than a dip in your snatch. Pick one and get it over with. Go home and cry and then bury it away. In two years, you'll be set."

I swore my vagina clenched shut. I'd have to separate my brain from my penis flytrap if I were going to get through this. Like any job, it would take time to learn the rules and shortcuts. Taking a deep breath, I decided to take her advice. I scrolled through my invites and accepted Paul Yoder's offer to have drinks on Friday. I would deal with Donald Zane's request tomorrow.

"I got it, first encounter is Friday. Drinks are what he offered. I imagine I'm dessert."

We hugged and went our separate ways. I was off to an analytics class. She had yoga. Life was so unfair.

My phone dinged during class. It had to be Paul with the details for our meeting. I silenced it and listened to my professor drone on about something he called data blending.

EXHAUSTED, I waited for the subway. I pulled the phone I'd ignored all day from my purse and scrolled through the messages. Several calls were missed while I was in class.

Paul left a message saying he would meet me at seven. I was to dress for a cocktail party. He told me to bring an overnight bag just in case. I texted him back and told him my schedule didn't allow for an overnight at this point. I didn't want to be stuck all night long on my first encounter. I might need a good cry, and having it in front of my mentor was unthinkable. Several requests had come in for initial meetings. There was also an update to my profile.

My eyes stared at the *yes* next to his profile picture. Finally, Jonathon had indicated interest. Of course, he had. The minute I picked someone else to be my first, he responded. I wondered if the mentors had each other on speed dial. It didn't matter; he was a means to an end. Like Jade said, these men only wanted a socket for their plug. Understanding that fact would save me a lot of heartache in the end. *In the end.* That was a funny thought. I could be getting it there on Friday.

Homework first, and then on to HGTV. Shows where I got to peek into people's homes and lives were my favorite. There was a voyeur in me.

Tired of watching the boob tube, I headed for the shower. The hot water cleared my head. All that managed to consume my thoughts were the feelings I experienced from a particular kiss. My mind kept going back to Jonathan. His kiss had made my core clench. Nope, I couldn't go there. If he called me right now and asked if I would go out tomorrow, I'd say no. To let an arrogant man have the upper hand would be stupid.

I shivered outside the shower, racing to dry my damp skin so I could climb into bed.

As if summoned, a message flashed across my screen. My heart raced, and my hands shook. I chanted *no* in my head. *No. No. No.*

River, are you available for dinner tomorrow night? I was thinking Japanese. Can I pick you up at seven?

J

He ended the message with a J, as if I was supposed to know who he was. Arrogant.

No. No. No.

My chant went on and on. I set my phone on the counter, picked it up, set it down, picked it up, and then I typed.

Jonathan,

That sounds lovely.

R

Chapter 8

"Cancel the arrangement, River." Jade's voice reverberated with authority. She looked around the coffee shop and whispered, "He's trouble for you."

Why was she acting so strange? I thought she would be happy my first paid lay would be with someone who didn't make my skin crawl. Instead, she acted like I was committing a horrible sin. "What? No. This is my first paid encounter, and I feel comfortable with him."

"That's the problem. This is your first experience, and you should be scared shitless, but you're not. You're acting like this is a first date. This is no date. This is a business transaction, period. Get that through your head." She may have been whispering, but the tone of her voice was serious. Take-no-prisoners serious. Ebola serious.

"I get it. Don't be pissed at me because my first encounter will be with a nice, handsome man who just happens to be a good kisser. Hell, he could have the tiniest womb broom around. Would that make you feel better? He doesn't make me want to puke, and that should count for something." God, I hoped he had some swag in the sack. There had to be a rainbow amidst this storm.

"That's the problem. He already feels too comfortable to you, and that's dangerous. You need to keep your distance. He's not good for you." Even though Jade was present, I could see her mind was being tugged in another direction by the faraway look in her eyes. She had one foot in this conversation, and the other was heading somewhere else.

"Where did you go? All of a sudden, you zoned out." Something was definitely up with her. She arrived looking like a hobo in sweatpants and a university T-shirt. What happened to the put-together girl who dined with me at Smith and Wollensky's, or the girl who met me for coffee yesterday? Where had she disappeared to?

"I was thinking of my first time. It was a 'hit it and quit it.' The experience erased any romantic notions I might have had. I was a commodity he'd purchased. I don't want you to think you're Julia Roberts and Mr. Broom," she giggled at the name she'd given him, "is going to sweep you off your feet. He's not. You're not his first, and you won't be his last."

I understood I wasn't special. I'd been reminded all my life of that fact. "Damn it, you're not listening to me. He made it clear he wasn't looking for a relationship. His exact words were, 'I don't want the entanglements of a relationship. I'm not interested in pleasing a woman in every aspect of her life. Blah, blah, blah.' He waited days to say yes to my profile. I'm not even sure he's really into me." My latte seemed less appealing now that the milk froth had evaporated, but I sipped at it anyway. I'd have to get used to things being less appealing.

"He's into you, or he will be." She graced me with a bright smile, making me feel less stressed. I would have felt more confident if it had reached her eyes. "I'm sorry. I love you, River, and I want this to work out for you. Don't fall for him. It's hard to distinguish between real and fantasy. Don't allow yourself to get hurt."

"I won't."

"Just keep telling yourself it's only sex. These men will never love you. They will love what you give them. Don't forget that."

"Good advice." My eyes fell on her university shirt. "Are you off to the gym, or are you trying to get in touch with your inner waif?" She looked bad.

Not only was she wearing sweats two sizes too big, her shirt was wrinkled and hung off her body. Her hair looked like she hadn't brushed it in days, but instead, she'd pulled it into a messy bun and left the house as if unaware. The mischievous spark that lived in her eyes was gone. She was still pretty, but it would be hard to compare her to the runway goddess she was the last time I saw her. Something was up. She would never leave the house looking like a street urchin.

"I'm tired. I had a rough night. My body and mind are exhausted." Her lips pressed together into a thin line, glued shut like she was trying to stop from saying something else.

"How is the dynamic duo?" Giving her boys a name made them real and gave me a way to ask questions without breaking protocol.

"Good, except that they are now more dynamic and not always a duo." A tear slipped from her eye, confirming she was holding back.

"It's time to come clean, Jade. I know you can't divulge names, but what the hell is going on? You look like Lindsay Lohan after a stint in prison. Pull yourself together and spill."

"Everything is all right. The dynamics of my agreement have changed. I thought I was signing up for one thing, and now it's different." The tear running down her cheek wrenched my heart. She had always been the rock of Gibraltar. *My* rock. Today, she was a shadow of her normal self.

"I call bullshit. Listen, I understand about confidentiality, but I'm here. I know your biggest secrets, and I've never told a soul. Now we share this huge thing together and…well…we need to share. Let's talk about the duo. Tomorrow, we can discuss Mr. Broom."

Silence filled the air while she appeared to contemplate my suggestion. She opened her mouth, closed it, opened, closed, and then spoke. "They shared me with someone else last night. I felt hurt and betrayed. I felt like they took our relationship and tossed it aside when they let another man mess with me while they watched. It was humiliating."

"Oh, holy hell, Jade. Is that in your contract?" Not that it mattered. She was a person, and her feelings should have been considered first.

"Yes. No. It's vague. I said I would participate in MMF, which I do with the duo, but my contract is with only one of them. So, he can bring in any other male he wants. He brought in this guy from the club. My duo treats me well. This man didn't. They didn't stop any of it. My ass is on fire from the whip, which is why I'm wearing clothes that fit like a damn tent."

"Oh shit, Jade, are you okay? What club are we talking about? Is this a BDSM thing?" My mind conjured up a dark room full of whips, paddles, and bondage equipment. I had no idea she was into kink. Maybe I didn't know her secrets like I thought I did.

"Yes, my mentor is a Dom, his partner is a sub. I'm a sub. I spend my public life wielding control over everything, but in the bedroom, I want to let go. I've always loved the power exchange, until last night. The power wasn't exchanged with someone I knew and trusted. I gave it up to a stranger, and it was a huge mistake."

My throat tightened at her response. It was hard for me to wrap my head around the situation. I only knew the strong kick-ass girl. I didn't know this broken woman in front of me.

"Have you always been attracted to the lifestyle?"

"Yes. Do you remember Colin Brown?"

"Yes." Wow. No hesitation whatsoever. Do I remember him? Who could forget him? He had the look of a serial killer in training. Hard. Cold. Relentless.

"He was my first. He would take me behind the gym and spank me before he screwed me against the wall. I loved it. I loved the loss of control, and I loved the sting. I loved the risk. It's been a thing all these years. I'm sorry I didn't share, but how do you tell your closest friend that you like men to slap your ass? Especially when her father is your pastor?"

We shared so many secrets; why would this one be any different? Another negative for growing up in a religious family. No one confided in you.

"You could have told me. I would have understood. Tell me now."

"My mentor wanted training on a particular implement, so he brought a master in to teach him. A lot of time was spent in instruction while I hung from the hooks in the ceiling. Look at my wrists." She pulled the long-sleeved T-shirt up her arm to reveal dark purple bruises encircling her wrists.

She winced as I held her hands and caressed the bracelets caused by bruising. "Shit, Jade, was there no safe word?" I'm not into BDSM, but I've read enough to know there should be a safe word.

"Yes, I refused to use it. I didn't want to disappoint the duo. They're important to me."

And there it was, the look that said it all. I'd seen that look before, but not since her sophomore year of college when she fell for that Italian exchange student, Paolo Bianchi. It had torn her to shreds when he returned to Italy.

She was in love. She loved her duo…and that was why she was adamant I didn't make the same mistake. *She* had broken her cardinal rule. Damn it.

"They need to take better care of you. Have you discussed it with them? Certainly, they can't repeat what they did. Did they let the man have you sexually?" So many questions ran through my head and out of my mouth.

"No, they let him have me mentally, which is worse. He didn't screw me; he screwed with my brain." Her shaking hands pulled back and wiped the tears that spilled down her face.

It was easy to overlook vulnerability when someone seemed so strong, but in that moment, Jade needed someone to recognize she was fragile and weak. I slid into the booth next to her and cradled her head against my chest. She winced when I rubbed her back. If her wrists were the color of eggplants, I could only imagine what her ass and back looked like. I made a note to myself to remove bondage, spanking, *and* restraints from my list. The thought of physical pain held no appeal.

Her tears ran freely. I hoped she could cry her anguish loose and find the tough girl who had been buried behind her sequestered tears. In the back of my head, many things became clear. Jade needed an ally, and her warnings to me about becoming attached came from her personal experiences. I was grateful she brought me on board, if only to support her.

"I'm sorry. I must be pre-menstrual. I'm not normally this emotional. We met this morning because you had questions about your first encounter. Let's talk about it."

And just like that, Jade turned back into the confident, no-nonsense woman I knew. I considered asking her to talk more about last night but realized she needed to feel in control. Advising me would give her something to focus her attention on.

"He's picking me up at seven, and we—"

"He's picking you up? Don't tell me he has your address. I'm such a shitty tutor. Never let them know where you live unless they're paying for your home. You don't want them showing up on your doorstep at all hours of the night. You take a cab. They can pay for it, but never let them get that close. Do you understand?" Possibly considering me reprimanded for my stupidity, she continued, "Obviously, Mr. Broom will know where you live, but don't let anyone else pick you up or send for you."

"Okay, duly noted." There was so much I needed to know, but something told me I would learn from trial and error.

"They can put their card on file at a car service. It's too risky. One night, you'll come home and find him drunk on your doorstep." She waved her hand between our faces as if she were shooing away a fly. "All right, enough of that. Where are you going?" Jade was back in control.

"Dinner, and then I don't know." He said sushi, but he didn't give me any details.

"Is it hourly, or the entire night?" She seemed to gain strength with every question.

"I don't know." It occurred to me how little I actually did know.

"You need to pry them for more details. The easy way to do that is to tell them you want to be prepared for anything. Ask if you'll need an overnight bag. Ask if you'll need a swimsuit. If they say yes, chances are it's a hotel with a hot tub or pool. What about condoms?"

"They're on my list. How many should I bring?"

"I never leave with less than six, especially if it's an overnight." Slack-jawed, I stared at her. My mind tried to process the information. Six? Who could go six rounds? "I know what you're thinking, it shows in your wide-open mouth, but three or four is average for an overnight, and if they take the little blue pill, they might be able to go all night."

I couldn't imagine going at it three or four times a night. Wouldn't a girl get dry and sore? "What about lube? Will I need it?" If properly motivated, my body slicked up like an oil-covered road in a rainstorm, but that took the right set of circumstances. Circumstances wouldn't be ideal in these situations. I'd definitely need lube.

"Will you? I can't answer that, but guys love it if they think you're wet for them, so inserting a bit of Astroglide inside before you head out the door will always be received well."

"I never thought of that." Clearly, I wouldn't need it with Jonathan, as he made me wet just thinking about his kisses.

"You'll go to dinner, then he'll take you somewhere and you'll do what you get paid to do. Wednesdays will be hard for you because you have Thursday classes. Keep that in mind when you schedule yourself. On the other hand, you can request a hotel close to campus so you can sleep in. You'll have to figure out a balance."

I stared out the window as I contemplated her words and watched people pass by. Not one person out there knew my vagina had become a rental property. A recent article I read indicated that one in five college students turned to the sex trade to help cover college costs. I scanned the crowd and tried to figure out who the twenty percent were. My motivation to enter the sex trade was singularly focused. The top priority was getting through school and chipping away at my student debt. What did Jade say? In two years, I'd be set. I wondered if the experience would change me. It was impossible to say at this juncture, but I couldn't imagine there wouldn't be lasting effects.

Jade reverted back to quiet contemplation. Her situation was disturbing on so many levels. First, she had been on this journey for months alone. Second, someone physically hurt her, and her mentors did nothing to protect her. Wasn't it their job to know her limits when she was not in a place to set her own? Third, she seemed a bit broken, and it scared me.

"What will you do about your situation, Jade? Will you stay with the duo?" She glared at me with a shocked expression.

"Of course. It was my fault. I'm angry with them for not stopping the situation, but I'm angry at myself because I held all the power and didn't use it. My ass is sore because I was hardheaded and stubborn."

She saw the almost imperceptible shaking of my head and frowned. "They had a responsibility to ensure your safety. I don't pretend to understand the D/s relationship, but I do know they failed you. You can be angry at me for saying so, but I don't care." I hated hearing her make excuses for them. The situation pissed me off.

"I'm not angry at you. I'm angry with myself. I let them change me. Don't let anyone change you, River."

Trying to lighten up the moment, I made a suggestion. "Why don't we get some Arnica cream, and I'll rub it on your ass? Let's go."

Her laugh filled the air. What once seemed heavy now seemed light and airy. "You would rub Arnica on my ass?" She gingerly slid out of the booth and hugged me.

"Of course. You're my best friend, and it's how we roll. Besides, I may need you to tweeze the errant hairs that have grown back between my legs."

Laughter continued to roll from us as we exited the coffee shop arm in arm. It was a well-needed and cathartic release for both of us. Despite my attempt at confidence, this was all so new to me, and I felt out of my depth.

Chapter 9

He said his favorite color was blue. I dressed for him. Would he notice? Would he care? Silver sandals were the perfect pairing for the navy blue dress I wore. My garter belt held the silk thigh highs Erica insisted I own. Twenty pairs came in the Bloomingdales delivery.

The lace undergarments felt soft against my skin. I always thought I bought nice undies. However, I'd never known lace to feel so exquisite. Usually, it itched and chafed my skin, but this lace caressed me.

There was something about having sexy lingerie under my clothes that boosted my confidence. Sex appeal oozed from every pore when I knew everything was the best it could be, from my hair to my underwear.

Visions of Jade's tear-swollen eyes helped to control my excitement. As I curled my hair and applied my makeup, I told myself repeatedly this wasn't a date, but a job. It would never be anything but a business transaction. Coating my lashes with a final layer of mascara, I wondered how many times Jade had told herself that *before* she fell in love?

I quickly sent her a message to say I loved her and was here if she needed me.

The buzz of the intercom silenced my thoughts. With a quick glimpse in the mirror, I gave myself a once-over before I answered the call.

"Hello." My voice sounded tentative and shy. A rumbling in my stomach felt more like a flock of birds than a handful of butterflies. This was it. Tonight, my life would change.

"It's me. Shall I come up and get you, or should I wait here?" His voice was like velvet sliding across every cell of my body. A lover's stroke without a touch. That's what he did to me.

Surprised it wasn't his driver again, I looked around my messy apartment and answered, "No, I'll be right down."

Condoms hung from the edge of my small bag. I tucked them deeply into the clutch. I was packing light. Given what I witnessed at the coffee shop today, an overnight experience wouldn't be wise for a first encounter. I didn't know this man. I only knew he made my insides tingle, and it wouldn't take an entire night to scratch that itch.

The elevator descended slowly, the wall-to-wall mirrors providing a full body view. Erica outdid herself with this dress. The scoop neck made it appear conservative. The back was obscene, but in a high-class vogue way. It was runway beautiful. The V cut down to my butt crack. No bra required. The dress had built in reinforcements so the back could be bare. A silver scarf hung over my arm just in case it got cold.

The ding of the elevator announced my arrival. My heart was running a marathon, my legs felt stuck in glue. When the doors slid open, Jonathan stood in front of me, dressed impeccably in a three-piece suit. He looked like he left the boardroom and came straight here. His eyes widened as I exited the elevator, but it was the roll of his tongue across his plump lower lip that told me he liked what he saw. My confidence soared while my anxiety fled.

"Wow." One word, and the strip of fabric between my legs was soaked. "Stunning."

I was so pleased with his response. My skin tingled in anticipation. I couldn't wait until he saw the back of this dress.

"You're looking very dapper yourself. I love the vest, and this gold tie is perfect." My hand brushed up his chest to straighten the knot at his neck. His hand folded around mine. He lifted it and gently rubbed his soft lips across my knuckles, causing a quiver to course through my body.

"Shall we go? Howard is waiting outside."

His eyes scanned the lobby. I'm not living large by any means. The only redeeming quality to this building was its security. Side by side, we walked to the door. He reached past me to open it and then stood back to let me pass. I swear he growled as I slid in front of him, exposing the back of my body from neck to bottom. Powerful—that's how I felt in that moment.

Howard stood with the door open. I moved across the back seat and waited for Jonathan to follow. He spoke to Howard for a few minutes before he climbed in and sat next to me. I looked past him and saw Howard on the phone.

"Change of plans; you look entirely too lovely for sushi. How about La Grenouille? It's close to our hotel."

Hotel. So, we were going to a hotel. What had I expected? He certainly wasn't going to bend me over a trash can in the alley and take me from behind. At least I hadn't considered it going down like that. I suppose anything was possible.

"That sounds great. Sushi sounded great. Isn't it hard to get reservations last-minute at these places? How did you ever get us into Per Se?"

I told Jade about our first meeting at Per Se, and she nearly fell over. There was a four-month wait if you were somebody. A nobody could wait forever. Obviously, Jonathan was more of a somebody than I thought.

"It's a lot easier when you hold the future of their finances in your hands. I find a lot of doors open when you're juggling people's money."

"That makes sense. Money is a powerful tool." I would probably go out with Jonathan even if he weren't paying me. For other girls, his money would have probably been the lure. Hell, who was I kidding? His money was what got us together. In what lifetime would I have had the opportunity to hang out with a man of his wealth and stature? Never. Dressed in my Forever 21 jeans and H & M T-shirts, he would have never given me a second glance. Tonight would be my first real lesson in the buying and selling of commodities.

"Money, used for the right purposes, is a powerful tool. Put in the wrong hands, it's a dangerous weapon. Don't forget that. And while we are speaking of dangerous, *never* give your address to a client. It's not smart." He had a drill sergeant quality to his voice. A tone I wouldn't argue with.

I pinched my mouth shut. I would love to find a comical retort, but he was right. I wasn't thinking, and I had put myself at risk. Thank God he appeared to be a good guy. "You are the only one who has my address," I said quietly.

"Good. You can trust me, River. I won't be camping out on your doorstep."

Did he talk to Jade? They sounded like a song on repeat. Sadly, the thought of him camping out on my doorstep sounded appealing.

THE CAR CAME to a stop in front of the restaurant on 52nd Street. The heat of his hand scalded my back as he helped me exit and led me upstairs to the posh French restaurant. Just like Per Se, the staff knew him by sight. We were taken to a table tucked in a dark corner. The flicker of the candle danced across his gold tie. King Midas came to mind as I watched it sparkle in the light. Everything Midas touched turned to gold; when Jonathan touched me, I turned to liquid. He offered the maître d' what appeared to be folded bills before he sat next to me. His hand glided over my knee and settled on my thigh. My breath hitched. Prickles of sensation pinged through me. My nipples hardened, and my thighs quivered under his touch.

"Wine?"

"Yes."

"Red or white?"

"You choose."

With a single brain cell left, I couldn't choose anything to save my life. Why was this man's touch so intense? Was it the forbidden circumstances that surrounded us? Was it my lack of recent sexual partners? My senior year kicked my ass. I didn't have much time for a social life. The homework nearly killed me. I certainly didn't have time for men.

The waiter delivered and poured us a glass of red. We perused the menu. Jonathan chose some kind of beef, and I selected the lamb chops. Dinner was the last thing on my mind when his hand gently caressed my thigh.

"How was school yesterday?" Talk about out of left field.

"Good, although it's hard to get back in the swing of things. I have a full load, but I'm piling them into two days. So, Tuesday and Thursdays are devoted to education. I have this analytics class that will more than likely bore me to death. Do you know Professor Pollard?"

"Professor Ralph Pollard? Yes, the man's a genius. Pay attention to him. If you can forecast financial trends, you can write your check at any company. Trends are important because, like history, everything repeats. It's the smart ones who know when to jump on board, and when to pass. If you want to manage portfolios, then analytics should be your bedmate."

"How about you be my bedmate, and I'll solicit advice from the master?"

His hand crept under the edge of my dress to caress higher on my thigh. He was distracting me, and my filter was gone. I'd just asked him to sleep with me in exchange for inside information.

"Being my bedmate is a given, River. As for information, I'm your mentor, and I will guide you, but I won't give you an edge. You will earn what you get, as far as your career is concerned. You can use your body to get you in the door, but only your brain will keep you there."

I loved that he was direct, as it cleared up a few things for me. I would get in a door somewhere, but once there, I was on my own, and I was good with that. I would never want to be accused of sleeping my way to the top. I would have to figure out how I felt about being accused of sleeping with the top to get my foot in the door. Once I graduated, no one would ever know what I did to get a ticket to the party. I could see why all ties were broken after graduation.

"I'm not asking for an edge; merely a chance. How was your week?" My snarky inner bitch took over my thoughts. *Yeah, Jonathan, how was your week? What kept you so busy, you couldn't take the time to push yes on my profile?* I so badly wanted to know why he dragged his feet, but I would never ask. I was happy to be with him—to have him as my first.

"Things were busy. I signed a few new clients and played golf with a few long-term patrons. I went to a charity auction for disabled veterans. Speaking of which, are you free Saturday? I need a plus one for an event. It's a crazy opera mixed with an art auction. I'm not a big fan of opera, so I need a distraction while I'm forced to sit through the event. I have a private box." His look was so seductive, it made me press my thighs together, trapping his hand between them. His chuckle sent a blush to my face. I could feel the heat of my embarrassment warm my cheeks.

"I'm free Saturday and would love to be your distraction."

I released his hand from between my legs. Instead of pulling it free, he slipped it between the juncture of my thighs. My initial thought was how mortified I was to be soaked with arousal, but I remembered Jade's words this morning about men loving that you got wet for them.

A sexy, slow smile spread across his face as he pulled my panties to the side and dragged his fingers through my heated flesh. Painfully slow, he circled my bundle of nerves with deliberation. I'd never had public sex, but I could see myself spreading my legs and falling back to let this man take me. Everything he did was with control and purpose. The power I felt before was gone. His fingers controlled the situation.

The arrival of the waiter stopped the exquisite torture. As Jonathan's plate was set in front of him, he pulled his hand free and licked his finger. The man licked his finger like it was a delicacy. He didn't wipe my arousal on his napkin, but rather he savored my moisture like it was caviar. Was it possible to come from simply watching a sinfully sexual man lick my essence from his fingers? If so, I was almost there.

When the waiter left, we stared at our plates.

"Eat up, Princess, you're going to need your strength."

Without a glance in my direction, he sliced into his medallions of beef. I stared at my lamb chops and wondered how I was going to get through dinner. My ravenous appetite had nothing to do with food.

"Is Saturday's affair formal? If so, I will have to shop for something appropriate."

I should get paid on Friday, so getting a dress for Saturday shouldn't be too much of a problem. I knew of a few places I could shop. Maybe the consignment shop on Madison would have something appropriate. My mind ran through my options.

"Who's your personal shopper?" He sipped his wine and scanned my body. I had a body made for men's pleasures. *And* it seemed Jonathan liked the full-bodied woman. Lucky me.

"I'll have her send you some options."

He set his glass down and brought his hand to cup my face. His eyes sparkled, but I didn't know if it was passion, reverence, or mischief behind his look. I didn't know him well enough. Any conclusion would be a guess at this point.

"I don't need you to do that. I'm capable of coming up with something appropriate. I just needed to know the details." Why did I ask? I could have googled the event and looked up the dress code. I certainly wasn't trying to get him to buy me something to wear.

"River, it's my job to make sure you're prepared for whatever I throw at you. This won't be the last formal event we attend together. You have enough to worry about with school, so you don't need to add shopping to your list. I'll take care of this. It's my pleasure to spoil you. I hope you return the favor when we're alone."

Soft lips pushed against mine. The kiss lingered for minutes. He had kissed the fight out of me. Who was I to argue if this man wanted to dress and undress me?

"I want to go," I said breathlessly. His mouth traced my jaw to my ear.

"You haven't eaten. Eat, and then we'll discuss dessert."

Disappointed, I hung my head slightly and whispered, "I thought I was dessert."

His roar of laughter surprised me. "River, you and I are going to be amazing together. Now eat. I wasn't joking when I said you were going to need your energy."

Jade's statement about three to four times being the norm repeated in my head. Oh hell, I would need to eat. I sliced into my perfectly cooked lamb chops and savored the first bite.

"I have to confess, I googled you. It said you lived on Center Island. How is that commute every day? I can't imagine trying to get in and out of the city during rush hour." Mundane conversation was how I would get through dinner.

"You googled me? Good. It's important to find out all you can about a person you do business with. Did it say I own a property in the city as well?" He slid his fork into the creamy potatoes and placed the bite into his mouth. I was obsessed with his mouth and lips. I felt jealous of the damn fork.

"No, it just mentioned you had a house on Long Island, and I thought about your commute."

He shook his head. "That's what I like about you. There are so many other things you could focus on, and you worry about my commute. I like that. I offered to buy you a dress, and you try to fight me on it. You're not typical."

"What's typical?" It was probably not a question I wanted to know the answer to, but I couldn't stop myself from asking.

"Girls who enter this type of service say they need help with school, but they get drawn in by the money, and often their focus changes. I hope you don't change, River. I like you just the way you are."

"Everyone changes, Jonathan. After tonight, I will be forever changed. The question is, how can I remain the same?" The next few bites of lamb chop were eaten, and my wine glass was almost empty.

We ate our dinner and chatted about superficial things like the market and movies and music. As it turned out, we had a lot in common.

He studied me for a few minutes. "I see you didn't bring a bag. From now on, I'll expect you to spend the night. An hour or so with you will not be enough. I'll need time to savor you. What I want from you can't be rushed."

Holy shit. Clench, quiver, and gush. My already wet center was drenched from his words. They were a promise of things to come.

"Okay." My breathy whisper was almost as unrecognizable as my voice. My ability to form a complete sentence was gone.

The waiter was called, the bill was paid, and I was helped to my feet. All I felt was his hand on my bare back leading me to the car. Nothing in-between registered; just the heat of his hand on the small of my back and his lips on mine the minute the car door closed.

"What time is your first class tomorrow?" he asked as he pulled from my lips.

A shake of my head cleared the cobwebs from my brain. He said something about class tomorrow and time. "Ten. Thursday classes are at ten."

"Nice, we have plenty of time to explore each other. Are you okay with moving forward?"

It was a bit late to ask now. The man slid his fingers through my wetness before dinner and set my parts aflame. The rest of the night, I watched his mouth and fantasized about the ways he could make me squirm with that alone. Not once did I think about not moving forward with the night.

"Jonathan, let's be honest. We have this incredible chemistry. It's hot, nearly volcanic. If we don't get to your room fast, I may erupt. Mount St. Helens will look like a puff of smoke compared to how badly I want to let go." Thank God for the divider between Howard and us. I couldn't imagine him listening to our conversation.

"River, spread your legs." I didn't think about disobeying, so I did what he asked. I separated my thighs for him. On his knees before me, he shimmied my blue dress past my hips.

A gasp escaped his mouth the minute my garters and stockings were revealed. In the confines of the restaurant, he didn't get the full experience. Thank goodness for the space a town car provided. Kneeling before me, he buried his head between my legs. The heat of his tongue brushed against my drenched panties. "I've wanted to taste this all night. That little teaser before dinner only made my appetite bigger."

A moan of frustration broke from my lips. I wanted more.

"Jonathan, I need more."

Pulling the wet fabric aside, he assaulted me with his tongue. I had no idea what was hotter—the slip of his tongue across my lips or the plunge of his tongue deep inside me. I had thought his lips were delicious. His tongue was heaven-sent. Then there was the primal growl that escaped his mouth. Hot. Hot. Hot.

Holy. Hell. Heaven-sent might be an understatement. The man's tongue matched his tie. Gold.

Chapter 10

Was the car stopped for a while, or did we just arrive? I wasn't sure. Jonathan straightened my dress and sat back in his seat. A single knock on the blackened window alerted Howard of our intent to exit. The smell of sex filled the air, but there was nothing I could do about that. Taking Jonathan's hand, I followed him into the foyer of the Four Seasons Hotel.

The lobby didn't disappoint. Granite floors that shined with the luster of a diamond and marble pillars that stretched to the sky greeted us. When we approached the front desk, we were greeted by name.

"Good evening, Mr. Ferris, Ms. Roberts. Welcome to the Four Seasons. Your suite is ready. Do you need assistance?"

They knew our names. Jonathan thought of everything. He had made me feel special, not like the girl he was paying to have sex with him, but like a woman who was spending a romantic evening with a wonderful man. Like somehow, I mattered. This alone would change me. The bar was just set higher. How were normal men supposed to compete with this?

"No, we can find our way. Thank you."

With the key in his hand, we walked to the elevator and entered. It zoomed to the fiftieth floor in seconds. My knees were shaking. Not from fear, but from anticipation. His long, slender fingers gripped the key card confidently. As he pushed it into the slot, I imagined all the part As that could go into part Bs. My imagination ran wild.

The door opened into a beautiful suite. Floor-to-ceiling windows framed the Manhattan skyline. The king-sized bed dominated the room. In the living area, a bottle of champagne sat chilling in a bucket of ice on the coffee table. I didn't expect this. I expected a decent room with a bed and bathroom. I imagined the event would be quick and I'd be sent away. I didn't expect the man to care about my pleasure. I didn't expect him to entice me with words like *devour* and *savor*. I expected him to take care of himself. Deep inside, I wanted more, and that was why I needed Jonathan to be my first. Somehow, I knew he would be generous.

The windows drew me in. I dropped my bag and scarf on a chair along my way to them. The bright lights of the city were hypnotic.

"Lovely," he said from behind me as he moved my hair to the side and kissed my neck.

"Yes, it is. The city is quiet and peaceful from the fiftieth floor." My head tilted, giving him better access to that sensitive area between my shoulder and neck.

"No, you're lovely. The skyline has nothing on you." His lips grazed my neck until I shuddered.

"Oh, Mr. Ferris, do you flatter all the women?"

"No, Ms. Roberts. I usually screw other women and move on, but you're special. You deserve more."

I was crushed by his words and buoyed by his intent. He screwed the others, but I was special, so something *was* different about me. Jade's words came to the forefront of my mind.

You are not his first, and you won't be his last.

She was spot on. This wasn't a date. It was business. A transaction —a sale of goods and services.

It was going to be an amazing sexual experience, but that was all it would be for both of us. How special could that be? Only time would tell.

"I wasn't trying to pry into your relationships. It's none of my business."

I needed to keep reminding myself I didn't have a right to information. My rights ended at the door. Thankfully, he didn't appear fazed by the conversation. He continued to worship my neck.

One would think a side zipper would be inconvenient, but the minute he pulled it down, the dress simply fell from my shoulders and pooled on the floor. Standing for all of Manhattan to see, I faced the glass wearing garters, a thong, silk stockings, and heels. Scratch that. With a tug at my side, the thong was torn from my body.

"Damn. You're so beautiful. You have a perfect ass. These," he held my torn panties in front of my face, "won't ever be needed when you're with me. Knowing you're bare for me is a turn on. Next time I bury my face between your legs unexpectedly, I don't want to hit a barrier. Next time we're at a restaurant and I crave a taste of you, I want to be able to slip my fingers inside you and pull your essence from deep down."

His words filled me with heat. Labored breaths fogged the window in front of me. My forehead rested against the cool glass. He skimmed my arms and pulled my hands to press my palms against the glass. He positioned me where he wanted me. My legs were spread. My arms were spread. His hands skimmed my body as he began to speak.

"I will never strike you. I'm not into that. I will have you—sometimes hard and fast, sometimes hard and slow. There are times I will take you for hours, times I will take you quickly. I will always see to your needs first. I find great pleasure in giving pleasure. I don't want to hear of other men. I won't tell you about other women. Tonight, it's just you and me, and not having you immediately will drive me insane." His hands slipped between my legs and floated across me from slit to crack. He stopped on my ass. "Your profile says you do anal. How many times have you done it?"

Panting, I exhaled the word, "Never." His hands pressed between my ass cheeks to touch my tightly puckered flesh.

"Take it off your list. No other man will have this part of you. This belongs to me alone."

His words stunned me. He wanted a part of me to be kept exclusively for him. Was I crazy to be flattered by that? Should I be angry he was setting expectations? Shouldn't I be the one to decide?

His words made me pulse with need, though. I sucked in a breath as he pressed a long finger into my dripping sex. Slow strokes built heat and a second finger joined the first. My legs opened wider on their own. Unbidden moans floated through the air. Were they his or mine? I stood in front of the window for all to see, but the only eyes I cared about were his.

"Jonathan, I need…" I tried to turn, but he held me against the cold, hard glass. My nipples pebbled painfully against the coolness of the window. Need overwhelmed me. The warmth of his body called me. "I need—"

"I know exactly what you need, and I'm going to give it to you again and again. You will feel me until Saturday, when I can sink myself into you again. You may be with others, but it will be me you will remember. It will be my tongue and my dick you will see and feel every time."

Holy shit, the man's an arrogant bastard.

But I had to admit, it was part of what made him so damn sexy. His fingers left me, and I felt empty. I didn't move from the window because that was where he had placed me. The pop of the champagne bottle startled me, and my mouth began to water. The heavy breathing had dried my tongue. His heat snuck up on me, his body pinned mine to the glass. The rigid length of him pressed against me.

"Turn around, River. I want to see all of you."

He stepped back to give me room to spin. My nipples stood erect under his gaze. He sipped his champagne and brought his liquid-filled mouth to my needy breast. Sucking the pink bud inside, the heat of his tongue battled the bubbly frost of the drink. The sensation was incredible. Rumor had it that men drank champagne from women's shoes. I wondered if any had sipped it from their most intimate parts. How would that feel?

My hand found its way to his length. With slow, deliberate movements, I wrapped it around the bulge in his pants and stroked. Growling, he ground himself into my palm. The man was hung. When he said I'd feel him until Saturday, he probably wasn't exaggerating. Relieving him of his glass, I drank the remainder and dropped to my knees. It was time to let this beast loose.

He assisted by pulling his belt free. I worked on his button and zipper. Who would have thought the conservative-looking man in the custom suit went commando? He stepped out of his shoes and pants and stood in front of me in a dress shirt, vest, tie, and jacket. I began to giggle when I looked at the black socks. Humor lit up his eyes when he saw his reflection in the window.

After a good laugh, I focused my attention on his magnificent length. The plush tip of his head had a bead of his desire pooled at the tip. My head tilted back, and my eyes searched his for the answer to the question I refused to ask.

"I'm clean," he said.

I licked the salty goodness that seeped from his tip and slid his length past my lips and into the wet warmth of my mouth. I explored him with my tongue, trying to memorize every dip, every vein. Out of the corner of my eye, I watched articles of clothing hit the floor around me. God, was he big. There was no way I could take him in completely, but I endeavored to try. My hands found their way to his ass. I kneaded the firm globes and pulled him to me, forcing him down my throat. This man could choke a seasoned pro. He backed away and pulled me up to stand in front of him.

My eyes scanned the goods. For forty-two, he was in really good shape. His time on the golf course showed. A lean, muscled torso tapered into narrow hips, strong thighs, and defined calves. When I got to the black socks, I laughed again.

"Get rid of the socks. They're not doing it for me."

"I'll show you what I'll do for you." He quickly pulled off the socks and dove toward me. In one smooth movement, he lifted me over his shoulder and took me to the bed.

I bounced across the top when he released me, coming to stop near the head of the big bed. Dressed in heels, garters, and hose, I felt sexy under his heated gaze. I stared at his body and thanked the heavens he was my first. If the night ended right now, I would walk away feeling positive about the choice I'd made.

My shoes hit the floor one after another. Next to go was the hose, and last, the garter. His eyes ate me alive before he turned and walked away. His firm ass flexed with each step. I lifted up on my elbows, curious to see what he was doing. With champagne-filled glasses in one hand, he walked toward me. Stopping at his trousers, he pulled a condom from his pocket. It struck me as funny how I'd suck him bare, but I would never let him go skin-to-skin inside me.

I never heard the wrapper tear or saw him slide the latex over his length, but he towered over me, dressed in his latex slicker, ready to go. He handed me a glass of champagne and toasted to new beginnings. With the flip of a switch, the lights were dimmed and the glow of the city blanketed our bodies. He removed the champagne flute from my hand and set it on the nightstand. My heart began to pound. Every quiver, every pulse had led to this moment. He climbed my body, nudging my legs apart. I felt him press at my entrance. Hot lips traced up the column of my neck and lingered at the place where my blood pulsed.

He nudged gently at my opening, pressing just the head inside. Words slipped from my mouth. "Oh...yes."

"Yes?" he questioned. I looked into his eyes and saw them darken with lust.

"Yes. It's so good. I need..."

I didn't have to say it. Jonathan knew what I needed. He covered my mouth with his lips and plunged deep inside of me. In spite of his size, my body adjusted readily. After hours of teasing, he had me primed, wet, and waiting for the exact moment he entered me.

"Damn. So good."

His words almost mimicked mine. Slow, powerful thrusts pulled sounds from me I never knew existed. A cat-like purr rumbled from my chest. His lips bruised mine in punishing kisses. Hard strokes pulled me to the edge. Soft strokes calmed my trembling body. Up and down, in and out, he took me until all I could do was shake beneath him.

His warm palms grabbed handfuls of my ass until my bottom no longer touched the bed. The position placed him in the perfect spot to massage my sex. He knew exactly what he was doing. His thrusts became stronger. His pace quickened. My body tightened, clenched, and squeezed around him. The build-up was exquisite. I closed my eyes as I fell.

"Open your eyes, River, I want to see you."

My eyes fluttered open as I cascaded over the edge. I can't say I saw him. My vision was lost the minute I broke into a million pieces. My body was still pulsing when his own orgasm took him. He called out my name and let the weight of his body fold over me.

Sweaty and sated, we lay together until our breaths steadied. He rolled over, leaving me alone in the bed. This was the awkward moment where I had no idea what to do. Did I get up and get dressed? Did I lay here and relax? He did say we were going to do this over and over again. His shadow fell across the bed, the bathroom light framed his silhouette. I sprawled across the bed naked while he stared.

"Beautiful."

One word, and my body reacted. He pulled back the covers and climbed into the bed. Patting the space next to him, I pulled back my side and pressed my body into his. With my head on his chest and his arms wrapped around me, I fell asleep.

My body was on fire. My nipples ached. Round two began in my slumber. He poked and prodded, licked and laved until I woke up in need. Once awake, I took over. I suckled and squeezed, nipped and nibbled until he was begging me for release.

The sound of his alarm woke us up the third time. Who got up at five-thirty? Apparently, Jonathan and his broom. We had sex in an unhurried fashion. He ordered room service, checked his e-mails, and left me while he took a shower. Dressed in the hotel-supplied robe, I answered the door and guided the waiter to the table. Pulling a twenty from my purse, I tipped the man as he left.

"You signed for it, right?"

He stood in the bathroom doorway, wrapped in a towel. Droplets of water fell from his hair to his chest. I was mesmerized by his beauty, and blown away because that beauty had been mine. All. Night. Long. He was gorgeous, skilled, and an extremely generous lover, and I was thankful he had been my first.

"Yes. What did you order?" I pulled the covers from the plates and found bacon, scrambled eggs, potatoes, and toast. He put on the other robe and joined me for breakfast.

"The tip could have gone on the bill." He obviously saw more than I intended.

"Yes, it could have." That's all I said as I picked up a piece of bacon and bit into it. I was famished.

"I ordered scrambled eggs because it's the least risky. I prefer over-medium eggs, but I hate it if the whites are runny, so I settle for scrambled when I'm out. It's safer. What classes do you have today?"

"International Business is my first class, then I have Accounting and Entrepreneurship."

"That's a lot."

"Yes, but I have all night to do homework." If his grin was any indication, I think he liked the fact that I wasn't going out tonight with another man. "What about you?"

"Oh, I'm meeting with some top-level planners to talk strategy. I'm having lunch with a friend, and then I'm heading home."

"Thanks for a great night last night. It was a wonderful experience, and I enjoyed your company. I'm looking forward to Saturday." I'd really like to throw myself into his arms right now, but that was something a girlfriend would do. Not something I should.

As if reading my mind, he scooted his chair back and patted his lap, inviting me to crawl into the comfort of his arms. How did he know?

He smelled fresh, but not like him. His cologne was washed away, and his scent was unfamiliar. His lips soft and supple brushed against mine. His hands slipped inside my robe to fondle my breasts. His presence in my body lingered, the tenderness he created would stay with me for days.

"River, you're incredible. I knew you would be. I'm already hard thinking about Saturday." He pulled my hand down to feel his erection. My eyes grew big. He couldn't possibly want me again. "Don't worry, I won't take you again. Your body has given so much already." With a kiss to my lips, he set me on my feet and began to dress.

"You didn't bring a bag either." It hadn't dawned on me last night that we'd both walked into the hotel with nothing. He put on his pants and proceeded to pull himself together.

"I wasn't sure how the night would go. I had hoped, but I didn't assume. I have a spare suit at the office, so I'll change there. Don't forget to update your limits list. Selfishly, I want that one thing reserved for me." Anal. He was referring to anal sex and his desire to be my first. Well, it looks like Jonathan will be my first for a lot of things. "Go take advantage of that big shower."

I did as commanded and walked into the massive multi-jetted steam shower. The water massaged my sore body. Every part of me ached, but in a good way. I stepped out and wrapped the plush robe around my body. The entire time in the shower, all I could think about was Jonathan and his reference to anal sex. Surely, I could ask him when he planned to do that. It was going to take both mental and physical preparation. I would take care of the mental and pray that he eased into the physical portion.

"Hey, Jonathan," I called as I walked into the empty room.

He had snuck out while I was showering, and my heart squeezed ever so slightly from his dismissal. Carefully laid out on the bed were my clothes. A note with several hundred dollars sat on the nightstand. Up until now, I felt like a normal woman having a sexy time with a virile man. Looking at the money, the reality of what I was hit me. I was officially a whore.

Chapter 11

Something about the money on the nightstand sucked the air from my lungs. Three hundred dollars lay out in a fan. A tip for a job well done. Most girls would have been pleased. Not me. I felt dirty. Not because I had sex for cash, but because I'd loved it, and loving it made me a whore. Every single kiss. Every single caress. Every single thrust was perfect. I would have done him for free.

I dressed and stared at the note he left me.

You are sunshine. Looking forward to Saturday.

Jonathan

Was I sunshine? I don't think I'd ever been compared to sunshine. I'd been called a lot of things, but no one had ever called me sunshine. The thought warmed me. I scooped up the cash and walked out the door. I tiptoed across the lobby, afraid everyone who glanced my way would know what I'd done. They would know I just screwed my way to a three-hundred-dollar tip. Hurriedly, I exited the front door to flag down a taxi. When you were at the Four Seasons Hotel, hailing a cab was easy.

The morning commute was a bitch. It took forty minutes to get home. Even though I'd already showered, I forced myself to do it again. It wasn't about scrubbing Jonathan from my skin; it was about scrubbing the fact that I'd just prostituted myself from my brain. I'd enjoyed it, and that made me feel dirty.

In an attempt to feel like myself, I tossed on my favorite red oxford shirt and my old, worn jeans. Sliding into my Tom's loafers, I dashed out the door to meet Jade for coffee. I hoped her evening had gone better than the one before. If she showed up sullen again, I'd be tracking the damn duo down. No one was going to beat the spirit out of my friend.

I relaxed in the corner booth with two vanilla lattes and a cranberry scone, waiting for Jade to show. I sent a note to Sandra, asking her to remove anal and any BDSM-related items from my profile. I imagined she thought I had tried it and decided to pass. I didn't care what she assumed. I was not getting beaten, and I promised my ass to Jonathan.

Jade walked in the door looking more like herself. She was dressed in slacks and a long-sleeved silk blouse. The bruises around her wrists wouldn't be going away anytime soon.

"Hey, ho," she said before she collapsed into the booth across from me, her crooked grin another sign that all went well at home last night.

"Who you calling a ho?" I puffed out my chest and did my best gangsta impression. I could play "girls from the hood", too.

"I calls 'em like I sees 'em." She took a drink from her latte. Her tongue swirled the edge of her lips, sweeping at the foam.

"Are you visually impaired?" My comeback made the liquid squirt through her nose. We both began to laugh, and it felt so good to let loose the way we used to.

"Tell me about your night. Was it awful? Did he live up to your expectations? I want details. How big is the broom?" Reaching over, she stole a piece of my scone.

"You first. I want to make sure you're okay. How were things with the duo last night?"

Her answer whooshed out. "Good. Everything is good. More than good."

"Come on, Jade. Yesterday you were despondent, and today you're different—happier. What gives?"

"The duo made amends. We sat down last night and talked about what happened. They know they failed me. They feel awful. Anyway, we won't be inviting others into our play. The problem is solved."

I would never understand the dynamics of their relationship. What did they call it…an exchange of power? I've found over the years that my power either lies in my sense of humor or my silence. It wasn't easy to gain power when you were invisible. Working with The Dean's List was the first time I'd felt like I had any kind of control. I got to decide who, and when.

Ping.

My phone chimed with an incoming message.

Sunshine,

Thank you. Sandra sent out your new limits list.

Jonathan

"Your face just lit up. Who's texting you?" She looked like she was going to pounce on me or my phone.

"J…I mean Mr. Broom. He asked for something, and I agreed to give it to him. He just thanked me."

She said my face lit up. Maybe like sunshine? My inner joy must be oozing out of my pores. My emotions are all over the map. This morning, I felt sullied by what I was but satisfied with what I did. How does one come to terms with the opposing forces?

Jade leaned into the center of the table. She glanced around the room. "What did you promise him?" Her whisper was barely audible. I felt like we were spies planning espionage.

Leaning toward her, I whispered, "My ass."

"Holy shit," she yelled, not caring who heard. All eyes were on us. "Exclusively?"

"Yep. He's a good guy, Jade, and he made me feel like I mattered. He didn't hide me, he was proud to be with me. I appreciated that." Leaning into the center where all secrets were shared, I said, "The only time I felt like a whore was when he left a tip on the nightstand." I pulled the note from my purse and pushed it toward her. She began to shake her head.

"I'm warning you. This is like when you were a virgin. Your first is always special. Don't get attached to him. He's probably married and has a half-dozen kids living in a house in Connecticut."

"I'm not attached to him. It was very clear what I was, especially when I saw the note and cash. I'm a girl for hire. There's no denying it now, but I'm glad he picked me. If I'm going to take part in something like this, at least he can be my rainbow."

"Well, apparently he thinks you're like sunshine. What do you have down there? A magical vagina?" She said the word vagina with a bit too much enthusiasm. The older couple seated at the booth across from us looked down their noses with a *shame on you* look.

"Oh, shut up. I don't have a magic vagina," I whispered at a volume barely audible. "I had a good time. Does that make me an awful person? I can hear my father's sermon about loose morals and the sins of the flesh." It was strange how my mind remembered stuff I never gave my full attention to.

Jade inhaled all the oxygen in the room, and then blew out her disappointment in a rush of air. The power of it displaced my hair. "Stop. You never cared what your parents thought before. Hell, outside of the church, were they ever even invested in you? I swear you are going to drive me nuts."

She reached for my hands. Her long sleeves rode up her arms to show her bruises. They appeared to have faded slightly and were taking on a green tint. I hoped never to see anything like that on her again.

"You're right." The family mantra, *children were to be seen and not heard,* didn't leave a lot of room for conversation or interaction. I was the perfect pastor's daughter until I wasn't. That first act of defiance had set the stage for my life now.

"Did you go home and cry last night?" What would she think when I told her I'd loved it, but I'd hated myself anyway?

"No, I went home and took my second shower of the morning. I'm struggling to come to terms with being a..." I whispered the word *whore*, "...and the feeling I had around the experience. I loved every second with him. Holy hell, Jade, three times, and each time my needs were met. Never in my life have I experienced that."

Her eyes grew wide. I wasn't sure if I saw shock or envy. "Wow, you ended up with a good one. So the broom is adequate?"

"It's a push-broom, not a tiny hand-broom. He knows exactly what to do with it. He also has a bit of an oral fixation."

"Give me something to hate him for. Is he ugly? Does he have moobs? What about bad teeth or foul breath?" She was searching for a negative, but there weren't any besides the fact that he paid me for sex. He was the kind of man I would have taken on for free. He was dating material. Marriage material. Father material, and yet he couldn't see past his past and into his future.

"Sorry, none of that. He's just a guy, and he knows what he wants. He's direct, demanding, and he makes me feel special." I fidgeted with the napkin in front of me. Was this where she would tell me to drop him again?

"He sounds lovely. So, you're seeing him again Saturday?"

"Yes, some auction and opera combination. He told me he needed a distraction." He also told me he had a private box, which only meant he intended to use it privately. Hot moisture seeped into my panties. My cheeks began to heat.

"You're blushing. What's going on in that dirty little mind of yours?" She pushed her hair off her shoulders, revealing a silver chain connected to an infinity symbol. I'd never seen it before.

"He has a private box." I bit my lip and waited for her to razz me, but she didn't. She gave me a somber look and changed the subject entirely. She looked into my eyes and in all seriousness said, "You're not a whore, River. I tell myself, and anyone who asks, that I work in hospitality. Convincing yourself is the toughest part, but convincing others is easy. It took me months to get over feeling dirty. When I went exclusive, it helped because I could honestly say I was in a relationship. Now that I've been in this relationship for a few months, I'm not sure what's better: going from man to man without expectations, or doing what I'm doing. All my eggs are in their basket, and that leaves me vulnerable." She stared into the foam of her latte. She was in a private place in her head, and she hadn't invited me in.

"You have money, right? You still get paid?" How *did* the compensation work when you became exclusive?

"Yes, I receive a monthly stipend, plus clothes, housing, and miscellaneous. Don't worry, I have money in the bank, and I'm well on my way to paying off my student loans."

Relief washed over me. I would hate for her to have gone through all of this and not come out on top. "So…do you want to tell me about the necklace?" Her surprised expression told me she didn't expect me to notice.

She pulled her bottom lip between her teeth and rolled it back and forth. "It's a collar. The duo gave it to me last night. It signifies the beginning of a journey. It's a public symbol of their commitment to me." She touched the metal softly. Her fingers stroked the figure eight in the center. The gesture had more significance than she was letting on.

"It seems to make you happy, and that makes me happy." I drank the remaining coffee in my cup and prepared to leave. We could talk later about the symbolism of the necklace. Right now, I had to get to class.

"I think Mr. Broom got it right. You are sunshine." She beamed at me. The light had found its way back to her eyes.

"No, I'm not. I'm River Roberts, and I work in commodities." I spoke in my best boardroom voice.

"Nice to meet you, River. What firm do you work for?"

"I'm an independent, seeing to the individual needs of each client. My services and contracts vary."

"Sounds like an interesting job."

"Oh, you have no idea."

We rose from the table together and embraced. What would I do without Jade? My mind answered the question with a vision of me dressed in a bikini behind the counter at The Grind.

LUCA SAUNTERED into my International Business Studies class like he taught it. I slunk down in my seat, hoping to become invisible. Pulling the syllabus in front of my face, I prayed he didn't see me. As the minutes passed, I tried to relax. Afraid to peek over the pages, I remained hidden by an eight-and-a-half by eleven-inch paper shield. The seats filled to my left and right, but I focused on the words in front of me. I didn't see the words, as they were a blur of letters. Slowly, I pulled the page down. The lecture hall was nearly full. An older woman sat to my right. To my left was none other than Luca. He was staring at me. His eyes were laughing, but his mouth was silent.

"Nice to see you again?" The rich timbre of his voice fell over me like a fresh blanket of snow. A chill coursed down my body before the heat of desire raced to replace it.

I had to decide in an instant if I wanted to pretend I'd never met him, or if I wanted to acknowledge him at all. I glanced around the hall and saw several women straining their necks to get a glimpse of the dark-haired man-candy sitting next to me. His bluebird-colored eyes danced with curiosity. I imagined he was wondering the same thing.

"It's Luca, right?" I'd never been one to play games, so why start now?

"So, you do remember me. I'm so glad." He licked his thumb and brought it to my nose and swiped. "You had a smudge from the papers you were hiding behind. You don't have to hide from me. We share the same secret," he said in a tone only meant for my ears.

I assumed that meant he got the job. I was still trying to decide whether I liked him rubbing his spit across my nose. Now I would have to digest the fact that one of my fellow students knew what I did. My once large world was shrinking by the minute.

"You're a business major, too? What's your emphasis?" Small talk seemed to be the best option at this point.

"Finance. You?" He gave me his playboy smile—the one that was destined to earn him big bonuses.

"Same. How weird is that?" That means there was a good chance I would see him in more of my classes. "What other classes do you have today?"

"I have Accounting and Entrepreneurship." I could have fallen out of my seat if I wasn't completely contained on three sides. "What about you?"

"Same. How weird is that?" I repeated my exact response from his earlier question.

"That's awesome. We're officially homework buddies. We can meet Thursdays at the student union after class." He said this like it was a done deal.

"We'll see. I haven't worked out my study schedule yet. I'll let you know." Like a high schooler, he pulled my hand in front of him and wrote his phone number on my arm.

"Give me yours. I'm serious, I need a buddy."

He could get any of the ogling women, and probably some of the men, not only to study with him, but also do his assignments. Some men just had that aura. He was one of them. Like an idiot, I gave him my private number and, just for fun, drew a smiley face next to it. It felt just like high school.

Luca and I traipsed from class to class together. I learned he'd earned his undergraduate degree in Chicago. He came to New York to be closer to the financial district. Although we had not discussed work, we danced around the subject several times. Eventually, one of us would be brave enough to start asking questions. My mind was full of them.

He came from a large family of Italian descent. That explained the dark hair and bronze skin, but his blue eyes were a surprise. Like me, he was on his own for college. In his case, it was simply a matter of numbers. With five siblings and an electrician as a father, there was no way his parents were financing higher education.

He asked about my story. I told him I was the only child of a poor couple. I didn't elaborate. He left it at that, and I was grateful. The groundwork for friendship was laid. I could see Luca becoming an ally. Everyone needed allies.

Chapter 12

"Someone has a sugar daddy," my roommate yelled from her room. Shit…shit…shit…did she know? How was I supposed to handle this?

"What are you talking about?" Clueless wouldn't have been my go-to plan, but it seemed the only option at this point.

"You got another delivery. It's on your bed." She walked into the living room dressed to kill. Her wardrobe consisted of a strip of fabric around her hips and one around her chest. She worked as a cocktail waitress at a nightclub. We hardly ever saw each other, as she was usually leaving as I was getting home. "I swear, River, if you stiff me for rent, I'll kill you."

"When have I ever stiffed you for rent?" If she only knew I was getting stiffed so I could pay my rent, I wondered what she would say. "I'm attending the opera, and I needed a dress. I have a friend who works at Bloomingdales, and she sent over something for me to try. She's been instrumental in finding some incredible things that fall within my budget." Everything about that statement was the truth in the loosest sense. I refused to out and out lie. This job was going to change a lot of things about me, but I'd be damned if it would make me a liar.

"Opera, I hate the opera. Let's hope your date can provide a distraction." Little did she know, those exact words were used to describe my role. She walked out the door, and I raced to my room to open the packages.

Two zippered bags were on my bed. Several bags sat on my floor. Erica went overboard. The woman obviously worked on commission.

Like a kid at Christmas, I quickly unzipped the first bag and gasped. I removed the single-shouldered dress from the bag. A simple brooch gathered the silver material to one hip, where it flowed in layers to the floor. It was elegant and sexy and would go perfectly with a black tuxedo. When I opened the next bag, I nearly fainted. The vivid blue gown had a low-cut, V-necked bodice with thin shoulder straps. The light chiffon material hung from a high cinched waist. A bold slit came midway up the skirt.

My clothes were discarded in seconds flat. I dumped the contents of the bags from the floor and found matching shoes, wraps, and clutches. Erica had thought of everything. Jonathan must have called her first thing this morning. That meant he was thinking of me. I reminded myself this wasn't a relationship, but I couldn't help rushing to my phone to send a quick text to him. I knew I shouldn't contact him. It seemed wrong, but I wanted him to know how happy he had made me. I wondered if he cared.

I found his earlier message and typed in a simple thank you. After a quick glance, I saw I had a lot of messages, none of which were from Jonathan. I'd get to them later. With a toss, my work phone landed on the bed. Right now, I was giving myself a fashion show.

Standing nearly naked, I debated between the silver and the blue. Which should I try on first? They were both beautiful in their own right. My eyes shifted between the two, but I spent more time eyeing the silver. I removed it carefully from the hanger and slipped it over my head. It fit my curves like it had been custom made for my body.

My phone pinged.

You're welcome. Do you like them? Wear the silver one on Saturday. We'll come up with somewhere to wear the blue.
Jonathan.

How did he know what they looked like? I figured he would have called Erica, and she would have selected everything.

Jonathan,
I just slipped on the silver dress. It fits perfectly. How did you know what Erica sent?
River

I anxiously awaited his reply.

I picked them myself. Take a selfie and send it to me.

He didn't sign the last message. I stared at the screen and read it over and over again. What did he mean he picked them himself?

No selfie. You have to wait until Saturday. You have excellent taste by the way, but you sent way too much.
River

He didn't reply right away. Just when I tossed the phone to the side, it pinged again. I rushed to pick it up.

You please me. See you Saturday. Howard will be there at seven.

I pleased him…somehow, that made a difference to me. I spent my whole life trying to please one person or another, with no success, but I'd spent one night with him, and *he* was pleased.

I spent the next thirty minutes trying on everything. Each piece was important because he'd chosen it.

A STREAM of moonlight peeked through the window beside me, its glow highlighting the scarred tabletop where I sat doing my homework. The Four Seasons seemed a distant memory. A text from Sandra flashed across the screen of my phone.

River,
You need to return your mentor's calls. I'm getting complaints. I know this is new to you, and you may be trying to adjust to your sched-

ule, but we pride ourselves on providing excellent service, and that includes expedient follow-ups. A yes means yes, River. Don't disappointment me.

Sandra

Well, shit, I was in trouble. I hadn't checked my inbox for second encounter inquiries all day. After last night, the thought of being with anyone but Jonathan made me queasy. No one could possibly live up to last night. I typed a reply to Sandra that simply said,

I'm on it.

River

I found a message from Paul Yoder, confirming our "date"; he asked me to meet him at Sir Harry's Bar in the lobby of the Waldorf Astoria. The man had lovely taste in hotels. I confirmed the place and time and then attempted to answer the remaining requests. I made my next meet-and-greet for Monday afternoon. John Strickland and I would meet at a swanky oyster bar in Times Square.

Ben Daniels wanted to meet for dinner. He was a nice old man. I looked at my calendar and set up a meeting for Monday night. I prayed he didn't want a sleepover. I didn't want to schedule anyone on school nights, but since I was quickly going to the top of Sandra's naughty list, I did my best to accommodate everyone.

Donald Zane wanted to meet, but I told him I wasn't available until the following Friday. I penciled him in until I heard back from him. The only one I hadn't heard from was Craig Hagen, and I was relieved. I had two new requests for meet-and-greets. I scheduled one lunch meeting for Wednesday. I was reluctant to schedule Wednesday evenings, just in case Jonathan asked for a permanent day. My last request was scheduled for Saturday morning. Since I was not doing a sleepover with Paul, I would be able to meet with Anthony Baldwin for breakfast without a problem. My life had never been so busy.

My personal phone rang, and as I didn't recognize the number, I answered it with a question in my voice.

"Hello?"

"It's Luca. What are you doing?"

"Homework. You should be doing the same." He better not expect me to do his homework.

"I'm done. I was bored, so I thought I would call." How could this hunk of a man be bored? I was sure there was a bevy of beauties happy to entertain him. He called me because he was bored? What did that say about me?

"I'm surprised. I thought you were going to ask me to do your homework."

"I always do my homework right after class. I don't know what my schedule is going to look like." There was an underlying message there —one I completely understood.

I hesitated for a moment. "Have you managed to find a balance?" I didn't have to elaborate. He knew what I meant. Even though Jade worked in the same field, her situation was completely different. Rather than shuffle clients, she submitted to one or two.

"No, not yet. My phone rings off the hook. I don't have enough nights. I refuse to work Mondays and Thursdays. The rest of the nights fill up like I'm selling crack in Queens." I couldn't tell if he was pleased or puzzled. I didn't know him well enough to decide.

"Yeah, I got a kick-in-the-ass reminder from Sandra today to get on my appointments."

"Really?"

He sounded surprised. I bet Sandra wouldn't be calling Luca. I wondered if the rules were the same for him. What did his limit list look like?

"Yes. Hey…can I ask you a personal question?" I knew I shouldn't ask, but curiosity was killing me.

Silence.

"Luca?"

"Yes?"

"Yes, I can ask?"

"Yes."

I was almost embarrassed to inquire, but the question had been in the back of my head since the first time I saw him. "Men and women?" I added a questioning inflection at the end. He would understand.

"No, I'm a man's man who adores women. I can't believe you considered I would swing that way." I listened carefully and recognized the sound of disappointment in his voice.

"My reality has been tilted this week. If you had asked me last week what I would be doing this week, I'd have told you eating Ramen and peddling coffee. Never in my life would I have thought I'd be doing what I'm doing."

"Are you okay?" There was concern in his voice, and I was touched he cared.

"Yep, my first encounter was positive. What about you? Are you okay?" I wondered if he was going through the same emotions. Did he feel dirty? Did he enjoy the experience? I wouldn't ask, not until we knew each other better.

"Yep, I think I'll survive. Do you want to have lunch tomorrow?" The question took me by surprise. It was like he plucked it from the ether. He could have said, *Hi, River, that's a lovely dress. What do you think about meatballs?* One had nothing to do with the other.

I quickly considered the benefits and downfalls of befriending Luca. In the end, I agreed to lunch because I could use an ally, one who was in the same arrangement as I. We agreed to meet at a little cafe in my neighborhood at noon.

WHEN THE MORNING GREETED ME, I walked to the bathroom and stared at the dark circles under my eyes. A restless night and abnormal amount of anxiety made sleep nearly impossible. In spite of placing my first experience solidly under my belt, this "date" tonight felt different. I wasn't filled with anticipation, but something akin to dread.

The lunch I enjoyed with Paul in Rockefeller Center was pleasant but unremarkable. Positive qualities had to be present, or I wouldn't have said yes to a follow-on. His blue eyes and talk of movies and music were all I could recall. Knowing Jonathan couldn't be my one and only, I vowed to focus on the positives. Jonathan had made it clear he wasn't interested in a relationship, so an exclusive agreement wasn't an option.

Still, the thought of another man's hands on my body niggled at me. Could I back out now? I could convince myself that being with Jonathan was a lapse in judgment, a one-night thing, like many I'd had before. But once I met with Paul, there was no doubt what I was.

How many times are you going to justify this? I asked myself. *You are what you are, a commodities broker specializing in private funds.* Jade would be proud.

Dressed in slacks and a silk blouse, I put on my new Kate Spade loafers and walked to the cafe a few blocks away. The sun sat on my shoulders, and the wind blew through my hair. This was the normal I needed. I needed friends like Luca and Jade. I needed to cut myself a break.

Waiting at a front table was the delectable Luca Gregorio. Sitting in the seat across from him was our waitress. I wanted to laugh at the absurdity of the situation. Luca was doing the top-earning women in business. The woman he was sitting across from and flirting with could barely afford to pay for his coffee.

Luca rose when he saw me. His perfectly cut suit hugged his lean body. I wondered who his personal shopper was. He approached me, leaving the waitress alone at our table. With a kiss on my cheek, he said, "You made it. Valerie was just going to get us both some iced tea, unless you prefer something else." What a clever way to dismiss her. Direct and to the point, but not mean.

"Iced tea is perfect," I said with all the sweetness I could muster. One look at Valerie, and I could see she wanted to gut me with a dull paring knife. Luca ignored her and pulled out my chair. That training would go a long way with his mentors.

"You look tired. Didn't you sleep well?"

"No, I tossed and turned all night."

"Thinking about our date?" He showed me a party smile, his white teeth like Tom Sawyer's perfectly spaced pickets. I could see why women swooned; he had a movie star quality, but a boy-next-door demeanor. He was the untouchable you wanted to touch.

"Don't flatter yourself. This is not a date, and I wouldn't lose sleep over you." Not completely accurate. I could see myself losing sleep over Luca, particularly if he were the star in one of my nocturnal dreams.

"Wounded." He swayed in his chair as if I'd slain him.

"I'm ignoring you." I turned my head just as he gave me a firm nudge with his foot under the table.

"If I wanted to be ignored, I could have…actually, I've never been ignored. Is this what it feels like? I'm not sure I'm a fan."

As if scripted, Valerie approached from stage left with two iced teas and eyes only for Luca. She barely glanced at me as she took my order. I'd be surprised if anything was delivered.

"Oh, my poor baby, it must have been rough to have a gaggle of girls at your beck and call."

"Oh, come on. You're a stunning woman. You can't tell me that you don't have your own throng of men drooling at your feet. I bet they kneel before you as footstools." He sure had an active imagination. Maybe he missed his calling. I could see him on stage with the bright lights beating down on his tawny skin.

"Oh, please. If my nights weren't reserved, I'd be sitting home alone most of the time. Are you free tonight, or are you…?" I tilted my eyes and gave him a *don't make me say it* look.

"Are you interested? I can give you a discounted rate." He wormed his brows like a silent movie star. He didn't see the ice cube coming his way. Bull's-eye. It hit his chest and fell down his shirt. Watching him squirm was going to make my day.

"Oh, I'll get you back. It'll be when you least expect it, and it'll be ten times worse." Valerie managed to save the day for me. Not only did she interrupt his diatribe on revenge, she actually got my order right. The girl had earned her tip.

Leaning to the center of the table, I positioned myself for secrets. "I'm serious, Luca, what does your schedule look like? I'm drowning here."

In the center of the table, he held my hands and told me what his week looked like. "I work tonight, and Saturday, too. Sunday is a twofer. Monday, I'm off. Tuesday is currently free, but I have a lunch meeting on Wednesday. Thursday I'm off, but you and I are meeting for coffee at the student union, and I would be devastated if you didn't show. You can bring Blondie if you want."

Valerie pressed us apart with her pitcher of tea. Luca leaned back in his chair, cool as could be. No one would think we were talking about his stud services. I wondered if I would feel more comfortable if I had a penis. I'd been told an erection had no conscience.

"What about you?" It was only fair for him to ask.

"Booked tonight and Saturday night. I have a new meeting tomorrow morning, as well as lunches on Monday and Wednesday. I have dinner plans Monday night, but I'm off Thursday."

"Do you ever wonder what you were thinking when you said yes?"

"Every day, and I do know what I was thinking. I was thinking I needed to be able to eat and get through school. I needed books I couldn't afford. I needed a place to call home. I didn't have much choice."

"You've had your first experience, and that's supposed to be the hardest. Why are you so stressed? The worst is behind you."

"My first was wonderful. I liked him, probably more than I should. We have incredible chemistry, so he's set the bar high. What about your first?" Did I really want to know? Yes, I was curious. "Jade—the girl you call Blondie—and I exchange bits of info using nicknames. She calls my first Mr. Broom because I asked her what I should do if he had a tiny womb broom."

Luca chuckled. "Does he, have a tiny...?" He dug into his salad. It was my turn to laugh.

"No." Embarrassed that we were talking about Jonathan's parts, I looked away. I stabbed at the chicken in my salad. I knew I had to eat, but the food sat uncomfortably in my tummy. "What about you? Isn't it hard to perform on demand? With women, we have open-all-night equipment. You…well, that's another story." Several bites later, he set his fork down and leaned to the secret bubble in the center of the table.

"I've had two experiences. These aren't young, stunning women. They are women who put off dating to break through the glass ceiling. One of them looked like she went headfirst. In all honesty, I thought it would be fine. I have a penis, and it's never been picky. I was wrong. Thankfully, most of the women aren't only interested in my junk. Women love the tongue, and I'm good at it. One of the women just wanted to cuddle."

My eyes must have bugged out by his candor. He volleyed with his own *get to know you* questions. "Don't you get sore?"

"I imagine I will, but with my clientele of one, I'm doing okay." We continued to toss questions back and forth.

"What about oral…do you actually go skin to mouth?" I whispered in the center of the table. To the average person, I imagined we looked like lovers sharing an intimate moment.

"No, I use really thin dental dams or plastic wrap. If they become a regular, I would consider flesh to flesh. What about you?" I stalled for the moment. I sucked Jonathan's while bare, but I was changing my policy tonight. No glove, no love.

"Same as you." I hoped Jonathan became a regular so I wouldn't have to feel like I'd fibbed.

Throughout lunch, we laughed and shared far more than I thought we would. In some ways, it was comforting. He was just as new to this as me, and I was surprised he wasn't as confident as I'd thought. That helped my insecurities a little. As we left and promised to meet at school, I felt lighter somehow. I had a friend, one who was as honest as Jade. Someone…real.

I arrived home in time to shower, shampoo, shave, and shine. Dressed in a little black number that hit mid-thigh, I was confident I could rock any cocktail party. Instead of wearing silk stockings and garters, I put on black lace underwear and a matching bra. Slipping on my black Jimmy Choos, I was ready.

A bead of sweat dripped from my forehead. I swiped it off and took a final glance in the mirror. My face looked pale. I pinched my cheeks, trying to pinken them up. My stomach lurched, and I raced to the toilet, where I relieved myself of lunch. Why was I so nervous? This was my new life. I needed to pull myself together.

To get through this night, I would need wine and courage.

Chapter 13

Ping. My private phone signaled an incoming message. Jade's face showed up on my screen.

Good luck tonight. Keep your eye on the ball.

J

Thanks, coach.

R

If you want some motivation, look at your bank account. It's payday! I gotta run. Text me when you get home so I know you're okay.

J

Oh my God, I totally forgot today was payday. I opened my banking app and blinked twice. I logged out and back in. *Yep, still the same.* Sitting in my account was nearly six thousand dollars. There was no doubt I could pay my rent and cover my student loan. It finally dawned on me that puking my guts out and feeling a little skanky would be infinitely better than being homeless and hungry. Jade's encouragement had come at just the right moment. She was right. It was the incentive I'd needed.

ROLLING up in front of the Waldorf, I settled my bill with the taxi driver. I was definitely going to have to set up a car service. Taking taxis would quickly eat into my profits.

The valet opened the door and helped me exit. I was feeling much better now that I had a solid reason to continue. Nearly six thousand solid reasons. I reminded myself that the money, although the end result, wasn't what drove me. Debt-free with a foot in the door did.

I found Paul Yoder sitting at The Oak Bar. Tucked off to the side, I watched him sip at the amber liquid in his glass. He appeared calm and confident. He laughed at something the bartender said, then turned toward the door as if looking for me. I stepped out of the shadows the minute he turned back around.

"Hi."

I tried to make my voice sound calm, but I could hear the slight warble. I wondered if he detected it. In spite of my pep talks and reminders to focus on the prize, I was nervous. No, I was scared shit-less. Jade would have been happy with me at this point. This was how she told me it should be.

"Hey, glad you could make it. You look stunning."

He pressed a kiss to my cheek and pulled out the stool next to him. I slid through the cloud of cologne and into my seat, carefully positioning my body so he was the focus of my attention. I learned that from my dad. Men of the cloth are as savvy as politicians. They pretended you were their sole focus, but they barely gave you a second thought once you were gone. In all fairness, so many people wanted a piece of him, and there simply wasn't enough to go around.

Our knees touched when he seated himself beside me. The sparks I felt for Jonathan didn't exist with Paul—no tingle, no spark, no damp desire. Paul was just a guy at the bar.

"What would you like to drink?" The bartender stood in front of me and waited for my order.

I'd intended to have a glass of wine, but tonight I was going to need something stronger. "Vodka martini, with a twist." The man behind the bar left to fill my order.

"Liquid courage?" Paul asked as his manicured hand covered mine.

In a small, tremulous voice I asked, "Does it show?"

"Your anxiety? Yes, but I like it." He turned my hand over and rubbed the soft pad below my thumb.

Great, the man liked me scared. What did that say about him? The arrival of my drink broke the tension. I lifted my glass and proposed a toast.

"To liquid courage," I said as I tapped the edge of his tumbler.

He raised his glass and said, "To everything else."

I really needed to figure out a way to ask about details. What did *everything else* mean? I had no idea what the plan was. I might be more relaxed if I knew what the night had in store for me. At this point, my brain was coming up with a hundred scenarios. The realist in me said that only a few of those could actually happen, but the alarmist in me was playing every one like a detailed movie in my head. How did the average escort do this? I felt relieved to know Concierge Services checked out these men. Someone knew where I was and whom I was with so I shouldn't ever come up missing. My agency calendar listed my encounters. All the safeguards had been put in place.

I sipped at the martini, letting the burn of the alcohol warm me inside. "I would feel less anxious if I knew what the plan was for the evening. You have me at a disadvantage here. I'm new to this…lifestyle. Maybe you could mentor me." My choice of the word *mentor* was genius. He perked right up and stepped into his leadership role.

"I'm sorry, River, I forgot you're green. I should have been more considerate."

The words spilled from his mouth easily, but they didn't seem sincere. He was just going through the motions to get from point A to point B. Quite honestly, I would rather he took me upstairs so I could get it over with and get home.

"Thank you for your consideration."

With each sip, my vag seemed to dry up and shrivel—no chemistry, no connection. That could only mean no climax. Not only was I going to have to pull out the lube, I was also going to have to dig deep into my inner thespian and put on an award-winning performance.

"We will have a drink, two if you need it. We have a room upstairs." His words were direct and to the point.

No dinner, nothing. A cocktail followed by one without the tail. I tossed back the rest of my drink, grabbed my purse, and stood. "I'm ready, let's go." My words were succinct and commanding. Gone was the girl who sat there scared and uncertain. She was drowned in a Stoli Gold martini. I owned this, or at least I'd fake it until I did.

I'm not sure if his wide eyes were a sign of shock or excitement. He seemed to like that I took charge. Power exchange. This was what turned Jade on. When someone took your options away, there was a mysterious unknown, and it was what got people excited. The perception was, you lost control. The reality was, you had it the whole time. You had to decide if you wanted to yield your power or not.

I made it out the door ten paces before him. He ran to keep up with me. "Are you in a hurry, River?"

"No, we had our drink, now we'll have our fun. What room are we in?"

His shaking hand pulled the card from his pocket. It wasn't a suite, just a standard room, but at the Waldorf, nothing was really standard. I had never stayed here, but I had been intrigued by the history of the hotel since I found out one of its original founders was John Jacob Astor IV, the very same Astor who died when the Titanic sunk. At that moment, I almost felt as if I were drowning. How interesting.

Paul pressed the tenth-floor button with his trembling finger. What happened to the confident man at the bar? I'd knocked him off-kilter, and it gave me joy. I felt powerful in that moment. I'd been afraid, and he had gained something from my fear. Now he appeared afraid, and I understood what he'd gained. It was easier to gain confidence in the face of weakness.

Sandra had said to be me. Was this the real me? Did I enjoy the rush of power in relationships? Sexual relationships, anyway. With

Jonathan, I had desired his lead, but perhaps with other men, I had to be in control to do my job. I would have to ponder this later. It was showtime.

We entered room 1017. It was a pretty room done in beige, gold, and touches of red. I glanced around the space. No champagne. Nothing special. This was a man who would take for himself.

"Do you want to take a shower, Paul? I hear it's a good way to start." I tossed my purse on the bed and approached him. Inside, I was trembling like a mouse cornered by a cat. On the outside, I was the cat.

"Um, yes, that's a great way to start. Listen, I need to tell you a few things. Um…" He stared at me, perplexed. "Um…" His face turned red. I had no idea what he was holding back. "Um…I have a really small penis."

Oh, thank the Lord. Of all the things he could have told me, lacking the goods wasn't what I expected. I was relieved he was packing a filet, as opposed to a porterhouse. That meant I wouldn't be sore tomorrow night. My evening just got a whole lot brighter.

"That's perfect, Paul, because guess what? I'm small, too." Hell, I have no idea how mine compared to others, but it seemed to adjust to size. If it could accommodate Jonathan's stretch limo, then I imagined it would adjust to Paul's Mini Cooper. Building his confidence was the most important thing right now.

Pulling him by the tie, I dragged him to the bathroom. "Start the shower, Paul. I'm just going to find a hair tie."

My butt sank into the bed. I sucked in air and courage with each breath. This was so far out of my comfort zone. I reminded myself to find my inner muse before I found the hair tie and returned to the bathroom. He sat on the edge of the tub fully clothed. The steam billowed above the glass, fogging the mirror in front of me. Thankfully, I wouldn't have to watch him take me.

"Can I undress you?" the slight voice just above a whisper asked. I thought about his boost of confidence in the bar and wondered if he struggled to take charge. My fear seemed to excite him. The rush was similar to the rush of arousal. How would it feel for him to lead?

"This is your night, Paul. Do you want to lead or follow?"

His head sank into his hands. After a brief face rubbing, he raised his eyes and slowly surveyed my body, from my heels to my hair. His uncertainty disappeared, and for a brief moment, my fear resurfaced. With his body at my back, the zipper was slowly lowered. One shoulder fell before the other. Once the zipper cleared my hips, the dress sank to the floor. His labored breath tickled my neck. It didn't send shivers, it merely tickled, but I turned the sensation into part of my act. Apparently, both Paul and I were faking it until we could master our dance.

"You're so pretty."

I turned to look at him. Standing in a bra, underwear, and heels, I slowly undressed the timid man in front of me. I left him in his briefs. It only seemed fair he should do that little reveal himself.

In a single motion, I unhooked my bra and let my breasts fall free. He dove to catch one in each hand as if they might hit the floor. Heavy in his palms, he rubbed across the center to stimulate my soft nipples. Thankfully, they perked right up. I tossed my head back and closed my eyes. I pictured someone else, someone who made my body tingle with a touch—Jonathan.

The moan came unsolicited. The moisture built between my legs. In my mind, amber-flecked eyes undressed me. Strong hands pulled my panties. With a flutter, I opened my eyes and saw the glazed baby blues take in my body. His fingers ran the length of my slit. Satisfaction showed in all of his features, from the glint in his eyes to the grin on his face. I would never tell him it was another man who made me wet. He could keep this victory as his own.

In the shower, we soaped each other's bodies. I hadn't glanced at his package, as I was afraid to react in any way. Did I ignore it? Make a comment? Act impressed? What was the protocol for a situation like this? Soap in hand, I skimmed down his chest until I met the tangle of his pubes. Why did I have to have my hair ripped from my body, and he could sport a bush? At least Jonathan trimmed. Buried deep inside the tuft, I found his button. It more closely resembled a clitoris than a penis. Soft, I rolled it between my fingers and felt it rise. By the time it was at its peak, it was no bigger than my thumb.

One sympathy lay coming up.

"I'm sorry." He turned the water off and exited the shower.

"You're sorry? For what? Lots of men have…" Not liking where that sentence was taking me, I began again. "Men come in all shapes and sizes. Men of smaller stature often compensate with good oral skills." Happy to redirect the conversation, I led him to the bed. Glancing at the clock, I noticed I was into my second hour.

"How do you get good at that skill when you can't get past the first deficit?" He lay on the bed, turned to his side and waited.

"Can we talk candidly?" So, it looked like our roles were going to change. Paul would be the student, and I would be the mentor.

"Please."

"You are my second experience, so this is all new to me. I certainly wasn't a virgin when I signed on, but I wasn't a whore." There was a bit of irony to that statement. "Anyway, I like sex, but honestly, as a woman, rarely will I come from intercourse. It takes external stimulation. You may not have a large…anyway, but you have everything else you need to be an incredible lover." His eyes flashed with surprise.

"Are you going to teach me?" His pleading eyes and earnest voice tipped the scales in his favor. It wasn't like I had much of a choice. I belonged to him for the time being. And so, we dove right into role reversal.

On my back, I opened myself for him. In order to see where we had to go, I needed to know what we were working with. "Show me what you've got" might have been the wrong verbal pistol to fire, but it did get him off the starting block and sprinting toward the finish line.

He dipped his head between my legs. Rather than keep his pace slow and steady or his stride constant, he was all over the place. A sprint here, a hurdle there, once I thought he bent over to tie his figurative shoes. I stopped him mid-stride and began lesson one.

Floating in his condom, I asked him to analyze how everything I did to him felt. I flicked, sucked, stroked, pulled, and kneaded. Every time he was ready to blow, I stopped and changed direction. I felt the tension in his body. He grabbed my hair and tried to hold me in one place. The lesson was learned.

"See how one technique feels amazing, and another just so-so? When you go from place to place too quickly, your lover never gets an opportunity to enjoy where she's been. Start slow and gentle, like this." I pulled his penis into my mouth and gently stroked the underside with my tongue. I took the whole thing into my mouth and sucked gently. It was like sucking my thumb. He moaned. "I'm listening to your cues, and that moan indicates you're enjoying the experience. My hands on your body are another gauge. When you tense, I know you're probably close." I continued to work him into a frenzy. When his body stiffened, I changed the pace and rhythm.

"Fuuuuuck," he yelled. I pulled away.

"You want a woman to brag about how you made love to her for hours? That's how." I focused my attention on him again, and this time I took him to the moon and back. I felt his release pulse against the end of the condom, but instead of pulling away, I languidly drew every shudder possible from his body. I had the impression no one had gifted him with their time. I imagined he was a means to an end for most, but I felt differently. Paul had something more important to offer a woman than the size of his button. He seemed like a good man.

I climbed up his body and laid my head on his chest. He wrapped his arm around me and held me tight. Convinced this night was going to be awful, I was pleasantly surprised at the turn of events. I didn't feel anything for Paul but sadness. I empathized with his feelings of inadequacy. No one wanted to be a disappointment.

He wasn't a powerhouse in the sack, but as his firm's Chief Risk Officer, he was the last word when it came to recommendations. A reference from him could be my golden ticket.

"Thank you, River. I didn't expect our night to go like this."

My fingers mindlessly played with his chest hair.

"How do they usually go?" I needed to stop asking those types of questions. It was none of my business.

"Usually, I toss back a few drinks to get enough courage to enter the bedroom. I've been more of a connoisseur going from girl to girl, embarrassed to invite the same girl back for follow-on encounters. This relationship has to go both ways. Until tonight, I've never felt like any of the girls were looking after my interests, so I wasn't concerned with theirs."

"Do you want to see me again, Paul?" Lord, I could do worse than Paul. I could teach him how to perform oral sex like a champion—the way I liked it. In exchange, he could provide the connections I needed to excel.

"Yes, I do." There was no hesitation.

"I'll look forward to your call, Paul. In the meantime, I want you to buy a bunch of ripe peaches. Cut a slit from end to end and practice getting the tender flesh from the pit without destroying the fruit." I read that in Cosmo once. I had no idea if it would work, but it would keep him focused on a skill he *could* master.

Fifteen minutes later, I was in a cab with my self-esteem intact and a hefty tip in my pocket. Although I was with Paul for slightly over two hours, I rounded down and entered my time into the system. Paul Yoder was a man I could respect. He may be lacking below the belt, but he had business savvy and a big heart.

I texted Jade to let her know I was alive and well. There would be no crying tonight.

Chapter 14

Anthony Baldwin sat outside in the crisp September air, sipping an espresso. I knew it was him because he had the look of money. He was also wearing jeans and a lavender polo, just like he said he would. He deserved a closer inspection.

"Anthony?" Dressed in black slacks, a black and white geometric blouse and black flats, I offered my hand. Mr. Smooth stood, took my hand and kissed it, all the while checking me out from beneath his wasted-on-a-guy eyelashes.

"River, you're prettier in person."

I was going to have to talk to Sandra if people kept telling me I was prettier than my pictures.

"Thank you."

A chair slid out beside me, giving me a start. I didn't see the waiter approach. I ordered a latte and sat back to let the meeting unfold. It seemed like a lifetime since I had my first meet-and-greet, but in fact, it had been about a week. Grey hair and eyes stared back at me. Were we playing chicken? Who would break the silence first? I folded and began a discussion about the recent crash in Temtech stock.

"What do you think is causing the disruption in Temtech?"

My latte was delivered, and my order of eggs Benedict placed. Anthony pushed back in his chair. With one ankle resting on his knee, he leaned back comfortably and visibly relaxed. I never considered the men could be as nervous as me. Until last night, their feelings about rejection had never crossed my mind. I figured they would just move on to the next available girl.

"Losing half of your stock's value isn't a disruption; it's a crash. They were banking on their new app to pull its weight, but with all the glitches and Semtech producing a clone that works, I imagine they are going to be feeling the pain for some time."

"Isn't Semtech a family rival? That seems cruel to produce a clone and wait for your family to fail." Or maybe that was normal family dynamics. I had no siblings, so failure sat squarely on my shoulders, and so far, I was exceeding expectations.

"They are the modern Hatfields and McCoys, except they are brothers. Rumor has it, one sabotaged the other."

"No way. That's the stuff of movies."

He rolled his eyes and said, "Way," mocking me.

I scowled.

He smiled.

I sipped.

He stared.

"So, River, you're a business major with an emphasis in finance. I own a brokerage firm and shuffle people's money."

He didn't just own a brokerage firm; he owned a chain of them, with offices in every major city around the country. He was fifty-eight, twice divorced, and lived in Manhattan. *I loved Google.* We spent the rest of the hour eating breakfast and in deep conversation about investments. All in all, the meeting was...pleasant.

My phone began to ring as Anthony and I said goodbye. He kissed me on the cheek, and we went our separate ways. These meetings were always so weird: you met, ate, and marked your sheet. I reached for my phone and snarled. It was my mom.

"Hi, Mom. What's up?"

"Daddy and I are coming to the city tomorrow afternoon. There's a visiting pastor, and since we were free, we thought we'd come to see our girl." Inside, I was screaming *NO,* but I would never have uttered the word out loud.

"That's great, Mom. Tips have been pretty good this week, so how about I take you guys to lunch or dinner?" If I could meet them somewhere and get the interrogation over with, I could resume my normal parent-free life. Thankfully, my day was free. What would I have done if my Sunday had been booked?

"That sounds lovely. You know your dad and I are on a fixed income." Duh, I was well aware of how their finances stood.

"How about I meet you at Dim Sumptuous for a late lunch? Let's say one o'clock." I crossed my fingers, hoping the plan was acceptable.

"That sounds sumptuous," she said, like she was the cleverest person in the world. Like no one had said that before.

"Gotta go, Mom." I hung up before she could say another word. Better to leave her happy with herself than disappointed with me.

I rushed into the corner store to pick up a little joke for Jonathan. He said he needed a distraction. I bought him a Rubik's Cube keychain.

The rest of the afternoon was spent primping and packing.

Rather than wear garters and hose, I wore nothing. He asked me—no, told me—to never wear underwear with him again. I picked out a beautiful bra, a simple white lace with a silver satin ribbon that ran along the edge. Last time, I wore bottoms and no top—today would be the opposite. Between the two days, I'd worn a complete set of lingerie. I twisted my hair into a simple up-do, securing it with rhinestone-ended bobby pins. The one-shouldered dress screamed for an elegant hairstyle. I slipped my bare feet into jeweled, silver sling-backs and slid the gown's silky fabric carefully over my head.

At precisely seven o'clock, the intercom buzzed and Howard announced his arrival. I felt silly carrying a small university duffle bag while wearing a designer gown, but it was all I had. Tucked in the side was a small, white box containing the little gift I'd purchased for

Jonathan. It was a silly little thing, but I hoped he accepted it with the humor intended. We were blocks away before I realized I had forgotten my wrap.

The city lights blended into a kaleidoscope of colors and shapes. My head shuffled between the evening ahead and lunch tomorrow. Both affected my stomach. One gave me the flutter of a butterfly or two. The other gave me an ulcer. The butterflies won the battle when they multiplied and raced through my veins at the sight of Jonathan standing by the curb.

"Unbelievable."

One word, and I melted at his leather shoes. I knew exactly why he'd selected this dress, as it was split nearly to the top of my thigh. All it would take was a gust of air to show everyone my lack of panties. He took my hand and pulled me from the car. His tongue ran the length of his lips. Having been pleasured by those lips, I felt the heat begin where the butterflies left my stomach and descended to the area between my thighs. My girly parts were already beginning to dampen and throb.

"You are incredibly handsome in your tux, Mr. Ferris." I reached up to touch his silver bowtie. It was the perfect match to my dress. He was a details man. I turned my head and glanced at my bag.

"Leave it there. Howard will be with the car all night. I'm glad you remembered. That pleases me."

And pleasing him pleased me. I leaned into the car and pulled the small white box from the bag. "This is for you. It's a small distraction."

"A gift for me?"

"Don't get all excited, it's a silly thing."

He opened the box and began to laugh. "Are you trying to keep me occupied for hours? And I thought you liked me." He held the keychain by the ring and dangled it in front of my eyes. I grabbed it from his hand and attempted to toss it in a nearby trash can. He stopped me. "You can't throw my gift away. It's mine."

"It was silly." Standing in front of him, I felt ridiculous giving him a stupid keychain. I should have given the gesture more thought.

"It was considerate." He pulled it from my hand and placed it in his pocket. "I brought you something, too." From his jacket pocket, he pulled out a long, thin box.

The blood rushed from my face to my rapidly beating heart. I held the box gingerly in my hand. I didn't know why I was so nervous, as it could be a Rubik's Cube on a keychain.

Tired of waiting, Jonathan pulled the lid free to reveal a silver bracelet with a sun charm. Emotion threatened to choke me. When he placed it on my wrist, I didn't know what to say, so I said nothing. Instead, I rose up on my tiptoes and thanked him with a kiss. We stayed outside on the steps of the Opera House, connected by our lips for minutes. When we separated, I could tell he knew how pleased I was.

I whispered in his ear, "You please me."

The joy he appeared to be feeling reached his eyes first—the tiny crinkles lifted with his grin. The light twinkled off the amber chips embedded in his dark brown irises. On his arm, we entered the chaos of the evening. Once again, I was unprepared. I had no idea what I was supposed to be to him. He was obviously going to be with some of his peers, maybe people he knew socially. I should have asked him some questions. He noticed the moment I stiffened. All I heard were his words in my head telling me, *I know what you need.* And from that moment, I trusted that he did.

Several people approached him. His hand wrapped protectively around my waist, pulling me closer to his side. With my thoughts focused on the feelings shooting through my body, I barely caught the name of the woman in front of me.

"Grace, this is River." Grace eyed me. Her lips moved, but her eyes and forehead were paralyzed by vanity. I offered her a friendly shake. The charm sparkled under the venue lights.

"How sweet," she said, looking at the bracelet. Her hands were encrusted with diamonds. The weight of them must have accounted for a tenth of her body weight.

"Thank you." I pulled my hand back, letting it fall safely next to Jonathan.

"I found it at Tiffany's today. It's perfect for River. She's a ray of sunshine on an otherwise gloomy day." He firmed his hand around my waist. He must have known my knees were going to buckle at the mention of Tiffany's. *Tiffany's?* I should have recognized the blue box, but I was so surprised by the gift, it didn't register. I gave him a three-dollar keychain, and he gave me Tiffany's. Now I was even more embarrassed by the trinket I brought him. Mortified even.

We mingled with the other patrons and looked at the art for sale. Most of it looked like an angry child had thrown paint on a canvas, but there was one that resembled flowers in a meadow. Abstract in every way, it was the only one with warmth and beauty. The rest were cold and lifeless.

"Shall we find our seats?" His hand sat just below the small of my back, scandalously close to my bottom.

"Yes, let's hurry. I feel the need for a distraction." I pulled his hand toward the theater entrance. He pulled me to a stop.

"You are a beautiful distraction." And right there, for the whole world to see, he kissed me slowly and sweetly. He wasn't ashamed of who and what I was. He didn't treat me like a cheap bauble. He treated me like a treasure. I felt like the Hope Diamond.

We entered the theatre late, having been waylaid by the kiss. *A perfect kiss.* His box sat dead center. Walled in on three sides, private had been an accurate description. Two plush chairs sat in front by the rail. A bottle of champagne chilled in the corner. I scooted as far as the chair would let me, but the arm blocked me from getting to him. Just like at breakfast, he patted his lap and I crawled into his arms.

I peeked at the stage and saw the singers serenading the pictures that appeared at random intervals. Nothing happening down there interested me. Everything worth paying attention to was right here in this private box. The slit of my dress fell open, exposing my legs. My eyes looked around to make sure no one could see what we were up to. I knew where this was going.

He chuckled. "No one can see."

The feather-light touch of his fingers left a trail of goosebumps from my ankle to my thigh. He shifted in his seat. I wasn't sure if it was to adjust his hardness, or if the shift was a guise to spread my legs. I leaned against his chest and opened myself to his exploration.

"Mmmm, you listened."

His fingers slipped inside me easily, as there was nothing that hindered his progress. I moaned softly in his ear while he stroked me gently, but purposefully. His thumb rubbed the bundle of nerves until I shook in his arms. I labored to breathe, my moans muffled by his jacket.

"Come for me, Sunshine."

It didn't happen like in the movies, where someone commanded you to come and you detonated on the spot. It happened with a slow build to an incredible crescendo. I closed my eyes and let him take me to places I'd never been. The music played in the background while the world shattered around me. The explosion, an array of colors, only seen in the recesses of my mind. I lay in his arms until I gained the strength to move.

"I love the opera." My lips traced his ear, dipping down to nibble on his lobe. His growl, an aphrodisiac for the second act.

"I have a newfound interest in the arts myself," he said.

Sliding down his lap to sit at his feet, I adjusted his cummerbund and unzipped his pants. I was well below the rail, so there was no risk of exposure. I let him loose and began at the silken tip, where a bead of salty goodness sat like a gift. With gentle licks, I lapped it up like the gold it was.

He shifted in his seat, pushing his hips toward me, silently begging me to take more. I ran my tongue down one side and up the other, using his throbbing vein as a roadmap to his pleasure. His fingers played in the fallen tendrils of my hair. His eyes focused on every move I made. Pulling him in, I suckled his flesh until he squirmed in the chair. His body tensed.

"River."

His tone was a stern warning for me to pull away, but selfishly I wanted it all, so I sucked and pulled until he spilled inside my mouth. I swallowed every pulse and licked him clean before I tucked him back into his pants and zipped him up. Rising to my feet, I walked to the champagne and poured us both a glass. I sipped mine, swirled and swallowed. I crawled into his lap and covered his mouth with mine.

"How was the distraction? Oh look, there's an opera going on down there. I hardly noticed."

I leaned forward in his lap, looking over the rail. Hundreds of people watched the stage. I turned and watched him.

His chin sat between his thumb and finger while he stroked back and forth in contemplation. He shook his head and looked away.

"I didn't expect to like you this much. What am I going to do with you?" He pulled me into his kiss. Hard thuds beat in my chest as I processed his declaration. Was it good? Bad?

I moved from his lips to his ear and whispered, "Just be with me. Nothing else is required. Enjoy me. I'll enjoy you. We'll enjoy each other. It's that simple."

"Is it?" His words made me wonder. Without notice, he pulled me to my feet and led me to the exit. The cold air blew across my skin, making the small hairs stand on end. "I thought I sent a wrap with that dress."

"You did. In the excitement, I forgot it."

I wrapped my arms around my chest and shivered. I felt so silly now. He pulled his phone from his pocket, removed his jacket, and placed it over my shoulders. Chivalry hadn't died—it lived in this man. He placed a call and then pulled me against his chest. Moments later, Howard arrived with the car. I was curious why we had left the opera early.

"Were you tired of the opera?"

"I wanted to enjoy you, and I didn't want to share you."

Aww, how sweet was that? This would have been the nicest date if that were what it had been. But it wasn't, and I needed to keep reminding myself of that.

"Where are we headed?"

"The Ritz."

With my head on his shoulder, we traveled in silence to the hotel. He checked us in and led me into another beautiful room. My stomach grumbled, and he laughed.

"I'm going to have to feed you."

"Yes, you are, because knowing you, I'll need my energy."

He picked up the phone and ordered two steaks, wedge salads, and a bottle of cabernet.

The pins in my hair were the first things to go. He sighed as it fell in loose ringlets down my back. Next was the dress. He removed it and carefully placed it on a chair in the living area. In the center of the room, I stood in heels and a bra.

"We have about thirty minutes. Not nearly enough time for anything but an appetizer."

And just like that, I was laid on the bed and feasted upon until he had made me scream his name twice. The man was a god. When I could open my eyes and look into his face, I saw…joy? He seemed happy to have given me two spectacular orgasms.

Who is this man?

A knock at the door sent me scurrying from the room before the third could take hold.

"It's safe to come out." The clank of silverware meant he was at the table.

Cocooned in the robe I found hanging behind the bathroom door, I floated into the living area high from the endorphins running through my body.

"Who is Grace?" She had bordered between sweet and hostile. It would be great to know their connection.

"She's my sister-in-law, Claire's sister." Wow, I totally didn't expect that. I wondered if his wife resembled her. I was curious about the woman Jonathan had loved so dearly. "She was in charge of the auction. All proceeds are going to breast cancer research."

"Is that what Claire died from?" Not my business, but I wanted to know.

"Yes, years ago."

I chewed on that information at the same time as I chewed on my steak. One tasted delicious, the other bitter. I wondered if she'd called his name while he'd made her come over and over again. My jealousy was completely unreasonable. He had made it clear that Claire had been the love of his life. That is why, after all, I was with him tonight, and any other night he gave me. I wouldn't ever own his heart. I had to smash down the ridiculous urge to be more.

After dinner, we fell into bed and made love slowly and passionately. We lay entwined with my head on his chest, my hand in his hand.

"What was the best thing about your family?" he asked. I was baffled by his question.

I answered quickly, "Their absence." It was sad but true.

"Come on, there had to be something good."

"Donut Sundays." Memories of hiding in the kitchen with Jade, our faces smeared with chocolate ran through my head. I loved donut Sundays.

"Okay, now tell me the worst thing."

I had two very distinct feelings from my childhood. Living in a fishbowl does that to you. "Being invisible, and yet always on display." Saying it out loud was a revelation, but also painful.

"Your parents were probably proud of you."

"Never." Hot tears pooled in my eyes, but I willed them to stay away. There was no way I was ruining this night by crying. However, I decided to share one thing that would give him some insight into my childhood. "When I was a kid, my parents would hold these clothing drives. Clothes for the poor. My mom would rummage through the donations first and choose my clothes from the piles of everyone else's discards. I'll never forget the day a girl in high school told me she liked my outfit. Apparently, it had been hers the year before. I was made the laughingstock of the school." Jade had my back then, too. It took weeks for that girl's black eye to heal.

He squeezed me to his side and held me there. The comfort of his embrace smoothed the sharp edges of the razor stabbing my heart. Until I moved away from my parents', I never had a new outfit. Even my underwear had been hand-me-downs.

"You said you were invisible, but what does that mean?"

"I was a disappointment, and so eventually I was ignored."

He turned to me and grabbed my chin. "That's not possible. You could never be a disappointment, and you're too beautiful to ignore."

"I was expected to be perfect. When I wasn't, it was worse than a sin. I was locked in the chapel until my dad was given a sign I was forgiven. They would walk around me as if I didn't exist." I felt his muscles tense. "When Mom called today and told me they were coming to lunch tomorrow, I wanted to scream. I took comfort in knowing I would be with you tonight…" I hesitated before adding, "…as in your arms…I matter."

Was that too much? He'd said we'd enjoy each other, but what if me being so honest was not really what he wanted from me?

This was business, River. You wouldn't share that with a boss, would you?

Chapter 15

Whispers from the door woke me. I pulled the blankets over my head and hid. However, the smell of fresh coffee pulled me from my comfortable cocoon.

"Breakfast in bed, Sunshine."

I peeked over the blanket at the tray Jonathan had put in the center of the bed. Fresh croissants and raspberry jam, berries, and cream, lox and bagels. He ordered an assortment of items, a veritable smorgasbord for me. He handed me a latte and moved in for a kiss. I turned my head to avoid his lips. There was no way I would assault him with my foul breath.

"I have morning breath. Ewww." I rolled to the side of the bed and headed straight to the bathroom, where my toothbrush lay on the marble counter. Minty fresh, I returned to his bed and his kisses.

"I don't care about your breath. I just wanted to kiss you."

And he did for over an hour. By the time we finished, breakfast was cold and my latte was flat, but my lips felt wonderfully swollen, and my heart felt full.

We lay in bed for the rest of the morning, watched TV, and made love. I knew it wasn't really love, but it was the way I would want a man who loved me to have sex with me. When Jonathan had sex, he focused solely on me. It was beautiful to be seen, especially by someone so incredible. It was as if I were worth his time.

Time passed too quickly, and I was forced to shower and dress so I could attack the day ahead of me. I feared leaving him alone in the bedroom. Would I come out and find him gone with only a note and money to confirm his existence?

"Will you be here when I come out?" He smiled, which looked *so* good on Jonathan. Why did he have to be so attractive?

"Yes, I only left you the other day because I didn't want it to be awkward."

"Leaving me made it awkward." Without thought, my lower lip dropped to a pout.

"I'm sorry, that wasn't my intent." His expressive eyes lowered.

"You don't have to be sorry. I want to enjoy another kiss before you go. I don't know when you'll want my company again, so I have to make it last." I didn't wait for his response. I turned around and walked into the bathroom. The charm bracelet shone under the harsh bathroom lighting. A sun made of metal possessed with the power to warm my heart.

His thoughtfulness overwhelmed me. Never had I felt so comfortable in a man's presence. Take the extravagant trappings away, and I'd still like him. He was nice and incredibly sexy. The bracelet slid from my wrist to sit on the counter. I'd wear it today to remind myself of him. Although I would be surrounded by darkness, I had become sunshine to someone else.

When I emerged from the bathroom, he was sitting in the plush chair by the window dressed in jeans and a button-down shirt. In his hand was part of the day's newspaper, and the rest lay in sections at his bare feet. Reading glasses framed his eyes. I'd never seen him wear them before, but they looked damn sexy on him.

He lowered the paper. Tossing it to the side, he patted his lap and I crawled onto it. This had become my favorite place in the world.

"Are you going to be okay today?" His head tilted as he stared at me. He must be inquiring about lunch with my parents. *Would I be okay?* I could never be sure when it came to them. It all depended on the level at which they intended to wound me. My list of sins covered clothes to education, premarital sex to alcohol. It was never the same, and yet, it was always the same. Their intent was to crush my self-esteem and conquer my spirit. Short of becoming cloistered, I'd never be able to make them proud. After twenty-five years of trying, I'd just about given up.

"Of course. I'm meeting them at Dim Sumptuous at one. I'm hoping to be out of there by two and back home by three." The chances of that happening were slim. It would take my mother at least an hour to list my sins, and then she'd give me several ideas on how to earn back grace. I'd be lucky if I got away by four, but I didn't want to burden Jonathan with my issues. That's not what he paid for.

"River, don't let them dim your light." He gave me a firm, reassuring hug. He always seemed to know when I needed reinforcement.

We left together. I insisted on taking a cab so he didn't have to go out of his way. He kissed me before he placed me safely in the taxi. *Safely* was funny to think about because I had never considered riding in the back seat of a New York cab safe. I leaned out the window and waved goodbye. The sun glinted off my charm bracelet, reminding me that he thought of me as warmth and light.

<hr>

WHEN I TOLD Jade I was meeting my parents for lunch, she groaned and told me to step in front of a bus. It would probably be less painful. I laughed and continued to get ready. It took over thirty minutes to choose an outfit that wasn't sexy, too sassy, or a million other things my mother would find wrong with it. In the end, I chose the same outfit I wore the last time I saw them. I could remind her she'd seen it before, and maybe she would think I was being a good steward of my money.

Dressed in blue slacks and a conservative sweater, I stood outside the restaurant and waited. It wasn't easy to stick your head in the guillotine. I allowed myself a few minutes for my breathing to normalize and my heartbeat to steady. Every time I'd been forced to see them, I felt like a dead man walking. With my pride tucked away, I entered the restaurant to find my mother's face pinched, staring at her watch. I was five minutes early, and still, she frowned. *Five minutes early*. My father's air of superiority weighted the atmosphere. For two people full of grace, they were the most miserable looking souls I'd ever seen.

"You're pushing the time, River. I thought I taught you better. Timeliness is next to godliness." She rushed over to pull the collar of my sweater higher up my neck before she patted me on the head like a Cocker Spaniel. I wanted to roll my eyes, but that never worked out well for me.

The hostess seated us directly under the head of a dragon, and somehow it felt appropriate to have its open mouth leaning in to swallow me up. I fidgeted with my collar and looked at my mother, who began her diatribe on the sins of women in the workforce. Once she finished, she moved on to the loose morals of today's young women. I attempted to listen, but it was the same distorted voice on repeat. The only sound I heard was Jonathan's, calling me Sunshine. Holding on to his voice would help me through the afternoon. Every time she would remind me I was nothing, I would remind myself I was the ray of light that brightened an otherwise gloomy day.

A shadow loomed over me, and I swore the dragon had decided enough was enough. He would just swallow me whole and put me out of my misery. Quicker and less messy than the front of a bus, perhaps? That was when I heard *his* voice.

"Hey, Sunshine, sorry I'm late. I got stuck in traffic."

He slid into the booth next to me and pressed his lips to mine in a sweet, comforting kiss. His fist unfolded, and he set his keys on the table. The Rubik's Cube took center stage.

I was speechless, but he was not. I couldn't wrap my head around his presence. One minute a dragon was devouring me, and the next an angel was saving me.

"I should introduce myself. I'm Jonathan Ferris. I'm seeing your beautiful daughter." He emphasized the word *seeing*, and I knew it was purely for my benefit. My parents were silenced.

Chapter 16

Jonathan's hand disappeared under the table to rest on my knee. His presence reassured me. My parents acted like someone had cut out their tongues. It was mildly entertaining to see their discomfort. However, I would pay for it later.

"Sunday seems an odd day for a pastor to be away from his flock. How did you manage that?" Jonathan was a smart man, and getting my father to talk about himself was the smartest way for him to forget about me.

"We had a guest pastor step in today. Regina and I haven't seen River for several months. We wanted to make sure she was faring well."

Jonathan felt my leg tense. His hand rubbed gently, and his touch comforted me. I relaxed, and he patted me as if I had pleased him.

"River, I wasn't aware you were bringing a guest." My mother obviously didn't approve of the man sitting beside me. He could have been Jesus himself, and she would never have approved.

"It was a last-minute decision." I turned to Jonathan. "I'm so glad you could make it." We stared at each other until my father coughed to get our attention.

"What do you do, Jonathan?" My father knew quality when he saw it. Everything from Jonathan's hair down to his Italian loafers screamed money. When money was screaming, my father was listening. He saw money, and money meant donations.

"I do a lot of things, Mr. Roberts. My interests vary, from finance to property management. It's important to diversify. You wouldn't want to put all your eggs in one basket now, would you?" He stared at my father. His eyes were scanning him, much in the same way he did me the first night we met.

For whatever reason, I thought of Jade in that moment. She told me her situation was risky because all her eggs were in the duo's basket. It may be risky, but at least it was simple. Every time she went home, she knew what she was getting. Or did she? Obviously, the duo had thrown her a curveball. Was anything simple these days?

"Well, Mr. Ferris, I would say it depends on whose basket you're choosing. Are you a religious man?"

My father was digging. I wanted to grab a proverbial shovel and bash him over the head.

"I wouldn't call myself a religious man, but I've had a lot of heavenly experiences." He squeezed my knee again, and I wondered if he considered his time with me divine. I replayed the opera in my head and shivered at the memory of taking him into my mouth. The music hit its climax at the same time he did. It had been a thing of beauty.

My mother chimed in, ruining my perfect moment. "How do you know my daughter? You appear to be quite a bit older than River. Some would raise their eyes to your motives."

In my mind, I've now taken the shovel and smacked her in her puckered mouth. Her beady little eyes never wavered from Jonathan.

"I can assure you that when it comes to River, I always have her needs in the forefront of my mind. She is lovely and smart. You should be proud of her accomplishments. Earning an MBA is not easy. Where did you go to college, Mrs. Roberts?" He hit his mark.

"Education is wasted on women, Mr. Ferris. We've been telling River that very thing since she started college. She doesn't need a career. It's a waste of time and money," she said. My father earned his bachelor degree in Christian Ministry. My mother never went to college.

"I disagree with you. In this day and age, you need every edge available to make it. River was wise to enter into her master's program right away. As for how we met, we have mutual acquaintances who introduced us." His eyes turned to me, and in them, I saw the same look I saw when he told me *I know what you need.*

"One of the best days of my life," I murmured, hoping he would understand the depth of my intention in the comment.

"Hey, Sunshine, you don't mind if I order for all of us, do you? You know how I love Dim Sum." He looked at my parents. "Do you mind?"

They shook their heads, and Jonathan ordered a buffet of choices. My mother would have a conniption at the waste. I'd be hearing about it until I was thirty.

She continued to eye the man next to me. I could see her trying to figure out if I was sleeping with him or not. She was calculating her next move. Unfortunately, she wouldn't get the opportunity because Jonathan set the pace for the day.

"We hate to eat and run, but River and I had the day planned. She insisted we take the time to meet you for lunch. Unfortunately, our schedule is very tight, and we only have about an hour to spare. I'm sure you understand, given the pulls you must feel from your community."

Oh, the man was smooth.

I don't think my parents had ever been told that someone didn't have time *for them.* They had always been treated with importance, but it was obvious Jonathan wasn't impressed or intimidated by them. He had come to protect me, and that warmed my heart. I knew he had more important things to do, but for whatever reason, this man continued to validate me in the most wonderful and unexpected ways. If he was not careful, I might actually believe I mattered.

My mother began a retort, but my father silenced her by raising his hand. I'd always wanted to do that. Just once. To raise my hand and have her shut up would have been wonderful.

Adding insult to my mother's bruised ego, my father said, "Wouldn't it be nice if all women were seen and not heard?" No one appreciated my father's attempt at humor except for my father.

Jonathan's hand stiffened on my knee. I'd never seen him be anything but calm. To the unsuspecting eye, Jonathan always appeared peaceful and easygoing, but I felt something change.

"Mr. Roberts, I mean you no disrespect, but you're an asshole. Why exist if you have to be seen and not heard? In fact, it's my understanding you preferred River when she was unseen and unheard. I spent my time driving over here wondering how a man of God could treat a beautiful creation of God with such disrespect. Now that I've met you, I see you hide behind God not to serve him, but to pretend He serves you." I'm not sure if my mouth dropped open or not, but I swear the entire table was silenced by Jonathan's words.

My heart beat boldly against my chest. My eyes stared at my lover. As always, he *saw* me, and he knew what I needed. I needed to be free of my parents' interference. He knew I could never do it on my own, so he'd stepped in to help.

"You have no right to talk to us that way." My mother's face scrunched as she blustered. "You don't know River. She was an awful child, too pretty for her own good. She inflamed the boys around her to sin. We've been trying to save her all her life."

That's when I'd finally had it. I didn't need Jonathan to protect me, but I was grateful he was there.

"I've had it with you two. All my life, you accused me of being things I wasn't. You started calling me Jezebel when I was twelve. Do you realize my first sexual encounter was at sixteen—almost seventeen—and I did it to piss you off for locking me in the chapel for three days? I had nothing to eat but the grape juice and white bread left for communion."

My father piped in and said in a voice as cruel as a winter storm, but colder, "You were sucking that boy's joystick behind the pulpit. You shamed me in my own home."

"You've been calling me a whore for years. I figured if I was given the title, I might as well live up to the name." Jonathan wrapped his arm around me and pulled me to his side. If I had my way, I would have crawled into his lap.

"Are you ready to go?" He turned my head to look into my tear-filled eyes. His amber flecks danced in the light. Eyes that warmed me from the inside out.

"No." He looked startled at first but only nodded his head. "I have more to say."

My mother leaned across the table, and I flinched. I expected to catch the flat of her palm, but instead, I caught the edge of her sharp voice. "You will never be anything, River. You were never anything but ungrateful."

The table rattled as Jonathan's fist slammed down on the top. His keychain hopped several inches by the force alone. "Stop." Looking at my parents, he delivered his message with cool clarity. "River is everything that's wonderful in the world. She is brightness and light. She is compassion and hope. She is laughter. She's my sunshine, and I will not let you dim her light in any way. You will not call her or contact her. If she ever wants to speak to you again, it will be on her terms." He pulled a handful of twenties from his pocket and tossed them on the table. "Lunch is on me. The shame is on you."

Sliding from the booth, he offered me his hand. I placed my palm in his, willing to follow him anywhere. I didn't look back. No, from that point on, the only direction was forward.

By the time we were on the street, his hands were on my face, wiping the tears that fell freely.

"It wasn't my place to fight for you. I didn't want you to face them alone. They sounded awful by your description, but they were worse in person. How did you turn out so wonderful in spite of them?"

This crazy man just saved me from weeks of self-loathing and hate. And *he* stood in front of me and apologized.

"You were amazing." I was sure I looked like a fool. My eyes were glazed over with tears and affection. I fell into his arms and buried my head in his chest. "I love that you came. No one has ever stood up for me."

"It was an impulsive choice, and I should have asked. Shall I get you home? Howard is off, so you will have to trust my driving." He dangled his keys in front of my face, the Rubik's Cube held between his fingers.

"You used the keychain." It shocked me to see his keys hanging from the dime-store bauble. He'd placed it on the table like it was a trophy. Now he held it like it was a treasure.

"It means something to me. You took your time picking it out. It was thoughtful and humorous. I've tried it several times, but I'm awful at it. When I see it, I think of you."

Pulled next to him, he walked me down the block and away from the restaurant, away from my parents, away from my past. Despite what should have been devastation, I felt like I was floating.

He sounded like what we had was something more than what it was. It was sex. Great sex, but when it was broken down, it was an exchange of money for services.

Sitting with my parents today, I realized their taunts had become a self-fulfilling prophecy. For years they'd called me Jezebel, and I'd had no idea what that meant. I was young and thought it was a gypsy name, like Esmeralda from the animated cartoon. My dark hair and blue eyes always caught people's attention. At twelve or thirteen, I was happy to have that moniker. Finally, one day I looked it up and saw it was a biblical name associated with painted women and prostitutes. What parent starts feeding a young mind that crap early on?

"I can get home. You don't have to take me." He ignored me and kept walking.

"What do you think about Greek food?" It dawned on me that it was after two and neither of us had eaten.

"You mean like kebabs and gyros?" My stomach grumbled at the mention of food. I was famished. What a shame my parents would feast on dim sum and Jonathan's generosity.

"Yes, like hummus and falafel and pitas and tzatziki. I don't know about you, but I'm hungry and there's a great little Greek place around the corner. Let's get it to go, and we'll take it to your place."

Holy shit. He wanted to go to my place. "You don't want to go to my apartment. It falls well below your standards."

"How do you know what my standards are? Besides, I've seen the lobby, so my expectations are pretty low." His look of concern was replaced by a smile. A sweet, heart-warming, panty-wetting smile.

Smiling, I tried to sound indignant but failed miserably. "You didn't just put down my home without seeing it, did you? I'll have you know, my apartment is much nicer than the lobby."

"Let's get lunch and go hang out at your place." He knew he was getting his way, but it was funny to watch how excited he got when he did.

"My roommate might be home. Is that a problem?"

"Nope, happy to meet her." He continued to amaze me.

"All right, I'm buying since you bought the dim sum. Also, today is off the clock."

"Are you taking me on a date, Ms. Roberts?" I loved his playful manner.

"Yes, Mr. Ferris, I think I might be doing exactly that." Wouldn't that be wonderful?

"What are my chances of getting lucky? It's been a taxing day." When I looked at him, I saw a young boy instead of a man. He was happy and carefree, and I was charmed.

"What kind of girl do you think I am?" Obviously, he knew what kind of girl I was. He knew my body intimately. Next was my mind.

"My kind."

And with that, our trip to Greece was stalled with a kiss. Why couldn't this man be mine? Why couldn't there be a smidgen of hope to keep him? Why? Because I was a paid commodity and he was a client. But for today, I could pretend he was mine, and I would.

We rounded the corner and entered a hole in the wall called the Caspian Cafe. After purchasing two gyros, a bag of falafels, and a pint of hummus with pitas, we were on our way to his car.

A Maserati Ghibli. He drove a freaking navy blue Maserati. "You have this amazing car, and you let Howard drive you around? What's wrong with you? I would be in this car all the time. It's amazing."

"Do you want to drive?" He held out the keys.

I contemplated the option for a minute and shook my head. There was no way I would want to drive this car in the congestion of the city.

"No way. What's the point of driving a Maserati if you're forced to drive under forty miles per hour? That seems criminal." On the open road, I might have considered it. Closing my eyes, I could see myself gun the accelerator and go from zero to sixty-five in four seconds flat. Oh, the thrill of a fast ride.

"It's one of the reasons I use Howard. Also, while Howard drives, I get to do naughty things to your body." The man just made me soak my panties. The ones I wasn't supposed to wear when I was with him.

Beep, beep.

The alarm disengaged, and we both hopped in. The engine roared to life with the push of a button. What a turn on. Hot men, fast cars, and gyros. This day couldn't get any better. Not true…the minute we got naked, the day would get infinitely better. I wondered if he would let me lick hummus off him. He could be my human pita.

Laughter erupted from my chest.

"What's so funny?" He glanced at me but turned his eyes back to the road.

"I was thinking dirty thoughts. I was hoping I could dip you in hummus and lick it off. You know, hummus to make you cummus." There goes my lack of filter, but seeing his shocked expression made it worth it.

"You're killing me, Sunshine." He glanced my way again and frowned.

"What are you looking at?"

"I'm trying to find a distraction that will stop me from getting hard. That sweater is working for me. Please tell me that outfit is going in the trash the minute we get to your place. I've never seen anything less attractive."

"I'll have you know, my mother thinks this outfit is too revealing." I tugged at the round neck that could almost be called a mock turtleneck. Another inch, and it would sit under my chin.

"What the hell does it reveal? Your head? It's awful." He reached over and touched the material. "And it's itchy. How have you tolerated this against your body all day?"

The truth was, I'd been pulling at it all day because the rough knit chafed my skin. "It's been a challenge, but I'll happily toss it when we get to my place."

"There better not be others like it in your closet. You should be dressed in silk and cashmere, not a fifty-fifty polyester blend." He looked appalled at the thought.

I didn't respond. I had an entire parent-friendly wardrobe taking up real estate in my closet. 'Parent-friendly' was a loose term, since nothing I wore short of a gunnysack was acceptable. I'd been the perfect example of ugly-clothes-wearing good people.

"I have some sorting out to do." The truth was I had a lot of sorting to do, both in my closet and my mind.

"Hmmm, speaking of your parents, how are you doing? This must have been a shock to your system." He turned onto my street and began to look for a place to park.

"No, it was a long time coming. I was too much of a coward to call them on their shit like you did. I was afraid of losing them…when in reality, I never had them. I had their hate and disgust. I had their contempt and disrespect. Today, you set me free, and I will always be grateful." I felt grateful, but I couldn't help the feelings of mortification from what he'd learned about me today.

He knew about the blowjob behind the pulpit. He knew they'd locked me away for three days.

"I can't imagine what that feels like. I'm sorry for your loss."

"You can't lose something you never had."

In a swift second, I felt free. I'd tried for years to be the perfect daughter. I floated between angel and devil to be seen, and all along I was a prop for their benefit. I was used as an example, a teaching element. I don't think my parents meant to be cruel, but they were. I think they used what they had to teach others. Too bad I was created to set the example. Sadly, *their* lie became *my* truth.

Chapter 17

There was no use feeling ashamed of where I lived. My life was a string of dismal facts. I lived in a mediocre neighborhood, in a rent-controlled property. I attended the university and now paid for it with the only thing I had to barter—my body.

What appeared to be a hellhole from the lobby actually opened into a charming apartment. The eclectic mix of furnishings gave the place a delightful cottage look.

Led Zeppelin's "Stairway to Heaven" blared from the stereo, about ten decibels past hearing loss. At the kitchen table, Tiffany sat clipping coupons. With a push of a button, I rescued our hearing by cutting the volume in half.

It was out of character for me to bring men to our apartment. Tiffany flashed me a smirk shortly after scanning Jonathan's body from head to toe. Jealousy ripped through me as I watched her eye-fuck him from her chair.

"Who's the hottie?" *Mine.*

Inside, I was screaming he was mine, when in reality nothing could be further from the truth. I watched him to see how he would react. He looked mildly amused. The crinkles in the corners of his eyes shifted before he did. He wrapped his free hand around my waist. His other hand held the bag with our food. The arm around me felt possessive. It was such an incredible feeling to have someone claim me, even if it was for show.

"This hottie belongs to me, and his name is Jonathan. We'll be in my room if you need us."

I pulled his hand from my waist and led him through the living room and down the hallway to my room. It wasn't much to look at, but it was tidy. Some habits were hard to break, and making sure my room was perfectly in order was one of them.

Cleanliness was next to godliness.

"I belong to you?" He closed the door behind us and set the bag of food on my dresser. "When did you decide that?"

What should I say? My heart decided the day I met him, but my head knew the reality of the situation. Maybe I should joke around and say my parts decided on our second encounter, or my lips decided on our first. It could have been the day at the opera when my body burst apart in his hands while strains of La Traviata provided the sublimely passionate background. I could have said all these things, but I didn't.

"Of course, you don't belong to me, but she doesn't know that. Besides, I don't like the way she looked at you."

Yep, I said something stupid. If this was what jealousy felt like, I'd have none of it. My stomach twisted from the emotion. A few minutes ago, my hands twitched to slap the look off Tiffany's face. Jealousy was an ugly beast, and I had no right or desire to feel it.

"Jealous? Really?" He slipped his arms around my waist and buried his head in my neck.

"I can't help it. You did an incredibly selfless thing for me today. You see me like no one ever has, and that's a powerful aphrodisiac. Call me crazy, but the whole thing that went down at Dim Sumptuous was foreplay. Totally sexy and powerfully arousing."

"How hungry are you?"

He walked me backward to my bed and pressed me to the

mattress. The weight of his body pushed me into the soft comforter. My body thrummed with excitement. This was so different from the hotel. He was on my turf, and somehow the rules had changed. This wasn't a paid-for adventure, but rather an experience to be enjoyed.

"Famished."

My lips sought his. My hands explored his body. Too many clothes. Tucked into his pants, his shirt sat snugly. Tugging and pulling, I slid it up and over his head. The hair of his chest demanded the attention of my fingers.

"Famished, huh?" His breathing had altered. The pace quickened with each kiss. His hardness pressed against me. Soaked were the ugly cotton briefs I'd put on for the inquisition.

"Starving."

His belt buckle slowed me down, but I managed to pull it free. Frantic, I pulled at the button and zipper of his jeans. If I didn't get him inside of me in seconds, I might perish. It was a silly thought. Of course, I wouldn't perish, but for some reason, he anchored me. He called me Sunshine, but in reality, he would be the light in my life. The days I spent with him would warm me from the inside out and give me the strength to get through the days without him. I realized I was treading on dangerous ground. Jade was right—my first would always be special.

"You are insatiable."

He rose to remove the rest of his clothes. Naked in front of me, I stared. My mouth watered at the sight of him. He was amazing. Seemingly chiseled from granite, his hard body called to me. I reached and pulled him toward me with an urgency and hunger I wasn't familiar with.

"River, what's wrong?"

His body balanced on his strong arms above me. Concern was etched on his face. The only thing wrong was he was not inside me. Everything would be perfect once he was.

"Nothing. Nothing is wrong. Everything is right. It's just taking too long to make it perfect."

I began to pull at my own clothes. The ugly sweater felt like sandpaper against my flesh, particularly since my skin was hypersensitive from arousal. He stood up, pulled me to my feet, and lifted the material from my body. It was disposed of in the corner.

"Throw that piece of shit away. I never want to see you in it again. Don't ever hide your beauty." He quickly divested me of my pants. With a shake of his head, he stared at my white cotton briefs.

A ripple of fear ran down my back. He told me never to wear underwear when I was with him. Certainly, he'd overlook it this time. I had no idea he was coming.

"Jonathan, I'm sorry. I didn't know you would—"

His placed a finger over my lips and silenced me. "You're not in trouble. I can't say these please me. I don't recognize the girl who wears them." He tugged at the panties until they fell to the floor, then picked them up and tossed them onto the sweater. "This is the girl I know, the one with a smile in her heart that shows on every part of her body. This girl pleases me. *Amazes me.* This girl turns me on."

Fire seemed to burn in his eyes as he took in my body. I could see his breathing quicken. I please him. I *amaze* him?

The condom he pulled from his pants was rolled on quickly, and he was in me before I could take my next breath. I wasn't sure who needed whom more. His lovemaking was desperate, like he was trying to fill a gaping hole. He'd told me sometimes he would take me hard and fast, sometimes hard and slow. Sometimes, it would take hours to get enough of me. Today, his pace was quick and focused. His strokes powerful but measured. All the while, his eyes never left mine. Something hid behind them that I didn't understand. It was something more than passion. There was a softness that resembled love, and yet I knew it couldn't be. Would never be.

His thumb circled around my bundle of nerves. The sensations were so powerful, I almost came right then. It was when his eyes shifted and watched as he pressed himself in and out of me that I broke apart. When his fingers slipped around his girth to feel me sheathe him, I exploded around him. He continued to tease my pulsing bud with his fingers until I could no longer stand the intensity of his touch. Bearing down, I squeezed him inside me, hoping to halt the torturous pleasure. He stilled and gave himself up to me. I relished in every pulse and twitch.

Sliding gently from inside me, he collapsed on the bed beside me. Pulling the edge of the comforter over both of us, I snuggled up next to his body in search of the warmth it offered.

"Why is it so good with you?"

Was that a real question, or simply a questioning statement? I had no idea how to answer him. I didn't know why it was so good between us, but it was. Our bodies talked to each other. My heart beat differently when he was with me. Its rhythm stronger. Chemistry. We had undeniable chemistry.

"It is good, isn't it?"

I'd love to tell him he was like no other man, but I wasn't allowed to discuss other men with him. I'd love to ask him how many women he saw. Was I really the only one right now? Unfortunately, it wasn't appropriate. It was at these times I was reminded of what I was. I was not his date, his girlfriend, or his friend. I was a paid companion. Although, today felt different.

"Your mind seems like it's somewhere else. Where did you go?"

He rolled to his side so he could see me. I felt him adjust himself and realized he was removing the condom. Reaching for the tissues on my nightstand, I handed him a couple so he could wrap it up and set it aside.

"I never left you," I said honestly. My thoughts always seemed to be on him. "I was just thinking about what you said, and I'm trying to figure out why everything with you is more. It's like my soul knows you, but I don't really know you very well at all. It's hard to explain."

"Ask me anything you want. Today is your day. We're on your time." He played with my hair, pushing it away from my face. I liked having it cover part of my face. With it pushed aside, I felt completely exposed.

"Why commando? I've never seen you wear underwear." I slid my hand down and rested it on his bare hip.

He lay silently beside me for several minutes. How hard could it be to divulge why he was always freeballing?

"Okay, I'll tell you, but I'm breaking my rule about talking about other women. Are you okay with that?" He watched my face for the truth.

Was I okay with that? Did I want to know about other women in his life? No. Yes. I wanted to know everything about him.

"Yes, I want to know."

I rolled my bottom lip between my teeth, biting the soft tissue inside. It was a nervous habit I'd had for as long as I could remember. I'd been known to chew a hole right through it if my stress levels were too high for too long.

"Stop chewing your lip, and I'll tell you. I'll chew your lip later if that makes you feel any better."

"Promise?" I might like him chewing my lip.

He leaned up on his elbow and began his commando explanation.

"Claire and I were trying to conceive for several years, but it wasn't working. We both went to the doctor, and they couldn't find anything wrong. Our parts seemed to be working fine. Her doctor told me to stop wearing underwear for a while because the heat from keeping my balls sacked up could reduce my sperm count. I tried it, and I've never gone back. I like the less constricted feel. Does it bother you?"

"No, I like it. It was just surprising. Had I known you were coming today, I would have disposed of my panties. I like to please you."

"You do please me, more than you'll ever know. What else do you want to know? I'm giving you free rein, Sunshine. You might never get it again."

Shocked by this revelation, my mind raced with all the things I wanted to know. Where did I start?

"This is a purely selfish question. I was wondering if you were ever going to ask me for a permanent day. I don't want to push you in that direction if that's not what you want, but I like spending time with you, and I want you to have all the days you want." I hoped I worded that wisely. What would I do if he told me he didn't want to see me again? Could that be a possibility? No, of course not. I still had a dress he bought me that he said we'd find someplace to wear. I wore his bracelet like Jade wore the duo's collar. A part of me belonged to him exclusively.

"I'm glad you brought that up. I hate to think of you with other men. It drives me crazy." Was it possible he would ask for an exclusive arrangement? I held my breath and waited for him to finish. "I can't offer you an exclusive arrangement, River. I wish I could, but that would be dishonest to you and myself. I can't talk about why, I just can't. Having said that, I would like to book your Wednesdays and Saturdays. Do you think you could stand to be around me two days a week?"

The disappointment of not being able to be exclusively his was heartbreaking. However, knowing I could be with him two days a week was a soothing balm. I pressed my lips to his and relished the softness.

"You have just made me the happiest girl," I whispered.

"I'm glad. You make me happy as well. All right, what else do you want to know?"

"What's your house like?" I was curious about where he went every night.

"My house on Center Island is a waterfront property. I don't get there very often. Some months, it's only once. I really should sell it, but I don't have the heart to just yet. I stay in the city most nights. I have a three-bedroom on Fifth Avenue. It's not too far from where Sandra runs her business. I'll take you there sometime."

"Really? I'd love to go to your place." Seeing where he lived would be amazing. I wouldn't have to lie in bed and wonder what he was doing. I could visualize it.

My next question might have ended all further questions, but I asked it anyway. "What brought you to Concierge Services, and how long have you been a member?"

"Loneliness brought me there about three years ago."

It shouldn't surprise me that he was a regular, but it hurt to know I was not as special as he'd led me to believe. He had been using girls from the service for years. I understood loneliness. I was no stranger to a solitary life, but he had so much to offer. I understood about using people for sex. I'd done it, but why did he have to? Any woman would be a fool not to want him long-term.

"Like I told you on our first meeting, I don't want a relationship. I don't need the complications of one. I can't go there. Concierge Services offers me what I want."

His words stung because no matter how you cut it, seeing me twice a week would put us into a relationship. Shit, my heart and head were there before he had committed to two days. He must have seen the disappointment on my face. He lifted my chin and stared into my eyes. I focused on the amber flecks because if I actually saw him completely, I might lose my composure. It was funny how my head could play games, creating the scenario I wanted. Two days a week would have to do.

"You're different, River." My head sarcastically said, *yeah, right.* My heart wished it were true. "I told you I chose you from your smiling photos. That's not entirely true. I looked at all three. The first two looked hollow. You were pretty, but the light wasn't in your eyes. The third picture, the one where you were laughing, showed something different. It showed a spark of something I wanted to get to know. The hollow girl tugged at my heartstrings. I hadn't seen her surface until today, when you said you would be fine at lunch."

"I would have been fine." The lie tasted bitter in my mouth.

"Bullshit. They would have extinguished the spark that shines so brightly in your eyes. I don't know how you are with others, but you shine when we're together, and it's contagious. I want that. I need that. What made you laugh that day when they took that picture?"

My head was trying to wrap around his words about wanting and needing a part of me. "Everything happened so quickly. One morning I was working as a bikini barista, and that afternoon I was in Sandra's office, being told my worries were over. The next day, I was sitting in front of the photographer. He told me to look sexy, and I wasn't sure how to do that. That was when Sandra said I was sex. It struck me as funny."

"I would agree with Sandra. Everything about you screams 'sexy'. Come here, beautiful." He pulled me into his arms and began to rub my back. I melted under his fingertips. I could feel his arousal press against my stomach. He wanted me again. Every cell of my body screamed with the need to have more of this man. "If you don't want to have sex with me again, just tell me."

Why would he think that? I wanted him as often as he'd take me. "I do, I want you so badly."

I reached into my nightstand drawer and tore off a condom from a new strip. Straddling him, I quickly rolled on the latex and slid my body onto his, sinking onto his length painfully slowly. I loved the feeling when he first entered me. My body hugged him tightly. My slickness built immediately. Rocking my hips, I established the rhythm and motion. I raised and lowered and repeated. He lay beneath me and let me control the moment.

His eyes were heavy and his breathing hard. My fingers traced his nipples, causing his hips to buck. The thrust increased my excitement. He pinched my nipples painfully, but the sensation only increased my desire. I sat on the edge between pain and pleasure. Rocking into him, I found the place that would send me soaring. Slow, steady movements drove me higher. I took him with me. We would fly together, and it would be magnificent. I moaned as my climax neared. He watched me. I was so close, so damn close. With his hands lowered to my hips, he pressed me into him as he thrust deeper inside me. I fell as the coiled tension released with a guttural cry. His name slipped from my lips as I crashed around him and he exploded inside me. We rocked until every quiver was leached from our bodies. Exhausted, I collapsed onto his chest. His fingers brushed gently across my back, sending prickles of sensation across my skin.

His breath became slow and steady. I gently lifted myself from his body, not wanting to wake him. I wanted to watch him sleep. Everything about him was so perfect in his slumber. I got one foot off the bed before he grabbed me and pulled me back.

"Where are you going? I'm not done with you yet." Surely, he couldn't be ready to go again? He pulled me to his side and kissed me with such passion, my heart nearly collapsed.

We sat in bed, eating cold Greek food. As famished as we were, anything would have tasted wonderful. Once finished, he leaned against my headboard, the sheet pulled up to his waist. If I could have, I would have snapped a picture of him.

"Your mind is racing again. What are you thinking about?"

"How do you know when my mind is racing? Hell, my mind is always racing."

"Your lip curls and twitches in the right corner. It's your thinking giveaway. So, 'fess up." He stretched his arms above his head. Every muscle rippled. How was I supposed to think when he was naked in my bed?

"All right, I was taking a mental picture of you since I can't take a real one. You are so freaking sexy in my bed, and I wanted to remember this moment forever. Are you happy? You squeezed the embarrassing truth out of me. I internally drool over you." I wanted to bury my head in his chest.

"What would you do with my picture?" He tucked the sheet around his hips.

I wasn't sure what he meant. What did he think I would do with his picture?

"I'd look at it. I certainly wouldn't share it if that's what you're thinking."

I never considered he might think I would use it in a malicious way. It was a moot point anyway. He would never let me snap a picture of him like this. Sandra warned me about nude pictures, but what was the harm in me having one of him? I knew I could trust me.

"No, it never crossed my mind. I might consider letting you take my picture if you reciprocate. I could use a naked picture of you to stroke away my tension when we're not together." Did he really just tell me he wanted a picture to jack off to? Oh Lord, if that wasn't the hottest thing. I knew I shouldn't allow him to take the picture, but I felt like I could trust him. "Get your camera, Sunshine." No freaking way. I hopped off the bed and raced to my purse in the living room before he changed his mind. I glanced around and realized Tiffany had left for work.

"We're alone," I said when I walked back in.

Not that it made any difference. The room could be filled with people, and I would feel like we were the only two people that existed. I pulled my phone from my bag and shot a picture of him all mussed and sexed up. He looked incredibly sexy. Little did he know, I might be using his picture to gain some relief on my own. Two nights with him was never going to be enough.

He rose from the bed, and the sheet dropped from around his waist. He grabbed me and tossed me across the mattress. Fishing through his jeans, he pulled his phone from his pocket. I was laughing at the situation, and he was snapping a picture of my body.

"How many did you take?"

He shrugged and began to scroll through his phone. I could see the passion in his eyes. My mouth dropped open when I realized he was getting hard again. How in the hell did he do that?

He looked down at his length and chuckled. "Don't be worried. I'm not sure I could do it again so soon." He tugged his jeans on and ended all notions that he would have me again. "Time to clean out the closet."

The next hour we spent analyzing my wardrobe. Anything that remotely resembled parent-friendly was tossed in the corner. When it was all said and done, my closet had a gaping hole in it, but my heart felt like it was healing. I wasn't aware how liberating purging my closet could be.

"Jonathan, thank you for everything. You were heaven-sent today. You liberated my closet and my life."

"I'm glad I could be there. I'm glad I could be here. This is one of the best days I've had in a long time. I'll have Erica send over some things to fill the gap."

"Please don't. I have plenty to wear."

My closet was three-quarters full. I had more clothes than I ever had in my life. I ran my hand over the silver dress I'd worn to the opera. It was too pretty to hide in the bag. I wanted to enjoy it for a little while longer.

"That day will be etched as another favorite. As for the clothes, I'd like to get you things. I'd...like to see you wear the things I chose for you." By now, the man knew saying those words would get him anything he wanted. "I should be going. I'll pick you up Wednesday at seven. We'll be having dinner with Grace and her husband. They wanted to go over the funds raised by the auction."

I faltered in my step as I walked behind him to the front door.

He wanted me near his family?

"What if she finds out who I am or what I do?"

"I would imagine she already knows." He brushed a soft kiss on my lips and left me. Brokenhearted.

Chapter 18

By the time I got up, Tiffany was in the kitchen. "Hey, how was the date? For an older dude, he's hot." She poured me a cup of coffee and set it on the table. "It was great. We…ate Greek and talked."

"Oh…is that what you're calling it these days? Well, I could use some Greek. Where do I get one of those? He's the one sending the clothes and stuff, right?"

"Yes, he's very generous."

She whistled loudly. "You got yourself a sugar daddy. Good for you."

And with that, she disappeared into her room. I probably wouldn't see her for the rest of the week. We rarely crossed paths, and when we did, it was mostly on weekends.

I hadn't checked my phone since yesterday. The only time I glanced at it was to shoot the picture of Jonathan. Looking at it now showed there were several missed messages from my parents. Of course, there was no way they would leave me alone. I pressed delete without listening to any of them. To let them back into my life would be a mistake. For the first time, I felt impervious to their ugliness. I actually stood up for myself, and it felt liberating. Scrolling through the rest, I found a message from Jade and one from Luca.

Hey,

How was lunch with the God squad?

J

Yesterday was a turning point for me in many ways. I finally let go of the hope I would ever please them. That was big.

How are things with you? We totally need to talk. So much has happened. Coffee tomorrow before class?

R

She replied instantly.

It sounds intriguing. Are you sure you want to wait? As for me, things are good here. My bracelets are fading, my heart feels lighter.

J

Thank God for that. Seeing my friend broken and bruised was one of the lowlights of the week. I wasn't sure I would ever stop worrying about her.

I wish I could meet today, but I'm booked. I have a meet-and-greet for lunch and a dinner appointment. It will have to be tomorrow. Same time, same place.

R

Luca's text was brief.

Just confirming our coffee date after classes on Thursday.

Luca

I replied back with a "yes" and got ready for my lunch meeting. I couldn't remember the guy's name. My calendar said, 'John Strickland'. I was supposed to meet him at an oyster bar in Times Square. I wish I could cancel. Now that I had a Wednesday and Saturday regular, I was kind of set. Jonathan might not want me as an exclusive, but who was to say I couldn't limit my appointments to him? Of course, I intended to finish with Paul Yoder. It would be cruel not to.

Speaking of Paul Yoder, my work phone pinged with an incoming message asking to set up the next meeting. Unfortunately, I was booked this Friday. I asked him if he wanted to meet tomorrow night.

It was really short notice, but it was all I had to offer. I was hoping he would find his self-confidence quickly. I didn't mind seeing him, but he needed more, deserved more than a woman he paid by the hour.

He responded with a "yes" and an address. I looked at the rest of the week and made an executive decision. I would see Ben Daniels and Donald Zane because we already had those encounters scheduled, but I was canceling Wednesday's meet-and-greet. Even if I liked him, I didn't know where I would put him in my schedule. This wasn't a career path for me; it was a means to an end.

John Strickland was already seated at the table when I arrived. He greeted me and shook my hand. Pleasant-looking, he was probably in his late sixties. Like Jonathan, he owned a company that managed the portfolios of wealthy clients. Estate planning seemed to be where the money was.

Dressed in a paisley printed dress and heels, I took my seat across from John. "Good afternoon. It's a pleasure to meet you."

"Nice to meet you, too. I don't have much time. My secretary double-booked me. I'm going to be honest. I'm a connoisseur. I'm not looking for a long-term thing. I'm more of a nail-and-bail kind of guy. So, I don't need to get to know you."

I liked his honesty, but his attitude was appalling. Nail and bail? Please. These types of men were not mentors; they served a different purpose. They were a single payday. Perfect for the woman without a heart or soul.

"I understand. I'm not opposed to single experiences. However, my schedule is limited at this point. I have regular meetings several days of the week."

His eyes widened.

"But you just started. How did you manage to secure regulars so soon?" He looked at me with surprise in his expression.

"I suppose we just clicked." I didn't feel anything for this guy. He would be perfect if I was desperate for three hundred fifty dollars, but some things weren't worth it. "I don't think I'm the girl for you, Mr. Strickland. I'm looking for consistency in my life, and I don't see you providing that. It was a pleasure meeting you, but I wouldn't want to waste any more of your time." I got ready to stand up and leave.

"You could at least have lunch with me. You are getting paid for it." I couldn't argue with that.

"Certainly." He had a valid point. "Tell me about yourself." That was truly the best question ever asked. People loved to talk about themselves, and he was no different.

He went on and on about his business and his clients. A name-dropper if I'd ever seen one. I listened attentively. If I had to make it through lunch, then I was going to use it as a growth opportunity.

We ordered oysters on the half shell and cups of New England clam chowder. When our time was up, I shook his hand and bid him farewell. He left first. I stayed behind to check my messages and texted Jade. Maybe we could meet for coffee.

J

Time for coffee?

R

While waiting for her reply, I opened my work phone and promptly put a *no* next to John Strickland. He could nail and bail else-where. What a slimeball. Craig Hagen sent a message requesting a second encounter. I figured since I put a *yes* next to his name, I owed him. I couldn't justify not seeing him again. Sandra would be all over my ass. With three nights taken, I had room for one more regular if I decided to go that route. The jury was still out.

Jonathan had warmed my heart with quite a few sweet actions and words, yet he'd managed to erase those feelings with something cold and uncaring.

Were his parting words intended to put me in my place?

Could he be that cold? We'd shared an amazing afternoon. The man had selflessly given me his time, and I'd given him mine. We called it a date, and yet when he left, he reminded me what I was.

Why did it hurt so much with him?

R

Can you come to my apartment?

J

There was no stall in my reply. I typed in a "yes" and hailed a cab. I would be there in twenty minutes if I were lucky. On the way, I answered the remaining messages.

My heart stilled when a naked picture of me flashed across the screen. Sandra's warning to never let anyone take pictures of me replayed in my head. I relaxed when I read the message that accompanied the photo.

Sunshine,

Missing you. Thanks for such a great weekend. See you Wednesday.

Jonathan

The photo, although sexy, wasn't pornographic in any way. The sheet was tossed in such a way that it covered my most intimate parts but offered a peek at what I was hiding. I looked sexy and carefree. I appeared lighthearted, which made me look happier than I had in a very long time.

I analyzed every nuance of that photo, from the way my hair hung over my shoulder to the silver chain that hung from my wrist. The camera flash caught the charm creating a starburst effect. It looked like I was tossing a magical orb. I glanced down at my wrist and admired the bracelet I'd yet to take off.

Jonathan,

I miss you too. Heading to a girlfriend's for coffee. Wednesday can't come soon enough.

River

And it couldn't. Time from this point forward would be measured by Wednesdays, Saturdays, and Brazilian waxes.

My correspondence was completed by the time I arrived at Jade's. It was hard to get over where she lived. The last time I was there, I was being prepped for my interview. It seemed like so much time had passed, but in reality, it had been just over a week.

She buzzed me in right away. My eyes scanned her apartment. I was looking at it through a different lens. When I was here before, I didn't know my friend was involved in a power exchange. I wondered if I would see everything differently now. What I saw was a beautiful apartment that looked like Jade. There was hardly a trace of the men who whipped through her life four days a week.

"What's up?" She embraced me fiercely.

"I have to tell you about lunch with the parents."

And so I did. She made us coffee, and we sat at the granite bar in the kitchen while I told her about the visit and how Jonathan had come to my rescue. Of course, I called him Mr. Broom. By the time I finished, she was mute. I've never seen her at a loss for words.

"You are in trouble with this guy, aren't you?" Her expression didn't look upset. She looked sad.

"Yes, I'm in trouble. He's everything I would want in a man, and I know I can't have him."

Sadly, the reality was so much easier to swallow when he wasn't around. When he was around, he enchanted me. For that tiny moment yesterday, it had felt like he'd needed me, too. But that would only be wishful thinking.

Stop now, River.

I needed to change the subject. "How is the duo?"

"Honestly, I don't know. We normally spend Thursday through Sunday together, but they exited early over the weekend, and I haven't heard from them. I'm not sure what to think." The light had dimmed in her eyes again. She sounded whiny, like she did when it was her time of the month.

"Are you on your period? Speaking of which, what do I do when I'm on mine?"

"What a shitty tutor. I can't believe how much I didn't tell you. You could buy a sponge, or you could get a diaphragm. I prefer the diaphragm. I was always honest with the men. Some men love it. The hormones often make the boobies bigger." If Jade's boobs got any bigger, she could be a human bouncy castle.

Argh. The thought of having to have sex on my period was unappealing. "Looks like I'll need another appointment with Dr. Chang."

"Do you want to tell me about the bracelet?"

"No." Absolutely not. "Do you want to show me your playroom?" I wasn't ready for her to ruin the beauty of the gift. Knowing Jade, she would tell me to take it off and put it away. Wearing it would only reinforce my feelings. Feelings I wasn't allowed to have.

Telling Jade about the death of the relationship with my parents had been cathartic and affirming. With each purge, I felt a little less exiled, but more...free. She'd been with me through the dismal, heart-breaking years of their relentless bullying. Although she raised her concern about Jonathan—and as my best friend, she should—I knew she also applauded my decision to be done with them.

We didn't discuss Paul Yoder. It would have been cruel to talk about his teeny weenie when he wasn't around. It was cruel to discuss it when he was around.

Question-and-answer time had officially ended. I told her I was meeting an older man for dinner and had to go home to get ready.

Jade's friendship was a treasure I was so thankful for. Her hugs and kisses as I left fortified my heart and soul.

THE ENTRYWAY WAS FILLED with packages when I arrived home. My roommate must have signed for the twenty or so boxes stacked neatly against the wall. The logo of Bloomingdales decorated each and every box. Jonathan had gone wild.

It took me several minutes to lug everything into my room. It was two hours before I had to leave for my dinner with Ben. Surely, that was enough time to check out the goods. I wasn't used to receiving gifts. In fact, this was more than I'd received over the span of my life. I wanted to savor each and every package.

One by one, I opened the gifts and pulled out the contents. When it was all said and done, I had six dresses, three cashmere sweaters, two pairs of slacks, five shirts of various bold colors, and four silk negligees. Everything was top of the line, not one garment was a fifty-fifty polyester blend.

Grateful to have someone so generous in my life, I picked up my phone and without thinking tapped in a message to Jonathan. Texting was the type of behavior that made everything seem so normal.

Jonathan,

You overwhelm me with your generosity. I love everything you sent my way. How did I get so lucky?

River

My eyes never left the screen. The wait was almost unbearable. How was I going to get through the night when this man was always in my thoughts?

Ping.

Sunshine,

You are long overdue. Isn't it time someone saw you? I wasn't able to choose those items myself, but I was told there were some sexy nighties in the mix. Bring one Wednesday. I can't wait to remove it from your body.

Jonathan

It didn't take much for my panties to dampen and my skin to tingle. One thought of Jonathan stripping me bare, and I was wet. Well, at least Ben would be happy. He didn't have to know my arousal came from a man not in the room.

I wanted to wear something from the items he'd sent me, but it seemed wrong—disrespectful to Jonathan. The clothes would be worn for him or when I was on my own. The only item I refused to remove was the bracelet. It was a constant reminder there were generous people in the world.

The flouncy edge of the orange A-line dress softened the bright color. I loved the movement it had when I walked. Racing around the room, I grabbed everything I would need for the evening. The taxi was waiting downstairs.

The ride to The Manor was quick and painless. Maybe because it was a Monday evening. Ten minutes early, I waited in the lobby. He lit up the room as he entered. Some people had that aura about them. Ben was one of those rare gifts.

"River, how was the trip over?" His false teeth sparkled under the light of the chandelier. I wondered if they were implants or the type that came out and were tossed in a cup of water at night.

"The ride was wonderful. Hardly any traffic, and there wasn't a crazy person in our path. I would say that's pretty darn amazing." His grandfatherly look put me at ease.

"We need to set up a car service for you. It would be more convenient and definitely safer. I would feel better." Apparently, Ben had plans for future meetings. There wasn't a reason to talk about car services if he didn't.

He placed my arm on his and walked us to the hostess. We were seated in a secluded booth. It reminded me of the night Jonathan and I went to Per Se. Everything reminded me of him. This was Ben's night, and it wouldn't be fair to be with him while thinking of a different man.

The Manor had a menu heavy in seafood. I loved that Ben had heard me on our meet-and-greet. I loved living by the ocean because of the abundance of fresh fish that came our way. We quickly placed our orders and enjoyed a glass of wine while we waited.

Ben was seventy-seven. He had been married twice before, but his last wife passed away fifteen years ago. He had one daughter and two sons. He used to have a house in Oyster Bay, but he sold it several years ago. He now lived in Manhattan with his dog, Nasdack.

"River, before you get nervous about having to put out for an old geezer like me, I wanted to clear the air."

Oh Lord, don't tell me he's another little man. I sipped my wine and nodded my head. This was the weirdest job I've ever had. A psychology major would be better suited for the position.

He gave me a wink. I was waiting for him to divulge his dirty, dark secrets, and he sat there and winked at me.

"Ben, you're killing me. Clear the air already."

"I would be happy to make love to a beautiful young woman like yourself. My mind is willing, but my body is weak. I lost that ability two years ago when I got prostate cancer. I was hoping you wouldn't mind entertaining an old buzzard like me. I like having dinner with a pretty girl."

Well, I'd been surprised twice this week, first by Paul, and then by Ben. I wasn't looking forward to having sex with a man who was old enough to father Moses, but I would have done it. Ben was a nice guy, and I couldn't hold his age against him. Now I was grateful for his age.

"I would be honored to have dinner with you. How often do you think you would like that?" I was learning to play the game. I didn't want to force him into a situation, but I had a schedule to maintain, and I had to know.

"Crowded restaurants bother me. I don't want to wait hours for my food. I want it when I want it. If Mondays are good for you, I would love to schedule yours for the foreseeable future." He wanted a permanent day. I would get to enjoy dinner with a brilliant older man, and all he wanted in return was for me to look pretty and show up. I could do that.

Dinner was relaxing. We discussed politics in-between delectable morsels of perfectly cooked salmon. It was interesting that we had the same taste in food. Our view on politics was dissimilar. He came from a different generation, and therefore his thoughts were more conservative than mine. In the end, we agreed to disagree.

Nothing about tonight could be compared to Jonathan except the dark corner booth. Everything was friendly and completely non-sexual. I have had three second encounters, and only one has visited the inside of my vagina. I was feeling good about that.

Chapter 19

Dressed in red, I showed up to the Waldorf Astoria at the specified time. Paul was waiting at the bar, chatting with the bartender. His confidence seemed high and his demeanor positive. This was a very different man to the one I met on Friday. This man seemed relaxed. He wasn't ready to jump out of his skin. He looked ready to jump into mine, though.

He rose from his seat the minute he saw me. In a rush, he hugged me tightly and twirled me around. I nearly lost a shoe from the velocity of his spin. When he put me down, I had to grab the bar to stop the whirling.

Once righted, I greeted him. "Hey, you. Having a good day?"

"Not so much, but I'm looking forward to a great night." He was giddy like a child.

"Did you do your homework?" I wondered how many peaches he had eaten. I had a feeling he had been on a steady diet since Friday.

"Yes. I'm excited to show you what I've learned. Would you like a drink first?" He offered the drink, but I could tell he was excited to get the night started. I wasn't freaking out, so I saw no reason to delay. I felt comfortable with Paul. His gentle enthusiasm was charming.

I glanced around the bar and caught the eye of Craig Hagen sitting at the other end. He left a message, and I had not returned it. I looked in his direction while he picked up his drink in a silent toast.

Thank goodness Paul didn't notice. How crazy would that have been? How often would I run into the same people? They said the world was small, but I never expected it to be that tiny.

I would contact Craig when I got home. I'd hoped for a quick evening. I had lots of homework to do.

Paul walked confidently to the elevator. His fingers didn't shake as he pushed the button to our floor. Twelve. It looked like we were moving up in the world. As we reached the door, he pulled the keycard from his pocket like a gunslinger pulled his weapon. Paul was feeling self-assured, and I was happy for him.

I didn't know what to make of his newfound confidence. What would that mean for me? The room was similarly outfitted to our previous room. The only difference: a vase of flowers and a bottle of wine on the table.

"Thank you for everything you are doing for me, River." His voice cracked ever so slightly, and I wondered if I were going to see a grown man cry for the first time in my life. I'd seen plenty of women bawl their eyes out, but men seemed to be made of tougher stuff.

"I didn't do anything for you."

I believed it was the truth. I told him the facts. We all had short-comings. When you found yours, you had to depend on your stronger assets. Paul's button wasn't an asset, neither were his oral skills. We couldn't make him grow, but we could make his tongue perform better.

He poured us each a glass of wine and toasted to bigger and better things. Lord, I prayed he wasn't hoping for a miracle. No amount of pixie dust could help his tiny peter.

"Shall we start with a shower? I hear that's a good way to begin."

His words were perfectly scripted from our last encounter, only this time he didn't have to waste his time being embarrassed and nervous. We both knew what we were dealing with, and it made the whole experience easier.

"Sure, I'll start the water."

Without hesitation, I entered the bathroom and started the shower. I felt his presence before I saw him. His kisses trailed down my neck and ended at my shoulder. He lowered the zipper of my dress and carefully let it slip past my shoulders. As it fell from my body, I stepped out of it and stood before him in a bra, underwear, and heels. With him behind me, I couldn't see his face. I hoped he was pleased with my selection of undergarments. The red of my lingerie matched my dress exactly.

His catcall whistles validated my choices. I bent over and picked up my dress. I knew exactly what I was doing when I presented my ass to him. I wanted to drive the night forward so we could be done with it. There was only this night and tomorrow's meet-and-greet standing between Jonathan and me.

I felt his soft hand glide over the curve of my ass and fumble with my underwear. This poor man was going to need more than oral sex lessons. He needed to rewrite his entire playbook.

I took his hands and placed his thumbs inside the elastic band at my hips. "Slow, like this. Drive her crazy with the anticipation."

I helped him shimmy the fabric over my hips and down my legs. I coaxed him to lift my shoes one at a time while I taught him to glide his hand between my thighs before he pulled the fabric free.

When it came to my bra, I told him to pay attention to the garment. The woman probably had taken her time to select it for him. He should appreciate the gift. I had him run one finger under the lace of the cup and skim my nipple. I asked him to press his lips to my lace-covered nipples and make them beg to be set free. Once they hardened like pebbles, he could release the hook and eye one at a time. Again, I tried to teach him patience through seduction. Or was it seduction through patience?

In nothing but heels, I worked on his clothes. One button at a time, I seduced his body. The only way I knew he was affected was his breathing. Most men would have a bulge in their pants. Poor Paul had nothing to work with, so I listened to his body, which said he was totally turned on. I, on the other hand, hadn't felt the slightest tingle.

A shower was a nice way to start. It was warm and relaxing and clean. It washed the filth from my body before anything took place. Thankfully, I'd been lucky enough to have men who had various needs. Ben wanted company, Paul wanted confidence, and Jonathan wanted...what did Jonathan want? Everything? Nothing? I wasn't sure.

We began the night lying in bed and talking about peaches. My original thoughts were confirmed when he gave me a list of peaches and told me which were still good this late in the season.

I gave him the option of using a barrier. I'd brought several with me just in case. It wasn't something I'd considered until I talked to Luca. Apparently, my recent medical exam was posted online with my profile, and I was given a gold star.

He climbed between my legs and began. This time, his approach was slow and methodical. I would be lying if I said it wasn't arousing. Who would have thought peaches could do the trick? Clearly, Cosmo did.

He had listened to everything I'd told him. He placed his hands on my thighs and felt for my response. He knew I was aroused simply from my breathing. He pulled me to the edge, and when I began to shake, he retreated. I wanted to pat him on the head like a good child.

That thought led to a thought about my mother and how she'd always patted me on the head. Was that her way of telling me I had done okay? I would have to give that more thought. Right now, I had to focus, and the errant thought of my mother had completely obliterated my tingle.

It didn't take long for him to pull me back into the moment. I swear, the man was softly manipulating my flesh from the seed—the hard knob of tangled nerves. He focused and then sucked at the flesh of my fruit until I was panting and begging for release.

He pulled me close and pushed me away for over thirty minutes. I closed my eyes and pictured a head of dark hair peppered with gray settled between my legs. I sank into a soft place and floated there for eternity. The burning in my belly was the first sign I'd reached the point of no return.

He knew it, too. My body quivered and quaked. I closed my legs around his head, afraid he would pull back before I selfishly accepted it all.

"Look at me."

The voice didn't match the picture in my head. I wanted dark, slow molasses, not a Hampton lobster boil. It was all wrong, but it was too late. My eyes had opened and caught the joy of the baby blues in front of me. He felt wonderful, and I was the one who came. I should have felt on top of the world, and yet, I felt polluted. It was so wrong, and somehow it was exactly right.

My mind and body came back together. I was the mentor, and my student deserved praise. "Oh my God, that was amazing. Who would have known you had it in you? Are you sick of peaches?" He looked proud. I wondered how many years this man had felt inadequate. "How old are you, Paul?"

The bed sunk under his weight. He climbed in next to me and pulled me into his arms. I would have to set his passion free soon, but for now, we would cuddle.

"I'm thirty-five, and I think that was the first time I've made a woman come."

I could hear the pride in his voice. I wasn't going to take the accomplishment away from him because I hadn't come to terms with what I'd become.

"Really?"

"You didn't fake it, did you?" His body stiffened at the possibility.

"I never fake it. What good would that do? Did you feel my body quake? That can't be faked." I wasn't sure if it could or not, but I said it to give him something to hold on to.

He proceeded to tell me everything he thought and felt while savoring me. I listened intently. At times, it felt like he was the only one who had participated because I didn't pick up on half the stuff he did. At the end of his story, I was positive I'd checked out of his room and into Jonathan's halfway through. What the hell was I doing?

I lay with my hand on his chest. My hand followed his chest hair down his stomach to the thatch of curls between his legs. It was time to pony up so I could go home. He stopped my hand when it reached his button.

"Sadly, I have something else to work on. The minute you came, so did I. Last week, I would have felt ashamed. Today, I feel accomplished." I suppose he could chalk himself up for two orgasms: one for me, and one for him.

"I should get going." I peeked at the clock and saw an hour was almost up.

"Can you stay another hour? I want to bask in the afterglow, and it wouldn't be as pleasant alone."

How could I say no? He had given me a gift. When it came down to it, I didn't feel dirty because of the orgasm; I felt dirty because I felt like I was cheating on Jonathan. However, that scenario wouldn't ever be a possibility. I didn't belong to Jonathan, and he didn't belong to me. I belonged to whoever was willing to pay three hundred fifty dollars an hour. Paul was that man tonight, and I would give him his money's worth.

We ordered room service because neither of us had eaten. When it arrived, we ate in bed with me cuddled up to his side. He was comfortable and safe.

"Well, Paul, what are you going to do with your newfound skills?"

He sipped the soda he'd ordered and turned to look at me. "I feel great about what happened with us tonight. I feel comfortable with you. You didn't judge me or make me feel inadequate in any way." I could tell something was on his mind.

"Spit it out, Mister." I saw his confidence was wavering. One time didn't make a master. It was written all over his face.

"This could have been a fluke." His body stiffened, and not in a good way.

"What you did took skill. A fluke would have been if I'd primed myself with a vibrator and you happened to touch me in the right spot at the right time to send me over the edge. You were the vibrator. You did the priming *and* the finishing touch. Own it, Paul. You made me fall to pieces in your mouth. *With* your mouth."

Again, the truth. It didn't take a particular person to make me come, but it had felt different. Every nerve in my body sang with Jonathan, but only the nerves between my legs sang with Paul. They were different songs.

"Thank you for that. Still, I want to build my confidence. I want to master this thing before I subject myself to rejection. Can I have your next few Tuesdays?" He looked at me like a kid looked at his parents when the ice cream truck was passing by.

"Of course. You want some more homework?" This time, it wouldn't be eating peaches.

"Do I need homework?" His head fell to his chest.

"No, your oral skills took a one-eighty. How do you feel about masturbation?"

"I like it."

"Good, do it a lot, but don't let yourself come. This isn't for your woman; this is for you. The longer you wait, the more powerful your orgasm will be. I'm sure you know that, but you deserve earth-shattering, too."

"Is that what I gave you? Was it earth-shattering?"

"Yes." All orgasms seemed to crack the earth around me. Some more than others. "Also, I want you to trim your freaking bush. You don't have to hide your man parts in a forest. In fact, you would look larger if you manscaped."

"Yes, ma'am. I really like you, River. You have been good for me." He set the room service tray aside and pulled me into his arms. He felt comfortable, like a plush throw in the winter.

"I like you, too, Paul. You're a good guy, with a big heart."

And a little penis.

Chapter 20

Hunter Glendale was my Wednesday meet-and-greet. He was a jumbo man. Not large, but supersized. He took me to an all-you-can-eat buffet outside Union Station. The staff looked nervous the minute we entered. I'm pretty sure the hostess ran to the back and told them to keep it coming.

In spite of his size, he was nice-looking. He dressed in a custom suit and wore a Cartier watch. His nails were manicured, and his skin was nice. If he dropped a hundred pounds, he would have looked like an older Ryan Gosling.

We chatted about the stock market and how volatile it was. We discussed oil futures and energy costs. At the end of the hour, he looked at me and said, "River, you're sweet, and I like you. But you remind me of my granddaughter, and I just can't go there."

Relief washed over me. I didn't want to pick up new clients. I wanted to stick with the few I had. Jonathan, Ben, and Paul were the perfect mix for me. I still had Donald Zane and Craig Hagen to get through.

I hoped my feigned look of disappointment was believable. I

wanted him to think I wanted to be with him. One of the things I'd learned since my journey began was that powerful men didn't always have matching egos. Often, they were insecure and stayed hidden behind the power of their positions.

Once we parted company, I looked to the sky and thanked the universe. The heavens had blessed me.

My phone pinged with an incoming message. I presumed it would be Craig. I'd left him a message when I got home last night, telling him Thursday was open. I knew I would be sore from tonight's encounter, but I wanted to tie up loose ends quickly. The faster I adjusted my schedule to three, the easier it would be to adjust to my new lifestyle.

I quickly calculated my earnings. Two overnights with Jonathan would be twenty-eight hundred dollars. Add an hour each with Ben and Paul, and that would take my weekly earnings up to thirty-five hundred dollars. I would be making fourteen thousand dollars per month before taxes. That was more than enough to make ends meet and pay off my student loans. When Paul dropped me, I would still be fine. I would be more than fine.

My guess was correct. Craig was delighted I had Thursday free. He gave me an address and told me to arrive at eight. I didn't recognize the address and wondered in what area of town it was located. My best guess was a boutique hotel somewhere downtown. I tapped in a confirmation and headed home. I had to be ready for Howard to pick me up in a few hours.

I texted Jade on my way home. She didn't meet me for our before-class coffee on Tuesday, and I hadn't heard from her since.

I'm worried about you. You didn't show for coffee and you didn't answer my text last night. What gives? Are you okay?

Why was it when you were waiting for someone to text you it took forever, but when you didn't want to hear from someone, they were always around? I was worried about Jade. Her text came in a few minutes later.

I'm fine. I wasn't feeling well yesterday and slept most of the day. I didn't text because you were meeting with a mentor. I'm fine. I'm sorry to stress you out. The duo is coming into town Thursday and I'll be busy all weekend. Let's meet for coffee Tuesday.

Tuesday? That meant she wouldn't be meeting me for coffee tomorrow. Something was definitely up. She texted she was fine twice, which meant she was anything but fine. Jade was great, fabulous, stupendous, but she was never fine.

I'm worried about you. Let's meet for coffee tomorrow. I'm going to worry until I see you again.

She responded immediately and included a selfie. She looked fine. Not fabulous, not great or stupendous, but fine, and I had to assume fine would be okay for now.

All right. Tuesday it is. I'm not liking it, but I'll deal with it. I'll be busy the rest of the week as well. Oh, I forgot to tell you. Luca is in most of my classes. We had lunch one day and we are meeting for coffee tomorrow. Join us if you can. He's a nice guy, but he's not you. Hugs.

She didn't reply.

Once home, I went about the task of choosing an outfit for dinner. Not knowing where we were going made it difficult to choose wisely. With three outfits laid side by side, I debated the disadvantage and benefits of each.

The pink dress was pretty, the flowers at the hem and neckline made it ultra soft and feminine. The green shirtdress was made from soft cotton and looked comfortable. Blue was Jonathan's favorite color. He would love the blue dress, but would the plunging neckline be appropriate for where we were going? Grace would be there, and she would be judging me. His mention of her already knowing what I did put a damper on the evening as it was. I may be a prostitute, but I didn't want to look like one.

Ultimately, I decided on the blue dress. My job was to please Jonathan, and that dress would do it.

I would have to get used to the reality of my situation. Could I justify what I was doing? Because no one but Jonathan had intercourse with me, it was easy to lie to myself. My mind compartmentalized the men and my role with them.

With Ben, I was a dinner companion, and no matter how you sliced that, it would never make me a whore. This was probably the closest example of the promised mentor relationship. I dined with him and benefitted from his time-earned wisdom.

Paul was a project, and no matter how I justified my actions, whether I considered it sexual tutoring or ego stroking, I was trading sex for money. We didn't have intercourse, but I did give him a blowjob the first time, and he wrapped his lips around my sex.

Jezebel.

Jonathan made it a cut-and-dried case. I spread my legs for him every time he asked. He deposited money into my account regularly. If that didn't shout 'whore', I didn't know what would. Ironically, I would have had sex with him for free. He was that good. Add that to his ability to make me feel valued, and I was lost in him. I could create every excuse as to why I wasn't a whore, but in the end, the exchange of money for favors made it so.

For the first time since I'd started working for Concierge Services, I cried. Tears flowed freely from my eyes because I knew I could never go back to the girl I once was. I knew my parents had been right all along, and I knew I'd made the biggest mistake of my life.

No amount of money was worth selling my self-respect. No amount of money was worth the raised glass by Craig Hagen. No amount of money was worth allowing any man to put their hands and tongue on my body, let alone their penis inside me.

Why did I allow this? What lies had I believed to make this okay?

From what Jade had said, and even Sandra, this choice was going to be lonely, and lonely is definitely what I felt now. I couldn't speak with Jade. I had to work through this on my own. After a deep breath, I thought, what was done was done. I'd do my time and move on with my life.

In spite of my tears, I was still looking forward to seeing Jonathan.

What did that make me? The happy hooker? The non-penitent prostitute?

It made me stupid, but the happy kind of stupid one gets when they eat too much candy. He was my sugar high. The other men were the bellyache.

To get through Donald and Craig was the plan. After the weekend, I would stay with Jonathan and Ben. Paul could stay as long as he needed me. This would limit my contacts, and potentially my opportunities, but The Dean's List served several purposes. The most pressing for me was money.

I typed a quick text to Sandra, telling her to close my account to new clients. She replied immediately with a not-so-nice message, telling me she was certain I had more time in my schedule to accommodate interested mentors.

Here was a woman who told me she didn't sell sex, and yet she was telling me my store could accommodate more customers. I didn't know if I wanted to scream, cry, or laugh. I decided to cry. On Sunday, I cried over my parents and their lack of everything. Today, I cried for myself. Tomorrow, there would be no more tears. Or so I hoped. Crying was a waste of time.

Anxious about the evening ahead, I waited downstairs for Howard to arrive. He showed up at the precise moment expected. I often wondered why Jonathan rarely came to get me and then realized I was falling back into my fantasyland of this being a date.

"Is Mr. Ferris at work?" I asked. Howard opened the door and helped me into the car.

"Yes. You will be meeting him at Lulu's." Of course, I would. He summoned me, and I came happily. I looked at the bracelet around my wrist, and everything seemed right in the world.

He was walking toward the car when I arrived. Today, he wore a black suit with a silver tie. It looked serious and intimidating. He had gone all Christian Grey on me. I could hardly wait to jump out of the car and hug him. That's how crazy the situation was. I wanted to be in his arms all the time. To be covered in his scent was as comforting as being tucked into my warm bed on a cold night.

Howard was taking too damn long. My fingers toyed with the handle, but I pulled them back. I wasn't an uncouth teenager. I had manners, and I was expected to use them when I was out with Jonathan.

When the door swung open, I offered my hand to the older man, who helped me exit the car. I wanted to hop out and dash the ten feet to my lover, but I exited the car with style and grace.

Jonathan told Howard he would see him tomorrow. I glanced at my overnight bag and was told Howard had it covered.

Seconds later, I was in his arms. His hands smoothed down my back and caressed my bottom.

"Good girl," he said when he felt nothing under the thin fabric. Stepping into his embrace, I ran my hands under his coat. I was certain I liked the feel of his body as much as he liked mine. "I missed you. How has your week been going?"

It was in these moments I had a tough time with the escort/mentor relationship. It felt too much like something else. Something real, but I gave in to it.

"I missed you, too."

With a tilt of my head, I glanced into his dark eyes. They were expressive, easy to get lost in. Easy to find yourself in. When his lips touched mine, the entire world ceased to exist. That was how it was with him. The minute our bodies connected, it was just us from that point forward.

"God, I can't seem to get enough of you." He cupped my cheek and kissed my forehead before he led me into the restaurant.

My nerves got the best of me as we entered Lulu's. The opera was easy, we flitted from group to group. I wasn't required to engage with anyone for longer than a few minutes. Tonight, I would be forced to endure an entire dinner with Grace and her husband. I hadn't liked her after five minutes, so what was I going to do in an hour or so?

She was sitting alone at the table when we arrived. I was hoping her husband's absence was because he was in the restroom. He at least could have been a buffer.

"Grace," Jonathan said curtly. There was no warmth in his tone, and I wondered why I hadn't noticed it the other night. "You remember River."

She looked down her nose at me and nodded. "Of course, she's the flavor of the month."

"Enough," he warned.

I'd never heard that tone come from him. It would have made me think twice about mouthing off if I had. He was firm when he dealt with my parents, but this inflection went deep. It was apparent he didn't like Grace, and that pleased me.

He pulled out the chair directly across from her. I would have to stare at her all night. If that didn't kill an appetite I had no idea what would. She reminded me of the gargoyles that sat on top of old churches. They looked stiff and mean. That was Grace. She had that Botox-infused look that did nothing for her face. Her scowl would remain forever.

Once again knowing I needed reassurance, from his position to my right, Jonathan slid his hand under the table and stroked my knee. Bliss. How could I *not* admire this man?

I sat quietly listening to the conversation. Grace's husband had been tied up at work, so he was coming late. Their conversation went directly to the fundraiser. They had raised two hundred and thirty-seven thousand dollars for breast cancer research. I thought that was amazing, but Grace found the number disappointing. I remember raising money for poor families in our community, and it thrilled me when we hit three digits. Six figures were phenomenal, but I kept my opinion to myself.

When Jonathan's phone rang, he excused himself, leaving Grace and me at the table. Alone. I wondered if she would continue to scowl at me, or if she would engage in some type of conversation. The silence was annoying.

"River, you realize he will never love you. His heart belonged to my sister. You are just one more in a string of young college girls he dates and forgets. I just thought you should know from the beginning." She looked really pleased with herself.

Her words should have stung, but they didn't. She thought I was a date. She didn't know I was an escort, and that made a difference in the way I felt about myself. When I arrived today, I arrived with the presumption that she knew what I was. That had eaten at my self-esteem, and I'd allowed her to glower at me the whole evening.

"I am completely aware of his love for your sister. I'm not looking to replace your sister. Thanks for the warning, but it was unnecessary."

She poured the red wine down her throat and went after me again. "You sit there with your smooth skin and perky tits and think you can win a man like him. Well, let me tell you. It's a losing battle. You may get him between your legs, but you will never share anything but body fluids with him. He's a cold, hard man, and my sister gave everything to him, including her life. He wanted a child. That was what killed her."

I should have been stunned into silence, but I wasn't. I felt like I had to defend Jonathan. "Let me clarify something for you, Grace. That man you called cold is anything but. He's the most generous, selfless man I know. As for being hard, you bet he is every time he sinks himself into my body." A shadow loomed over me, but I was on a roll. "More importantly, he's never been anything but honest with me. He's an honorable man, and I'm sure he was a fine husband to your sister. She was a very lucky woman."

I looked up to see Jonathan standing above me. His eyes were dark and hard. I wasn't sure if he was angry with Grace or me, but it was obvious he was angry.

"Are you ready to go?" His words were reminiscent of Sunday's conversation.

"No," I said. I wasn't quite finished with Grace. She had treated me with contempt from the minute she'd met me. Out of respect for Jonathan, I should have been afforded some type of courtesy.

He looked between Grace and me. "Okay." He stood back and watched.

"Grace, someday someone is going to come around and win his heart again, and you're going to want to be nice to that person if you want to continue to have him in your life. He's worth having. You don't have to mentor me. I've taken a spin around this world a time or two, and I'm not quite as stupid or naive as you might think. I know I'm not that girl. I'm just the girl who's blessed to have him in her life right now." I looked at Jonathan and said, "Now, I'm done."

I stood up, turned around, and walked out of the restaurant. I wasn't sure if I should hail a cab or wait. My limbs were shaky. The adrenaline of the moment had surged through my body, and I was coming down from the high fast. Concrete benches lined the concrete planters outside the restaurant. I found an empty spot and sat.

His eyes searched the area when he stepped out of the restaurant. It didn't take him long to find me. Air filled my chest as he approached. My breath stilled. I wondered if he would be unhappy with me. I'd overstepped my boundaries when I'd spoken to Grace. She was his family. I was nothing but the girl he would take somewhere to have sex.

His silence frightened me. He stood above me and stared. When I didn't look at him, he kneeled before me and laid his head in my lap. The air left my lungs in a long sigh. My fingers combed through his hair.

We both spoke the same words at the same time.

"I'm sorry," blended in perfect harmony.

He rose and pulled me against him. "Thank you."

I had no idea why he was thanking me. I'd lost control of myself. I'm sure I had embarrassed him. Somehow, I always managed to be a disappointment to those around me.

"Why are you thanking me? I shouldn't have been so outspoken. I'm sorry." My hands found their way into his jacket to wrap around his waist.

Would this be the last time he held me?

"Sunshine, you make me feel alive. I love hearing that I'm worth having, but you were wrong about one thing. You might just be that girl. Let's go home. I'll explain why Grace hates me, then you will understand why she dislikes you."

I wasn't sure what shocked me more: the word *home,* or that he told me I might be that girl. Did he mean he was capable of loving me?

Chapter 21

We entered his Fifth Avenue address and took the elevator straight to the top. The penthouse. Standing at the threshold of his magnificent home, I was in awe.

This is where he lives?

The floor-to-ceiling windows provided a diorama of Central Park. A million-dollar view he was sharing with me.

The clink of ice in a glass drew my attention. He stood by the bar in the corner and poured himself a scotch. For me, he shook the vodka and poured it into the Vermouth-spritzed glass. After tossing a few olives into the glass, he presented me with the perfect martini.

As he approached what looked to be a delectably soft, black leather sofa, he said, "Come and sit with me." I didn't need to be told twice. He patted his lap, and I crawled onto him, letting my shoes slip to the floor.

He said he wanted to explain about Grace. "You owe me no explanations." I leaned my head against his chest and relaxed.

"I may not owe you one, but I'll give you one." He leaned forward to pick up his drink. "Claire died from inflammatory breast cancer. It's a rare form of cancer that progresses rapidly. Grace blamed me for her death because I wanted children. Claire wanted children as well, but she was okay if it didn't happen."

He took a minute while he sipped the scotch. I tried to slide off his lap, but he held me tight. I wanted to see him. I needed to look into his eyes. He was telling me about his dead wife, the woman he had sworn to love forever. I wanted to see what that kind of love looked like. Instead, I leaned into his chest and listened while he spoke.

"Go on," I coaxed. If he felt I needed to know about his past, then I would sit wherever he wanted me to sit and listen for any length of time he needed.

"She started fertility treatments. They messed with her hormones and made everything feel out of whack. When her breasts became sore, she thought it was a side effect of the shots. It wasn't. The whole time we thought her hormonal, but in fact, she was dying from cancer. It was quick. We found out on a Friday, and she passed eight weeks later. When she died, she was four weeks pregnant, and we hadn't known."

Sorrow stuck in my throat and threatened to choke me. How was I supposed to comfort him? "I'm sorry" seemed like a ridiculous thing to say when he had lost so much.

"How old was Claire?"

"She died five years ago. She was thirty. I thought I'd mourn my whole life for her, and then I met you." He finished off his drink and placed his glass on the table.

"I don't know what to say."

"Don't say anything. Just make love to me. With you, I finally feel something again. Make me feel something."

I slid from his lap to the floor. His head lay against the cushions while I stripped him bare. He was mine for the night to do with as I pleased. We weren't in some swanky hotel; he had trusted me enough to bring me to his home.

I straddled his erection and pressed it against my bare skin. He hissed and groaned as I slid the tip in and out of my heat. I was playing with fire going skin to skin with him. He held my hips and looked into my eyes. I knew I was clean, as I had just been tested. I had no idea where he had been.

"Let me get a condom." I swear, the light died in his eyes the minute the word *condom* was uttered. "When was the last time you were tested?"

"The first day I called you. My tests came back clean." His hands sat loosely on my hips. He no longer controlled our movement.

My entire medical history, from my weight to any STDs I might have had, was available on my profile. Mine had a big, fat zero in every column. I'd never had a disease of any type. Not even a cold sore.

I spoke the words that filled me with warmth when he said them to me. "You please me."

As the last word was spoken, I sank myself onto his length. I swear, his eyes rolled back into his head. It wasn't smart, but it was my gift to him. I wanted him to feel everything—unhindered, uninhibited, unharnessed passion. It was his to take and mine to give.

The moment was incredibly special. He peaked several times, but I slowed the pace to pull him back. He had always seen to my needs first. Wasn't it time for someone to see to his? When I knew he could take no more, I lowered myself onto his rock-hard member and rotated my hips until he came so powerfully, he screamed my name. I'd never let a man come inside me. Tonight was a first, but I imagined it wouldn't be the last. Once we went bare, I was certain we wouldn't go back.

He lifted us both and walked us to his bathroom. He slipped out of me the minute he sat me on the counter. Naked, he stood before me in all his glory. I sat on his marble counter with my dress up to my waist. Damn, he was sexy. The man was seventeen years my senior, and I didn't give a shit. I would sooner date him than date Luca. Jonathan had maturity on his side, and that outshone youth any day.

He no sooner placed me on the counter before he started a bath and began to undress me. We hadn't said a word to one another, yet the silence wasn't awkward; it was comforting. Nothing had to be said. Something profound had happened, and it seemed we both recognized it.

The water was perfectly hot when we stepped into the enormous soaking tub. He cradled me between his legs and pulled me against his chest.

Home.

The first thought that crossed my mind.

Bliss.

The second.

"I've never taken a bath in here," he whispered. "I've not brought a woman here. What are you doing to me?"

"I'm pleasing you."

"Yes, you are."

His hands soaped my body and cleaned me gently. When his fingers grazed the area between my legs, my hips rose from the water. My body responded to everything he said and did.

"What are you doing to me?" I asked. This was more than sex. He was making me fall for him in the hardest of ways, and when I finally hit the ground, it would be painful. I knew it, but I couldn't stop it.

"I'm playing," he said. I could tell he was smiling by his voice. It had a happy inflection to it. "Are you on birth control?"

Now he asked. I answered by mocking him. "Your sperm is safe with me."

"Good to know. I'm going to be making huge deposits on a regular basis. I hate to ask, but do you..."

I knew what he was going to ask. He wanted to know if I let other men come inside me. "No, you were the first ever. I mean, ever. I've never allowed that kind of contact. I should tell you—"

"No, I don't want to hear about the others. I just want to know why now? Why me?"

"Jonathan, I trust you. I trust *in* you. I've never felt like this before...you mean something more to me." I wanted to tell him there were no others, but we had agreed early on that I wouldn't discuss that.

His fingers slowly circled the tangle of raw nerves between my legs. Long minutes of his heated touch had me squirming, and I reached for the pleasure that was so close.

"I'm lost in you."

And with his last word, I soared. He kept me tethered to him while I flew higher and faster than ever before. We sat in the tub until our skin was pruned. The only thing that made us stir was the grumble of our stomachs.

Starved, we had pizza delivered and curled up on the couch to watch the news. It was such a normal night. We did things normal people did, and it was my favorite night so far.

Thursday morning came much too soon. I didn't want to say goodbye to Jonathan, but he had to rush off for a meeting at the school. I wondered if I would see him on campus, and if so, if he would acknowledge me.

There was no reason to hurry. Jade wasn't meeting me for coffee. Luca and I were hanging out at the end of the day, but I didn't have a lot of time for him. I had to hurry home and get ready for my one and only encounter with Craig Hagen. I hoped he was the kind of guy Jade had described, the kind who liked to come on your boobs and be done. I had lucked out so far; maybe my luck would hold out.

Luca was saving my seat when I walked into Entrepreneurship. He sat there with a smile and a vanilla latte. I had wondered why he'd dashed off so quickly after our last class, and now I was touched he thoughtfully bought me my favorite brew.

"How's it hanging?" It was probably the wrong thing to ask the man-child.

"About ten inches down my leg. It was only nine inches until you looked at me. That sexy smile of yours gave me that little extra sumpin' sumpin.'"

"Glad to know I'm good for an inch." Our joking ended as soon as the instructor stood in front of the podium.

"I am excited to have a guest speaker today. Please welcome Mr. Jonathan Ferris, the founder of Integrity Financial Services."

"Shit." My voice might have carried. Several people turned to scowl at me. I slunk down in my chair and watched my Jonathan take charge of the room.

"Something I should know?" Luca asked. "Something you want to share?"

"Nope," I squeaked.

When I turned my head toward the podium, Jonathan was staring at me. He spoke for an hour about taking risks. He said you had to love numbers and feel passionate about finance. Every time words like 'love', 'passion', 'push', 'risk', or 'pulse' were spoken, his eyes were on me, and I felt him. It was as though his hands had been caressing my skin.

By the time class was over, my panties were soaked. Against my better judgment, I pulled my work phone from my purse and texted him a message.

Jonathan

You could have said something. My panties are drenched.

Sunshine

It took longer to gather my belongings than usual. I watched him pull his phone from his pocket. He may have been talking to my professor, but he was reading my text. He held up a finger to my professor, asking him to wait for a second.

Sunshine,

I wanted to see you in your natural environment. Who's the playboy? I'm not sure I like his familiarity with you.

J

PS What panties?

He glanced my way, and my knees nearly buckled. His look was feral. I knew I had to gather my things and run; otherwise, we would be screwing in the nearest mop closet.

Luca was waiting by the door when I exited.

"What the hell, River? I could smell your arousal. Who the hell was that guy?"

"Gross, Luca. You don't tell a woman that. Besides, I can't tell you. It's against policy."

"He's the broom?"

"Stop asking. I can't say."

"No words are necessary."

We walked to the coffee shop at the student union and sat down to talk. It's not like we hadn't talked all day, but we just hadn't talked freely.

"Luca, how are things going for you?"

"Oh, you know. Have prick, will travel." He laughed at his joke. I didn't.

I wondered if he was struggling with the situation as much as I.

"Seriously, do you feel dirty?"

"Nope, I feel all right. I think it's different for women. I sleep with a hundred women, and I'm a stud. You sleep with a fraction of that number, and you're a whore." Direct and to the point. I had to love that about him.

"I've been lucky, as only one actually has sex with me." I blush at the mention of sex. It's not something I would have talked openly about a month ago.

"It's him, isn't it? You don't have to say it…I can see it. You're, like, all swoony over him."

"I am not." I'm pretty sure I was. I couldn't help the way I responded to him. He made my heart beat faster and my thighs clench.

We chatted for a few more minutes before I told him I had to leave for an appointment. He knew my meaning. He was off tonight, and I was envious. For me, tonight was simply a means to an end.

On the way home, I sent a response to Jonathan's last text.

I like the fact that you might be jealous. However, there is no need. Luca is a friend and if you must know, a co-worker. Next time you're

coming to class let me know. I'll be sure to skip the panties and wear your favorite color.

Sunshine

He texted back with a short note, telling me I was killing him. I closed my phone feeling giddy.

ALTHOUGH I DID shower and shave, I didn't put much effort into my look. I let my hair hang loose, and I applied my makeup sparingly. Maybe if I looked plain, Craig wouldn't be interested.

I put on the dress I wore for the pictures and pulled on a sweater. As fall was coming, and the nights were getting colder, there was a chill in the air. I took the elevator down when my cab arrived.

My stomach roiled as I slid into the back seat and handed the driver the address. I kept telling myself it would be okay, but something in my gut told me it wouldn't. I finally convinced myself it was just like my meeting with Paul, and that had turned out all right, so this would, too.

By the time I reached the hotel, I'd talked myself into a false calm. I made my way to the room and knocked.

The minute he opened the door, I could smell the alcohol. *Shit.* I wanted to turn around right then, but I didn't want another call from Sandra telling me I'd disappointed her. Hadn't I disappointed enough people in my life? I would get through this night, and it would be smooth sailing from that point on.

The hotel was pleasant, not anything worth writing home about. It wasn't the Ritz, but it wasn't a Red Roof Inn either. It fell somewhere in-between.

He walked unsteadily to the coffee table and pulled a bottle of gin from a paper bag.

"No drink?" he slurred.

"No, thank you." Everything about this situation was wrong. The man was drunk and still drinking. We were in a hotel that was off the beaten path, and I wasn't sure what he wanted. "How was your day?"

"The day? Totally okay. The night, I expect to be amazing."

I walked at a snail's pace around the room. Gold fabric covered the windows, making it obvious we wouldn't be enjoying the view. One peek between the panels into the alley, and I could see why the curtains were closed. There was no view.

He snuck up on me, and I jumped. His fingers ran up my arm, leaving a trail of goosebumps. Not the kind that made you feel warm and fuzzy, but the kind that made you feel scared. Every cell in my body wanted to turn and run.

"Tell me, River. When you purchase something, do you think the seller should be able to change the product before delivery?"

His lips traced the edge of my neck while he unzipped my dress. This was obviously going to be all about sex. Relief *and* fear set in. It would be over soon, but how much would it cost me?

Could I do this? Think about the end goal. Think about the end goal.

"It depends if the seller offers a full refund should the customer be dissatisfied." Why was he asking this?

"So, what you're telling me is that the seller can change the rules anytime she wants."

"What are we talking about? I might be able to answer better if I knew what the product was."

"You."

His hands gripped my arms painfully as he dragged me to the bed. What had I promised him that I was reneging on? I was here against my better judgment because I refused to let down my boss or my client.

"You're hurting me. Let go." I struggled against his hold, but his grip tightened. His fingers dug into my flesh, and it felt like he was touching my bones.

"You owe me what I want…what I signed up for," he slurred. He pushed me down on the bed face first. I struggled against his strength. "I want that ass of yours, River. It's what I like, and I'm paying a lot of money for it." One of my arms was set free as he lifted my dress and pulled at my panties.

That's when I began to fight back. Up until then, I'd been stunned.

"Stop. What do you think you're doing?" I screamed.

I lashed out with my only free hand. I was at a disadvantage being pinned to the bed with a two-hundred-pound man holding me down. This was the kind of thing that wasn't supposed to happen. These men were supposed to be safe. *I* was supposed to be safe.

He growled as he tore my panties from my body and spread my legs with his feet. I felt helpless and trapped. He intended to rape me. The sound of his buckle being undone brought me out of shock and into action.

No. I wouldn't go down without a fight.

I felt his hardness press against me, and all the while he told me he paid for it, so he was taking it. Everything around me became silent. It was like my world was slipping away, and if he managed to penetrate me, it would be gone for good.

My self-worth would vanish. My self-respect would crumble.

I twisted and turned, but I was stuck. It was then I reached back and grabbed his package. I gripped and twisted until his hold on me was gone.

He swung angrily and connected to the side of my face. Stars floated around my head. I could have collapsed, but I knew this was my only chance to run. He was drunk and angry—never a good combination. I stumbled across the room to grab my bag and bolted for the door.

I could hear his shouting as I ran down the stairs. There was no way I was waiting for the elevator. When I got to the ground floor, I pushed the door open and landed on my hands and knees in the alleyway.

How I got several blocks away, I had no idea. I ran until I couldn't run anymore. Like a caged animal, I looked around me, waiting for the attack to begin again. With shaking fingers, I pulled my phone from my purse and called Jade. My tears burned as they poured from my eyes.

The phone rang four times and went to voicemail. I tried again and again, but I got the same result. The only message I left was a hysterical cry for help. I thought about calling Jonathan, but what would I tell him?

I was going to have paid sex with another guy, and it didn't work out so I called you to save me.

No, that would never work. I dialed the only other number I could remember.

"Luca." *Help me.* "I'm in trouble."

Chapter 22

I had curled up into the dark corner and collapsed into myself, and that was where Luca found me.

"River, I'm here." His voice was muffled. All I could hear was screaming.

The screaming in my head.

The sound wouldn't go away. It got louder and louder as the seconds ticked by.

"Make it stop," I cried.

"Make what stop?" he asked.

"The screams." I grabbed hold of my head and began to rock.

Somehow, I ended up in his lap in a taxi. The next thing I knew, I was being placed in a strange bed and covered with an unfamiliar blanket. The frost against my cheek gave me a jolt.

"Shhh, it's okay. I've got you. You're at my place. You have a pretty good egg on your cheek. It's going to be black and blue for days." Luca tilted my chin to look at my face from every angle before replacing the icepack.

I lifted my hand to feel my cheek, but the pain in my arm was excruciating. One glance told me why. I had purple bands that rivaled Jade's purple bracelets. Seeing the marks brought it all back. The alcohol. The vehemence. The violence. The escape. I broke down again. I don't think Luca was prepared for that. *Who would be?* When he befriended me, I was pretty sure this wasn't in his plan. Through the haze, he looked scared and lost.

"I'm calling the police."

"No! What do I tell them? I'm an escort, and things got out of hand?"

"Did he rape you?"

"Is that even possible, Luca? Can a prostitute be raped?" I wailed into his pillow.

"Yes, River. No means no."

I believed that. Luca believed that. But obviously, Craig Hagen did not.

Luca. I'm at Luca's. I was nearly raped.

"No," I said vehemently. I recalled his hands, his breath against my neck, and I shuddered.

I was going to be sick.

"He didn't get that far," I whispered.

Luca swore. I felt like I was emerging from a dark tunnel.

"He didn't get anywhere, Luca. He was violent from the onset...but I fought back." His gentle touch across my forehead soothed me. "I have been letting people beat me up for years, whether it was mentally or physically. I've had enough, Luca." A new torrent of tears streamed from my eyes. Would I ever cry myself out of tears?

"Yes, you have. I'm calling Sandra. She needs to know." I nodded my head and pressed my face back into the pillow to cry.

Whispers faded in and out. The distinct sound of Sandra's voice broke through my void. I preferred the nothingness of sleep. When I was awake, everything became a reality. When I was asleep, it was just a bad dream.

The bed dipped, and a gentle hand glided across my hair. The focus of my eyes was off. At first, I saw my mother, but I knew that couldn't be right. Things came into focus, and Sandra sat on the edge of the bed.

"I'm sorry this happened, River. In all my years, I have never had something like this occur. He's been removed from The List. He said you brought it on yourself when you promised something you didn't deliver. Is that true?"

Was she really sitting there, asking me if I deserved this? *Stupid bitch.* I couldn't deal with her now. I rolled over and covered my face with the blanket. The bed shifted again, and I hoped she left.

The next voice I heard was Dr. Chang's. He rolled me over and inspected my cheek and arms. His eyes told the story, and sadness blanketed his expression. He said something about giving me a shot to help with the pain. After that, I don't remember much of anything.

"Sunshine. Wake up, sweetheart."

His voice took over my dreams. I was glad my mind could grasp something positive amidst the terror of the night. My head ached, and my eyes burned. My body felt sluggish, and nothing made sense.

"Baby, look at me."

Eyes fluttering, I opened them to see Jonathan sitting on the edge of the bed, his eyes filled with concern. Behind the concern was darkness. Tethered by a thread, I could tell he was furious. I'd seen that look once before. I'd never wanted *that* look to be directed at me.

He'll never want me now.

"Jonathan? What are you doing here?"

I couldn't process the information. I was in Luca's apartment. I remembered Dr. Chang and Sandra visiting. I remembered Luca hovering but looking lost. I recalled trying unsuccessfully to reach Jade. I had no memory of calling Jonathan. I would never have done that. This wasn't his place. He didn't need to be tainted by the ugliness of my life.

The pain made me wince when I struggled to sit up. I looked down and saw I was still in the dress I'd worn to the encounter. I would throw it away the minute I got home.

"Luca called me." Jonathan's hand cupped my unblemished cheek while his thumb brushed my lips.

"He had no right."

The tears sprang to my eyes. Everything came crashing down. Up until this moment, I was still lying to myself. If I'd only had intercourse with Jonathan...if I'd just gotten Thursday and Friday over with. If...if...if.

"He did the right thing. I'm grateful to him. I'm taking you home. Howard is downstairs."

His tone was matter-of-fact. There was no arguing with him. It wouldn't have mattered regardless, as the fight had been beaten out of me. I was exhausted and emotionally spent.

I didn't want him to see me like this. We didn't discuss other men —it was part of our agreement. I'd pretended there weren't any because deep in my heart, only Jonathan existed. The evidence on my body told a different truth. Another man had touched me. The proof was plain to see.

I gingerly slid out of bed and rose slowly. The world spun around me. He steadied me.

"Bathroom?" I asked. "Just tell me where it is."

"I'll take you." He hovered over me like a hen watching her eggs.

It was tough to convince him I could pee by myself, but he eventually conceded. I did my business and washed my hands. Fear burned through me as I lifted my head to the mirror. I wasn't prepared for the girl who looked back. *Her* cheek was nearly black. *Her* eyes were hollow. *Her* skin was pale. *That can't be me.* I traced the fist-sized bruise. The swelling must have reduced because it didn't appear to be as big as it felt, but it was sore. The skin was intact, and for that I was grateful. There would be no physical scarring.

In spite of my parents' awful parental skills, they'd rarely raised a hand to me. I'd been on the receiving end of a backhand or two, but in general, their beatings were verbal in nature. This was the first time I'd ever been punched by anyone.

The experience was not one I would recommend. I needed to get my head on straight, but trying to knock it off wasn't the best-laid plan. I splashed some cool water on my face and exited the bathroom. Jonathan leaned against the wall, waiting for me.

"Can you walk, or should I carry you?" He leaned down to pick me up, but I stepped back. I was used to standing on my own two feet, and to let him carry the burden would be a mistake.

"I'm good. Thank you."

His hand sat gently against the small of my back. I exited Luca's apartment in a six-hundred-dollar dress, no shoes, and no underwear. Ironically, I was inadvertently following Jonathan's rules of no panties, but this time I was positive he wouldn't be pleased. They had been ripped from my body.

We climbed into the back of the car and headed toward home. At least that was where I thought I was headed. Imagine my surprise when we arrived at Jonathan's Fifth Avenue flat.

"I want to go home. My home."

A wounded look crossed his tired eyes. I hated that I'd hurt him. It wasn't my intent, but I needed time to think, time to plan. All I knew was, my life wasn't working out the way I'd intended, and things had to change.

Jade's idea of "two years, and we would have it made" was bullshit. It wasn't working out for either of us. She was losing herself in the same way I was. If we didn't do something soon, neither of us would recognize what was left.

I remember on my second encounter with Jonathan, he said he hoped the job wouldn't change me. I told him everything changed, the important thing to watch for was what remained the same. Could I salvage a piece of myself after *that*? I didn't want to feel dirty, humiliated or tainted.

He knocked on the window and asked Howard to take me to my home. I was grateful he didn't push. I wouldn't have had the energy to fight him. It would be easy to fall into his arms and allow him to carry the burden, but the burden was not his to carry.

I didn't want him to see me like this.

I leaned against his chest as the car moved toward my place. I loved his smell. He was sandalwood, and basil, and the scent would always exclusively belong to him.

When we arrived at my place, he insisted on coming up with me. I wanted to tell him no. I needed to tell him no, but I didn't have the strength physically or mentally. My roommate was gone, thankfully. One look at my face, and she would have jumped to all sorts of conclusions.

I checked my phone for messages and found one from Sandra and one from Luca. Sandra told me the best way to move forward was to jump into the saddle again.

Was she kidding me?

She had canceled my appointments through the weekend, but I was expected to keep my appointment with Ben on Monday. The woman was impossible. Luca wanted to make sure I was okay. There was nothing from Jade.

Tucked into bed, Jonathan spooned behind me, lending me the strength and warmth his body could provide. I wanted to cry. I wanted to stay like this forever.

"I know we have an agreement, but it's killing me to not know what happened. Who the hell did this to you, and why?" His voice cracked as he asked. He pulled my body against his chest and begged me to tell him.

I contemplated how to answer. He had come to my rescue on numerous occasions and had always managed to be there when I needed him. I owed him something. "I can't tell you who. You know I can't. I can only tell you he tried to take something that didn't belong to him. He tried to rape me. It wasn't consensual." In a softer voice, I added, "He tried to take what was yours."

I could hear him swallow hard several times. He was processing what I'd told him. I knew the minute the full impact hit him. He buried his head in my hair and cried. I was so glad he was behind me. I wasn't sure I could have handled his anguish had I been face-to-face with him.

Jonathan stayed the rest of the night and held me in his arms. I felt safe. He was the protector. I would survive, though. I *had* to survive.

Maybe my parents had done me a favor by raising me with an ounce of love and a pound of hate. I was resilient, and in spite of my softness, I had an inner resolve that required me to stand up and dust myself off.

When I woke, Jonathan was gone. I had expected to find a note or something, but there was none. I found Tiffany in the kitchen making coffee, and it was actually funny to see her out of her element. I was the official coffeemaker in the house. She searched the cupboards for the filters and grounds and managed to get the machine to spit water. Sadly, we didn't have a fancy coffee machine, just your standard model that poured water over inferior ground beans. In spite of its second-class status, the coffee smelled fabulous.

"Holy shit. What the hell happened to you?" Her eyes bugged out while she stared at the contusion on my face.

"Bar brawl," I said in a matter-of-fact manner.

I knew those two words would get me off the hook. As a cocktail waitress, Tiffany saw everything from fistfights to catfights on a regular basis. She shrugged her shoulders and left the room.

"You should ice that," she called from her room.

I checked my calendar to make sure Sandra had canceled my meetings. My schedule was blocked out through Sunday.

Next on my list: my parents. They had called nearly every day since our lunch visit. I hadn't listened to one of their messages. They didn't have anything I wanted to hear. They raised a girl who lacked self-esteem, one who was willing to sell the smallest remaining part of her to get what she wanted—an advanced degree. Like somehow that degree would fill the gaping hole in her life.

I was supposed to live in God's grace, but it was never given. I believed my father had the power to grant it and take it away, but the reality was, he needed it just as much, if not more than me. My parents had nothing I wanted to hear, but they were going to listen to what I had to say. Once I was finished talking, I knew they would be finished with me as well.

I tapped in the numbers and waited for them to pick up the phone.

No hello. Nothing. She just dove in. "River, do you know how many times I've called you, young lady?" Oh, my mother and her finesse. She knew how to make me feel all soft and pliable. Not.

"Yes, ten if you count the hang up. I didn't call to listen to the endless list of transgressions I've saddled you and Dad with. I called to tell you that you were right. Everything you ever thought of me has come true. I have to wonder if I became what you predicted because of you or me, though, Mom. In the end, it doesn't matter. I just wanted you to know I lived up to your expectations for once in my life. I became a whore."

Silence.

I loved that I could silence her. I'd been trying all my life to shut her up. If I'd known it would take the simple act of agreeing, I would have agreed with her fifteen years ago when she started calling me Jezebel. Sometimes life was that simple.

"River, are you okay?" Her concern surprised me. I couldn't remember a time when she asked if I were okay. How dare she start asking now?

"Mom, I'm finally fine. I called to say goodbye. Jonathan told you to not contact me, and it didn't work. I figured it was because it had come to you second-hand. So, from my mouth to God's ear and straight to your own, never call me again. Never contact me. I would hate to see what my life would turn out to be if I continued to meet your expectations. I expect more from myself."

I hung up and blocked my parents' number.

It was liberating to take my life into my hands. Scary as shit, but I felt like I'd grown up, and all it took was a punch to the head and a man who thought I was sunshine. Everything was clear. I'd been flotsam and jetsam floating in everyone else's current my entire life. I'd never rocked the boat. I went with the flow. Not anymore. From this point forward, I was the storm, and I would determine how the waves crashed and how the current would flow.

Chapter 23

Despite the two hours it took to cover the bruise on my face, a dark shadow was still prevalent. I packed up a duffle bag and headed out the door. Sandra wasn't expecting me, but she would receive me. I would pound down her door until she acknowledged my presence. I still couldn't get over the fact that she insinuated the blame was on me. The closer I got to the office, the angrier I became.

Merilee looked shocked when I entered the lobby. I didn't wait for her to call Sandra. With a push, the panel on the wall opened up and I was in.

Poor Merilee, with her eyes large and glossy, looked like I'd brandished a weapon and held her hostage. She looked at Sandra the way I looked at my parents, as if she were waiting for the disappointment to show on her face. She expected it. She had failed in her job, and Sandra would never let that go unpunished.

It was hard to believe I had admired Sandra.

I looked at Merilee in sympathy. "She'll get over it, Merilee. Go pull yourself up by your knickers. Tomorrow will be a new day, and you can do something else to make her unhappy. Today, it's all about me." I tossed my duffle aside and walked with purpose to Sandra's desk.

"You could have called, River. Why all the drama? I would have been happy to see you." She tilted her head and stared at my cheek. No matter how hard I tried, nothing short of spackle would have covered the bruise completely.

"Somehow, Sandra, I imagine that to be an untruth. You sat in this office and told me we could speak candidly. You sold me a bunch of crap, and I fell for it because I wanted to believe it could be true. You enchanted me with new clothes and spa treatments. You sold me on the job like you were hiring me to be your accountant."

"I was never dishonest with you, River." She looked nervous. She rearranged her desk constantly while I spoke and didn't look me in the eye.

"No, you weren't. You told me the way I felt about myself would be the hardest thing to accept, and you were right. I didn't think it through. My parents had called me a whore my whole life, so I didn't think it would be such a huge leap to become one. My head was already wrapped around the notion. However, I found out being called a whore and actually becoming one were two different things."

"Whore, prostitute, escort…it's semantics, River. It doesn't matter what you call it, the end result is the same. Some would call a stay-at-home housewife the same. Doesn't she profit from serving up her goodies on a regular basis? We all sell something."

"Yes, we do. You sell young girls to men. You're a Madame."

"I am not a Madame." Her tone was indignant and full of shock.

"Madame, pimp, procurer, facilitator, brothel keeper…it's semantics, Sandra." I tossed her words back at her.

"What's your point? You had a bad night? Poor River." Sarcasm dripped from her lips. "You'll survive. Like I said, get back in the saddle and ride on." She lined up the pens on her desk, once again, and she looked everywhere but in my direction. Coward.

"That's my point. I'm not getting back in the saddle. I'm finished with this ride." I could almost hear the snap of her neck as she raised her head to look at me.

"You can't quit. You can't afford to quit. I invested in you, and you made a commitment to stay a year."

"What are you going to do, take me to court?" The thought made me laugh. "I could see it all play out. 'Excuse me, Your Honor. I'm suing River Roberts because she reneged on our agreement to sell her body for tuition. I bought her clothes and had her pubes ripped out for free.'"

"Don't be silly. I would never involve the law. That would put our clients at risk. But I wonder how your parents would feel about your career path."

Naturally, she would go there, but I was prepared.

"Oh, you mean my zealot parents? I told them today before I came here. I prefer to keep things above board. They were really proud. Speechless, actually."

That was a bitter pill for Sandra to swallow. Her face distorted the way mine did when I sucked on a lime. She thought she could black-mail me, but I'd taken away her options.

"Why would you want to go back to your little life when you could have so much more if you stayed on with me? You do realize today would be your last payday if you quit?"

"Yes, I'm fully aware I will no longer have an income. I was making it before I met you, and I'll figure it out again."

"Let me know when you get settled back into your old job. I really do love a good latte."

The thing about women was, they were catty bitches. They would dig at you until you bled. When you scabbed over, they would scratch at you just to open the wound again. Sandra was a catty bitch, but her claws didn't wound. I'd heard worse from my own flesh and blood.

"I'll make sure to let you know."

I wasn't interested in a catfight. I just wanted to get it settled and get on with it. I was saddling up again, only this time I was riding a different kind of horse, and I was going in a different direction. I needed to slide back a step or two before I stepped forward.

Thump.

The phone banged as I tossed it across her desk. I had already pulled Ben, Jonathan's, and Paul's phone numbers from the contact list. I had to make things all right with them. I didn't owe it to them, but I felt like I owed it to myself. Standing up, I turned to walk out. As I got to the door, I glanced at the duffle bag near my feet.

"The clothes you purchased are in the bag. I imagine my purple cheek is worth the rest of what I owe you." Freedom was only a few feet away when she called to me.

"Oh, by the way, Jonathan Ferris called and said he had moved on. I was pretty sure the message was intended for you. He was always a bit of a connoisseur. It actually surprised me that he saw you more than once. That wasn't his style."

There was no comeback. Inside, I felt my chest crack. I struggled to find breath, but I wouldn't let Sandra know she had wounded me. Turning, I walked out the door. For the second time in twenty-four hours, I curled up on the sidewalk and cried. Jonathan was done with me. What did I expect? I'd been his good-time girl, nothing more. I looked down at the charm around my wrist. Part of me wanted to yank it off and toss it aside, but the rest of me held on to the memory of being his sunshine...if only for a moment.

When I was with my parents, his words had been the much-needed salve for my beaten soul.

River is everything that's wonderful in the world. She is brightness and light. She is compassion and hope. She is laughter. She's my sunshine, and I will not let you dim her light in any way.

He wasn't a man to play games, so I could presume he had meant those words when he'd spoken them. But I was tainted now. Ugly. No longer his sunshine. No longer *his* anything.

He'd moved on.

The minute the homeless person sat next to me and tried to console me, I knew it was time to get up and move on. I may have hit rock bottom, but I wasn't going to spend my days panhandling and hiding in dark corners. I thanked the man for his concern and handed him the change I had in my purse.

Next stop: Jade. She still had not returned my calls. I realized the duo had all of her minutes, but that was bullshit. I needed her, and she owed me. She got us into this mess, and I was going to get us out of it. Her voice echoed in my ears.

Two years, and I'd be set.

In two years, I would have been a shell of myself. My lower lips would have hung like elephant ears to my knees.

What the hell had I been thinking?

I walked several blocks to her apartment. Come to think of it, she didn't live that far from Jonathan. Did everyone live on Fifth Avenue? At the door, I buzzed her number. I buzzed, and buzzed, and buzzed until I heard her voice yell over the intercom.

"What the hell?"

"It's me, let me up." There was silence on her end. Was she debating letting me in? I swear, if that buzzer didn't ring to grant me entry, I was going to ring every flat in the building until someone opened the door.

"I don't want you to see me." Her voice sounded small and defeated.

"Open the damn door, Jade."

Rage blossomed inside me. I was in an ass-kicking mood, and if I found her in any condition short of perfection, I would be strapping a few men to the wall and beating them to within an inch of their lives. Jade was all I had left, and I'd be damned if someone was going to take her away from me.

The door buzzed open, and I flew through it. I didn't bother with the elevator. I took the stairs. What did she mean, she didn't want me to see her?

With my hand raised and ready to pound through her door, she opened it and pulled me in. She looked like crap. Her hair hadn't been brushed, and her face was as white as a marshmallow.

"What the hell?" I pulled her to the sofa and went in search of water. She looked like she might collapse at any minute. The refrigerator was full of apple juice, her favorite, so I grabbed a bottle and handed it to her. She looked at it and set it down.

"What do you mean, 'what the hell'? What the hell with you? What the hell happened to your face?" Her hand came up to touch my cheek, but I flinched and backed away. It was too painful to touch.

I grabbed her wrists and checked for bruises. She inspected the rest of my face for damage. I pulled up my sleeves, and she gasped. The bruises were thick and dark today, and the weight of my cotton shirt was nearly too much friction to bear.

"I called you last night. You didn't answer. I needed you, and you weren't there." The weight of that statement hung in the air. I hadn't realized I was crying until I felt the tears drip off my chin and onto my chest.

We embraced gently. She avoided my arms, and I circled her waist. It was then that I realized how thin she had become. I could feel her shoulder blades poke through her shirt.

"Oh my God, are you sick? You're so skinny. Where are these men who are supposed to be taking care of you?"

Her shoulders rounded as she slumped against the couch. "You first, then we'll discuss me."

If this was her way of evading my questions, she was crazy. I'd play along for now, but she was going to talk. We began with me. I told her about Craig and his anger about changing my limits list. I told her I'd fought him off and ran. I told her about Luca coming to rescue me, about Jonathan getting me through the night, and about how I had quit my job with Sandra, and the talk with my mom. By the end of my verbal barrage, her face was blank.

I kept trying to hand her the apple juice, but each time I did, she turned her face to the side, grimacing. *What the?* I pulled my phone from my purse and brought up the picture I'd taken the day this whole mess had started.

"This was us a few weeks ago." I leaned in next to her and took a new picture. "This is us now. Look at us. This isn't who we are. This isn't who we saw ourselves to be. Look at *you*, Jade. You're a shadow of yourself. You look like a refugee. I look like a prizefighter."

I scrolled between the two pictures. It was amazing how a few weeks could change a life.

"I'm going to be all right. I just haven't been feeling well."

"They aren't beating you, are they?"

"They never beat me. They have always been gentle and kind but in control. I like that. The bruises came from my own stupidity and hardheadedness. Look around you, River, do I look like an abused woman?"

I had to admit, she didn't look abused. Her residence was beautiful, her refrigerator was full of food, and her closet was full of designer clothes. She looked like the kept woman she was.

"Why aren't you eating? You need to eat." I wanted to spoon-feed her myself, but if I couldn't get her to drink juice, I would have never persuaded her to eat. "You need to quit this job. It's going to kill you."

"Sandra let me go today. It looks like we're both free."

"She let you go? Was it because of me? I can't say I'm unhappy about this turn of events. I'm sure we can get Tiffany to rent you the room again. Hell, she never moved anyone in since you left."

"She never moved anyone in because I still rent the room. I wanted to make sure I always had a place to stay. It was part of my negotiations with Eric and Todd." The duo had real names. I suppose if neither of us were part of The Dean's List then the rules that surrounded the club didn't really exist. We would never publicly divulge information, but we could talk amongst ourselves.

"Eric and Todd, huh? What will happen now that you're not part of the service? Will they keep you? Do you want to stay?"

"I'm pregnant, River. That's why I was released. I broke the rules by getting knocked up. I have been on my deathbed with morning, afternoon, and night sickness for a week. I'm sorry I missed your call. Eric took my phone so I wouldn't be bothered. He's worried about me."

I'd been so angry with her for not answering my call, and now it somehow seemed unimportant. She was pregnant, and that opened up the need for new discussion. "How does the duo feel about this new development? How do you feel?"

"Initially, I was scared. I knew they loved me, but I wasn't sure how far their commitment would be. We met through The Dean's List, after all. I used to think all men who bought sex were slimy little bastards. Then I got to know my two. What we have is untraditional, but it works. We have had some bumps in the road, but we have managed to pave our way through them. I'm in love with them, and I am in love with the idea of having their baby. To my surprise, they were thrilled."

I wasn't sure if I should even ask, but I had to know. "Who's the father?"

"They both are. I don't know whose DNA was deposited, and it doesn't matter. All I know is we are having a baby. What about you? You were enamored with Mr. Broom which I deduce from our earlier conversation is Jonathan. What will happen with him? Will you see him?" Was that hope I saw in her eyes?

"No. Sandra indicated he had moved on. I haven't had time to process that. I tried to talk myself out of loving him, but I couldn't." I'd tried, and I'd failed. Dismally. He was too much the whole package I wanted in a man. *How could I not?* "I fell hard, and it will take some time to get over him. Last night when we were together, he cried. I know he blamed himself for the whole event. But when I got up, he was gone. No note. No message. Just gone."

I closed my eyes and took a deep breath. I hadn't had time to process the stark reality of his departure, but I needed to get through this moment with Jade. Right now, she needed me.

I laid my head in her lap, hoping to find comfort and give comfort. Softly, Jade stroked my hair. She would make a great mother. Although tough, she was compassionate and caring. She was motherly. So much had changed in so little time.

"River, I might have an idea to help us both. Since Eric and Todd travel several days a week, they wanted to hire someone to be my companion. I refused, but since you don't have a job, and *I* need you, would you consider moving in here with me? You could help me turn the playroom into a nursery?"

"You want me to move into your fancy Fifth Avenue high-rise? What insidious acts will I have to perform?" I was teasing her, but I could see her eyes dim.

"I'm so sorry I got you into that. I was happy in my situation, and I thought you would be, too. I never expected it to end like it did. Let me show you your room before you tell me no." She led me down a hall into a beautiful bedroom. The king-sized bed sat center stage. The color scheme was bold just the way I liked it.

"Won't it be weird with me here when your men are here?"

"No, they are going to have to get used to you anyway. You will be my child's godmother and aunt. You're a permanent fixture. Besides, with everything that's happened, I think a change of scenery is in order." She led me to the attached bathroom and walked me into the enormous closet. "As a perk, when I get too fat for my clothes, you can have them. The Louboutins are already yours, as the boys banned me from heels until the little one is born."

"Shouldn't you ask them first? This is their place, after all." I looked around the bedroom and wondered if I could find the things I needed. Things like comfort, safety, and love. After glancing at Jade, there was no doubt. She had always been my rock.

"No, this place is mine. They signed it over after the Dom incident. The experience made them realize how much they had to lose. They were trying to make me stay forever."

"No way. You own a flat on Fifth Avenue, and it's free and clear? Wow, who would have thought that possible?"

I stayed long enough to make her scrambled eggs and dry toast. Just as she was sitting down to eat, her men entered the house. They stopped the minute they saw me. I wasn't sure if it was my face or the simple fact that a stranger was there that startled them.

I was surprised by their looks. Eric was tall and handsome, his hair sandy blond and his eyes sea-green. Todd was average height with dark hair and dark skin. In seven or so months, there would be no doubt whose DNA created their child. The men were like night and day, and yet their demeanor was the same. They doted on my friend, and I knew right then that she would always be okay.

They were ecstatic when they heard I'd be moving in. I told them it wouldn't be long-term, but just until Jade had the baby.

I hugged my friend goodbye and told her I would begin moving my things over the next day or two. The duo kiboshed that notion and arranged for a moving company to pick up my things on Monday. I would pay Tiffany what I owed her and move on with my life. Again.

Chapter 24

I probably should have erased the picture of Jonathan from my phone, but I didn't have the heart to do it. Looking at him was my guilty pleasure. He was still one of the nicest people I'd ever met, and he'd always seemed to know what I needed.

It was as if he had really cared about me.

Maybe him leaving was just another gift, a way to tell me I needed to figure out my life on my own.

How attached would I have become to him had I been able to continue what we had? There was no future for us. He'd made that clear from the beginning. Maybe if we had met under different circumstances it might have worked out. Here I was, lying to myself again. Under what circumstances could it have worked? None. It wasn't like we walked in the same circles. Someday we might, but not at this time.

I often wondered how he really felt about me. He said I was sunshine, but what else did he think? I treated our time together like a relationship. I was smitten with everything about him from his looks to his bedroom prowess. Did he see me as a beautiful woman or a

221

woman who had a price? How could a man who hired me for sex ever respect me? Hell, I didn't respect myself.

I stayed in bed from Friday until Monday. The door buzzed a few times, but I didn't answer it unless I was expecting Chinese take-out or pizza. Too much time on my hands created other issues. My mind replayed the last few weeks of my life. Weeks I never wanted to repeat and yet I would have jumped at the chance to have one more day with Jonathan. I stressed over my less-than-perfect finances. The extra courses I picked up cost money. Money I didn't have. The only good that would come from this situation was the time I would have to focus on my studies. And in the end, wasn't that the intent? I wouldn't be debt-free or guilt-free, but I was free, and I could work with that.

THE DUO HAD ARRANGED for the pickup of my things. All I needed to pack were my clothes. My closet was divided into two sections. My pre-Jonathan clothes were mostly second-hand or purchased from large box stores like Forever 21. My post-Jonathan wardrobe was brands that ranged from Tahari to Escada. There was a disparity between the two sections and yet I felt connected to both. I *was* the girl who went to college, and the woman who dined at Per Se and stayed at the Ritz. Never once did I feel out of my element, like I wasn't good enough. All my insecurities came from the voices in my head that had told me I was nothing. Why had I never considered those voices to be worthless?

I checked my phone before I placed the beautiful blue dress I never got to wear in the garment box. My belongings were ready to go. Luca checked in every day and today was no different. He always said he was thinking of me and hoped I was healing.

Physically? Mentally? I wondered which he meant.

We planned on coffee that Thursday.

I'll never forget the first time I saw him. He was buttered toast and I was hungry. I had decided then that I'd wanted him. In fact, I'd decided I would be wealthy enough one day to get me a Luca. The irony of the situation was that I had *my* Luca, and he was wonderful. His friendship was offered freely.

Despite my misgivings and unfortunate final experience, I did have some wonderful moments during my short tenure as a Dean's List student. My greatest joy and biggest regret would be Jonathan. I played with the charm hanging from my wrist and decided that from that point forward I would work on my self-esteem and confidence. I would become the woman a man like Jonathan would be proud to date.

I left a check on the counter for the remaining rent due on my lease. Tiffany seemed happy to have the place to herself.

I glanced over my shoulder and said goodbye to my old life. I was the new, improved me. The girl who focused on school. I had a shit-load of student loans, but they were mine, and I would chip at them like every other person did, one chunk at a time.

THAT NIGHT I met with Ben at his favorite restaurant. He was distressed by my experience. He kept brushing my cheek with his thumb as if he possessed some magic elixir that would heal my bruise on contact. I wished that were the case. The blackness had faded and now it was an ugly combination of purple and green. I did my best to hide it, but I lacked the skills needed for that kind of coverage.

"Tell me his name. I'll make sure he pays for that." Ben's voice was dead serious.

"You know I can't do that. Ben, I totally believe in karma and he'll get his. I got this, not because I deserved it, but because I needed the wake-up call. I needed to learn to listen to my instincts."

"What did your instincts tell you about me?" His question told me that no matter a person's age, we were all concerned with how others perceived us.

"I liked you from the beginning. You are a kind, gentle soul. You are a good man. I was in the process of limiting my schedule to three men. Only one of which I had intercourse with." I stared off into space and thought of the one man who made my body tingle simply by his presence. "Anyway, I wasn't cut out for this kind of work. I had no idea how much it would take from me, so I chose the people who didn't take from me but gave something to me."

"I liked you from the beginning, River. You have a sassy innocence. You were humble, and that was refreshing."

"I was hoping we could still meet for dinner, Ben. I do need mentoring, not the type The Dean's List offers, but real-world mentoring. We can still meet every week if you want, and we'll trade off on who pays the bill. When it's my treat, we may have to choose someplace a bit less fancy." I looked around the steakhouse he seemed to favor. I might be able to swing this about once a month. Maybe.

"How about we meet for dinner every week, and I pick up the bill? I can afford it more easily than you." His warm hand came to rest on top of mine. "Also, I have this political fundraiser to attend in a couple of months. I was hoping I could persuade you to attend. I would be the envy of all the old geezers having you on my arm." *Ben still wanted to meet with me?* The man was amazing, and I felt extremely thankful for his kindness and consideration. He was the Rx for my soul.

"I'd love to go." Lord knows, between Jade's closet and mine, I could come up with something to wear.

"So, tell me about these other men." He knew I couldn't give him details, but I thought he wanted to know what kind of men they were.

"One is a very nice man, but he lacks self-esteem." As I listened to myself, I found it funny that I was responsible for raising someone else's self-esteem when mine was so low. "He was so sweet and considerate. We spent our time learning about all sorts of things. He was working on his confidence and I was grateful I could help. I am going to meet with him one more time to say goodbye and thank him for his kindness."

"That's what's amazing about you. You could punish all men for the sins of one, but you're grateful to the few who showed you kindness. That's a real gift, my dear."

I hated to get emotional in front of Ben, but his affirmation touched me. I suppressed the tears that threatened to spill.

"The third man was actually my first and he was everything I could have hoped for in a mentor. He seemed to know what I needed, and he was always there to provide it whether it was a kind word, a vanilla latte, or a reassuring hug." Damn it. A rogue tear escaped and trickled down my bruised cheek. It would be the only one I would allow.

"It sounds like you have feelings for this man." It was impossible to get anything past Ben. Thankfully, we didn't have a romantic connection. I didn't have to worry about him being jealous.

"If I'm being honest with myself, I fell for him immediately. In spite of my efforts, my heart had a connection to his. It was like it beat at the same pace and rhythm."

"Where is this man now? Are you still seeing him?"

"Oh, no. He saw me through the night of the incident. For whatever reason, my friend Luca called him. Anyway, he was there for me that night, but I guess it was too much. And now that I'm not part of the 'club' I imagine he will move on to another girl." The thought of him with another woman twisted my heart so painfully it felt like I couldn't breathe.

As only a grandfather figure could do, he scowled. "The man is an idiot." His statement was direct and to the point. He warmed my heart. Maybe I would need to think that way to get through the pain. Putting him in the role of the idiot would be a stretch for me.

"I'm not sure who the idiot is at this point, but I'm thinking it might be me. The only thing I am grateful for is I never actually had sex with anyone I didn't care about. I'm coming to terms with that first, and once I move past that I'll focus on the idiot quotient."

We spent the rest of the evening talking about my career aspirations. He told me to go to his HR department and see if there was anything I might like to try. I was touched by his generous offer, but I wanted to make it on my own. Through hard work and due diligence, I would create my future.

With a kiss on the cheek and a promise to meet the following Monday, Ben put me in a cab and sent me home. There wouldn't be a form to sign to account for my time. This time I gave it freely, and I felt incredibly wealthy.

———

JADE WAS SITTING on the couch with a bucket in one hand and a plate of refried beans with cheese in the other when I arrived home.

"Hey ho…me," she teased.

"Hey, preggers. What's with the bucket?" I slid onto the couch beside her. Some of her color had returned. Her white skin and light blonde hair made her look see-through on a good day. The minute she was sick she looked downright ghastly.

"I have this craving for beans with lots of cheese, but I'm afraid it's going to come back up so I'm prepared because I'm eating these beans. They are the first food that hasn't turned my stomach."

I pulled the bucket from her hand and began to spoon the beans into her mouth. The first step was always the hardest.

"I'm going to continue to see Ben on Monday nights for dinner. I enjoy his company, and he enjoys mine. He's a sweet old man. I have no idea why he was paying such exorbitant fees to Sandra, as the man can't have sex anymore anyway." I continued to feed her beans keeping her mouth occupied. "I'm seeing Paul tomorrow. I have to break the news to him that he can't eat me anymore."

She choked on her beans, so I handed her the cup of water sitting on the table. She managed to get a "What?" out before I shoved another bite of beans into her mouth.

"Oh yes, he has a thumb tack between his legs, but he's the nicest man. Because he can't perform with his tool, I've been teaching him how to give oral sex like a master. He's a quick learner. He's going to be disappointed because he was hoping to improve his confidence. Sadly, my vagina has taken an early retirement."

She pushed the spoonful of beans I had tried to put in her mouth aside. "You can't mean that. Your vagina needs attention. I've seen you after months without sex and it's not pretty." She pushed the plate out of the way, indicating she was finished. I put it on the table and picked up the bucket just in case.

"I'm not giving up sex permanently, but I'm going to be selective. Honestly, Jonathan was the best lover I've ever had. I'm not sure anyone can live up to that. I figure if I wait awhile and get him out of my system, I may forget what good felt like, and then I can settle for mediocrity. Do you think that's possible?"

Her answer was direct and honest. "No. Once you have great, there's no going back. You should call him." She sat back on the couch and placed her hands on her concave stomach. It was hard to believe she had a baby growing in there.

"I can't. He told Sandra he had moved on. The message was clear."

"Sandra is a bitch. How do you know if she was telling the truth? Does he have your phone number?" She let out a burp that I thought was something else, and I quickly pressed the bucket against her chest. She laughed as she pushed it away.

"No, we always followed the rules. I used the work phone. The only thing I used my phone for was to take a boudoir shot for my own enjoyment."

"You have to share. I have a picture of Pierce Brosnan in my head. I'll be so disappointed if he doesn't look exactly like Pierce in Dante's Peak."

I pulled my phone from my purse and scrolled through my recent pictures. Just seeing him lying in my bed was painful. I missed him so much. He'd made me feel like I counted. He had been the only adult besides Jade who actually saw me. I handed her the phone and watched her. He wasn't Pierce Brosnan, but he was the perfect mix of Gerard Butler and Jon Hamm and I loved him. How was I ever supposed to move on?

"Oh, he's hot. I can see the attraction."

"It's not his looks I'm attracted to. He's an amazing man in every way." I traced the sunshine on my bracelet and thought of the night he gave it to me. I'd given him a keychain. He'd given me hope. Her eyes fell to the bracelet on my wrist.

"He may be amazing, but the fact he gave you up means he's not that smart." She shook her head and rubbed my back to comfort me.

"I'm going to bed. I have class tomorrow. Are you going?" I leaned over and gave her a hug.

"As long as I'm not puking my guts out. By the way, Todd has arranged a car for us. He wants us to ride in style." The mother of his child had to ride in style, and if he wanted to chauffeur me around, who was I to argue?

Chapter 25

In spite of sleeping in a strange place for the first time, I slept well. I wasn't sure if it was pure exhaustion or the painkiller that knocked me out. Dr. Chang didn't specify what type of pain it was designed for, so I took it anyway. I figured a heartache counted as pain, too.

I woke up to Jade placing coffee on the nightstand next to my bed. It was a sweet gesture, one I completely appreciated. She looked chipper and put together, more like her old self. The beans had done her good.

"Get up, we have school." She sat on my bed and bounced. Her movement guaranteed my obedience. Who could sleep through that kind of motion? She was like a 7.2 on the Richter scale.

"Argh," was all I could muster before I dragged myself from the bed. I headed to the bathroom to try out my camouflaging skills.

A bruise the size of Texas was a challenge to cover when you didn't have the makeup artist training to attack a project so large. I gave up attempting after three coats of concealer.

We started our day in the most normal way we could. Coffee at the student union. Decaf for Jade, fully loaded for me. It felt good to get back into our normal routine. I finished my classes and took the subway home. Jade stayed on to complete her day.

Luca called to check on me. How did I explain I was fine when I wasn't? Physically I would heal. In fact, the attack was the least of my worries. I told him I was as good as could be, and that was the truth. I would have to figure out how to extricate Jonathan in order to move forward. Just before Luca hung up, he told me Jonathan had been calling him to get updates on my recovery. I didn't know what to think—it was that type of behavior that made it impossible to let him go. I told him if Jonathan called again to tell him I was doing well and moving forward. Wasn't that what he had told Sandra? I was determined to follow his lead.

The rest of the day was spent puttering around the house and attending to the responsibilities that came with a move. I took care of address changes and made a new budget based on my current financial situation. The check I sent to the bank reduced my student loan by several thousand dollars, but it left my bank account in need of a cash infusion. Thank goodness I received a final paycheck from Concierge Services. It would have to last until I got a new job.

The duo had offered to pay me to look after Jade, but I could never take money for loving my friend. Jade refused my money for rent and for that I was grateful. I would be fine for a couple of months if I watched my money and paid the minimum balance due on my loan.

A glance at the clock told me it was time to get ready for my date with Paul, so I gathered my papers and returned to my room. This would be the last time I would see him. When considering what to wear to dinner, I rummaged through my closet. I nixed everything that Jonathan had bought. I decided to wear something from my existing wardrobe—my pre-escort wardrobe. A red dress that cinched at the side seemed appropriate for the restaurant he had chosen.

We had never met for dinner before, so this was something new. I walked into the restaurant and found him sitting by the bar. Paul looked...confident. From what looked like a soda in his hand, it seemed he no longer needed liquid courage to get through the night. I felt proud of him, and dearly hoped he would be able to continue in that direction after tonight.

His face fell when he saw me. In spite of my efforts, I couldn't hide the ugly truth that I had been hit. "Who the hell hit you?" His voice was a controlled roar. I sat beside him and ordered a martini. *I would need the liquid courage to tell him I could no longer be his girl.* I liked Paul and I would miss him. He hit my heart in a very special way. I understood him. We'd both had people telling us we were inadequate for most of our lives. Their lies had become our truths, and it would take some reprogramming to turn those thoughts around.

"Hello to you, too," I said. I leaned over and gave him a kiss on the cheek. It was funny that we had been intimate with each other's parts, but we had never kissed. Apparently, my kisses had been reserved for Jonathan as well.

"Our table is ready. Is this part of my training? Dinner?" He told the bartender to bring my drink to the table before he led me away.

"Yes, in a way it is." Truth be told, he did need to work on his approach. If he had a *let's just get it over with* attitude, then his companion would, too. Paul needed to slow everything down.

We were seated at a quiet corner booth. I was grateful for the privacy for two reasons. First, I didn't want people staring at my face and thinking Paul had done the damage. Second, I knew we would be candid about sex and his future, and I didn't want to titillate anyone with our conversation.

"What happened to you?" He reached for my cheek, but I backed away. The skin was still very tender and it didn't matter how gentle a hand was, the pressure was simply too much.

"I was hit. It's not pretty, but it's over. As I'm sure you already know, I am no longer working for Sandra. This dinner is not on the clock. We are two friends sharing time together."

"I was a bit confused about your message. You said let's meet for a friendly dinner, and no room." The concern showed on his face. "Are you dropping me?"

"Paul, I'm not dropping you. You were a quick learner. You graduated. You don't need me for what you have to accomplish." I could see a flash of fear in his eyes. He truly thought he needed me.

"I'm not ready to let you go. You make me feel normal." His hand reached out to take mine. It wasn't the touch of a man in love, it was the touch of a man who felt he needed to be tethered to something safe. I was his lifejacket while he waded through the deep end.

"You are normal. Look around you. What do you think the average penis size in this room is?" His head snapped back at my question. His eyes scanned the room.

"I have no idea. Should we have them drop their pants so we can inspect?" Humor. Paul was making jokes about penises, and I thought that was great. It was a huge step forward.

"I'm going to say five inches." I sipped at the martini the bartender had delivered to our table.

"Well, that's about three inches more than I've got." He tilted his head and frowned.

"You're right, but they depend on their five inches to work all the magic and honestly, no one has a wand that good. You have a secret weapon. He who has the best oral skills wins. Sure, a penis feels great, but so does a dildo or a vibrator. Nothing, and I mean nothing can substitute a man's lips on that tiny bundle of nerves. You got that down."

His pride shone as bright as the North Star. "River, I still want to see you. I don't expect it to be in a sexual way, but maybe we can have a regular dinner date. Would that be possible? What are you going to do now?" Why was it that the only man I wanted to want me was the one who had moved on?

"I'm flattered, but given the intimacy of our relationship, it just wouldn't work." Ben was different, he never seemed like a client but a friend. "I was never cut out for this kind of work. I thought I could turn my brain off and let my body take over, but my damn heart and head got in the way. So, I'm going to do what I've always done. I'm going to survive. I'll find a job and work on regaining my self-respect."

"I could get you a job where I work." He looked hopeful.

"I've taken enough risks for a while, Paul. I appreciate the offer, but working for the Chief Risk Officer sounds like more risk than I'm willing to take at this point."

We spent the rest of the night enjoying dinner and conversation. I noticed the waitress eyeing Paul throughout the night. Being the gentleman he was, he pretended not to notice, but he had. His occasional flustered blushes were adorable.

When she brought the bill, I pulled her into the booth beside me. Her name was Melody, and she was perfect for Paul.

"Melody, I want to introduce my good friend Paul." Melody lowered her head and blushed. The moment was too cute. "What day is your day off, Melody?"

Both Paul and Melody stared at me.

"I'm off Wednesday and Fridays," she said softly.

"Well, isn't that perfect? Paul wanted to see a movie on Friday night, but he didn't want to go alone. Isn't that right, Paul?" Like a man who had been Tasered, his eyes opened in shock but he didn't answer immediately. It took a kick to his shin to bring him into the moment.

I twisted my head and bulged my eyes. Melody and I stared in his direction. I was breathlessly waiting for him to ask her out. She was waiting as well.

"Melody, if you're free, I would love to take you to dinner and to a movie." If a drink had been available, I'm pretty sure Paul would have sucked it back in one gulp. He was so nervous.

Melody squealed with delight. "Yes, I would love to go with you. Wow, I thought you two were a couple."

I piped in, "No, Paul and I partnered together on a project that we recently completed. He's an amazing man." It was so nice to see him sit tall and soak in the compliment I was sure resonated truth with him.

Paul and Melody exchanged numbers and tentatively planned their first date. When I walked out of the restaurant, I felt good about everything. Paul and I agreed to stay in touch. He conquered a major hurdle in his life, and all it took was determination and a bushel of peaches.

With the weather being mild and the neighborhood one of the safest in the city, I decided to walk the six blocks home. Three blocks from my final destination I saw him out of the corner of my eye. Howard walked around the black town car and opened the door.

My eyes shot up to the address on the building. I knew Jonathan had lived nearby, but I didn't remember the building. I was so tied up in him, I hadn't paid attention to where we had landed when he'd taken me to his place.

Glued to my place across the street, I waited and watched to see who would exit the car. My brain told me to move on. How would I feel if a young co-ed slid from the back seat followed by Jonathan? In all honesty, I would feel devastated.

His dark hair rose above the roof of the car. His gaze turned to me, and I froze in place. Did he know I was standing there or was it the connection we had that pulled his eyes to mine? My heart felt like it had leaped into my throat. He looked beautiful, and I wanted to run across the street and throw myself in his arms, but I knew I couldn't do it. He had moved on, and I was trying to do the same.

Just when I thought he would cross the street, a second car pulled in front of his building. He looked to me and then to the car. He was torn. I could see it on his face. When he turned toward the car, I took off. I didn't want to see who would exit the vehicle. Why deepen the wound? I'd let the cut heal and prayed it didn't leave a permanent scar.

Chapter 26

The next several months passed quickly. Thanksgiving, Christmas, New Year's and Valentine's Day faded into the past. Jade was growing into her pregnancy, and the baby had begun to move. I spent most of my evenings with my hands on her belly. I was mesmerized by the whole experience. How my friend could grow a baby dumbfounded me. The woman couldn't hem a pair of pants or boil a pot of water, but she could make a human being. I was in awe.

Her men turned out to be good guys. I'd misjudged them. We all made mistakes and I'd forgiven them for theirs, but when it came to Jade, they wouldn't be granted clemency for any other missteps. She was all I had left, and I would take on anyone to protect what was mine.

Jade and I took the playroom, which was pretty boring compared to what I'd envisioned, and turned it into the cutest nursery known to humankind. It was easy to create the perfect baby space when we had unlimited funds.

Jade chose a neutral pallet and kept with a natural theme. She had a muralist come in and paint one wall with a realistic meadow scene.

High in the sky, the sun rose above the wildflowers and butterflies painted below. Ladybugs flitted through the air.

It wasn't until I inspected the mural closely that I saw the rays of the sun were sentences. The inscription read as follows:

The warmth in a life doesn't come from the sun.

The light in a life isn't from the sun's rays.

It's the people in your life that warm your soul,

The smiles in your life that dazzle your days.

The spirit shines through the darkness and gloom,

To illuminate life in so many ways.

A person should strive to be someone's sunshine.

The sunshine my friend River displays.

I collapsed in the middle of the nursery and cried like a baby. I was overwhelmed by her gift. Her child would grow up under a sun dedicated to me. I would have to up my game so I didn't disappoint him or her. I would do my best to spread my sunshine across the lives I came in contact with.

Jade stood in the doorway with her rounded belly peeking from under her T-shirt. She refused to buy maternity wear until absolutely necessary. I was beginning to think that moment had come sooner rather than later. I made a mental note to drag her to Bloomingdales for a shopping trip, but right now I had to get ready for my date with Ben. The man had become such a good friend, a father figure in some respects. Our date was the political fundraiser he had invited me to months ago.

***

We arrived at the venue at ten to seven. Ben liked to arrive slightly early. His generation had more courtesy in their pinky toe than any generation since, and he operated under a set of standards not known in this day and age.

He valued people more than money. He told me if you treated people right, everything fell into place, including money. He believed it was a courtesy to show up early and look eager for the event. People put a lot of time and effort into these types of things and others should recognize the effort by following the guidelines. A start time wasn't a suggestion, it was a rule.

He said manners would never go out of style, and quality people would always use them. Quality didn't mean rich in his book. A homeless man who had integrity had more value than a CEO with none. Character was more important than anything. It was the backbone of society. Riches came and went, but the essence of who you were would always remain the same.

Having not had strong male examples in my life, Ben's influence had been important. I felt stronger from our friendship, from his wisdom. I valued the things he'd taught me.

The teal dress I borrowed from Jade flowed freely to the tips of my silver heels. I owned two formal gowns, both of which Jonathan had bought for me. Both of which I would never wear. The silver gown brought back too many special memories, and the blue gown never made its debut. Keeping it hanging in my closet was another lie I told myself. It was a *maybe* lie. Maybe he would call someday and ask me out. Maybe he would find himself without a date to the opera and wish he could have a distraction.

Maybe.

Maybe.

Maybe.

Maybe the reality was when it came to Jonathan Ferris, I didn't know the truth. Maybe I was never his sunshine. Maybe he was the sunshine and his light had blinded me.

Ben and I entered the convention center arm in arm. I would never understand why someone was willing to pay twenty-five hundred dollars a plate for an overdone filet and a couple of grilled asparagus spears.

I suppose it wasn't the dinner they came for, but to support a friend or a cause. Ben worked the room like a politician running for office. At one point, I wasn't sure he wouldn't usurp his friend's place on the podium and claim to be the one running for office.

I didn't attend events. I went to school, worked at the student union coffee shop, and babysat Jade. Ben and I went out for dinner once a week if he was available, and that was all the excitement this girl had on a regular basis.

He was here. I could feel him. His gaze always heated me from the inside out. It never occurred to me that I might run into him at some kind of event.

My eyes traveled the room several times before I found him standing in the corner. *Jonathan.* I tried to ignore him, but my eyes continued to drift toward him. Each time they did, his were fixed on me. Uncomfortable under his gaze, I whispered to Ben that I needed the ladies' room.

I needed space and a splash of water on my face.

Ben kissed my hand and pointed me in the direction of the restrooms. I wound through the crowd and slipped into the stylishly appointed room. The attendant stood at the ready to hand me a towel, or spritz my neck with perfume. I simply patted my face with cool water and touched up my lipstick. I pulled my shoulders back and thought about my panties. If I'd been here with him, I wouldn't have had any on. With Ben, I was fully covered. In fact, I was squeezed together with the ugliest of coverings—Spanx.

Some would think I had fallen into a black hole when I entered the ladies room. If only I'd been so lucky. If the room could have swallowed me up, I would have gladly sacrificed myself.

"Perfume?" the attendant asked.

I shook my head, reached into my purse for a tip, and walked out the door. The scar I thought had healed had begun to fester. One look at Jonathan and my old wounds opened. My heart was breaking into pieces. I would never be over him.

I turned the corner and found him leaning against the wall. My heart stilled. His tuxedo was perfect. I wanted to reach up and trace the bow at his neck. I wanted to drop to my knees like I had at the opera and pull him into my mouth. I craved everything about the man.

"River." His one word, my name, was such a beautiful sound as it rolled off his lips.

I tried to breathe. I tried to speak. Everything in me leaned toward him. But I stood firmly where I stopped. "Jonathan."

"What are you doing here?" He sounded accusatory as if I had no right to be near him. I was hurt by his tone. That wasn't how I had envisioned our first meeting after…I couldn't really call it a breakup, but that is what my heart felt.

"I'm here with a friend." I looked to the right of Jonathan and saw Ben glance in my direction. I'd been gone a long time. I was sure he was wondering what had happened to me.

"I thought you had exited that line of work." His tone was flat, his body stiff.

"Ben is a friend," I repeated.

"Is that what you're calling them these days?" He wounded me deeply with his accusation. I wasn't a whore. I was never a whore. I was naive. I was stupid. I was desperate, but I was never actually a whore. It was a close call for me, but in the end, I made it out whole. Not unscathed, but complete, and I would never let anyone call me a whore again.

I wanted to reach across the distance and slap his face. When I raised my hand, the light glinted off the charm he had given me months ago. Both of our eyes slid to the bauble. I never took it off. Not wanting him to see that I carried him around with me always, I tucked my hand behind my back.

"Jonathan, you can believe what you will. I will never be able to convince you otherwise. I had encounters with three men before I was punched in my face." He winced, but I wasn't sure if it was because I told him there were three men or because I reminded him I'd been attacked. "One of those encounters was with Ben, the man I'm here with. We never had sex. Hell, we've never even kissed. He likes my company. He doesn't pay me, we're friends. Only friends."

I waited for a second and watched his jaw tense and twitch.

"It's none of my business." He pushed off the wall and stepped forward to leave.

Something came over me. I pushed him back against the wall. He wasn't going to leave me in the hallway after he just insinuated I was a whore.

"Oh, no you don't. You will stand here and hear me out. You don't get the privilege of disappearing again just because things are a little uncomfortable."

He leaned against the wall and crossed his arms. "Go on. Your date is waiting."

"Yes, he is. All you need to know is Ben is a nice old man who thinks I'm pretty and he likes to take me to dinner. He helps me with my homework and he gives me advice on various things."

Jonathan shifted uncomfortably between his feet. He may not want to hear what I had to say, but I needed to say it.

"My second encounter was with a nice guy who I also didn't have sex with, not intercourse anyway. He was the size of a tootsie roll and he wanted to learn oral skills. I fed him a bushel of peaches and let him make me come once with his tongue."

I glanced at Ben and held up one finger indicating I would be with him in a minute.

"You, on the other hand, were my only actual sexual experience, and the only man that ever made me feel like a whore. I spread my legs for you whenever I could. I loved what we had together, and if that made me a whore, then I was a whore, but only in *your* eyes, because when I was with you I felt like a cherished woman. Until you left me. *Then* I felt like a slut."

I swiped at the lone tear that ran down my cheek.

"The night I got my brain rearranged was a different matter. You had never asked me for an exclusive arrangement. You made it clear you never would, so I decided I would be exclusive to you. I would dine with Ben, get rid of the rest. The abuser was a loose end. He tried to rape me, but in my heart, I belonged to you. So, there you have it. The truth."

"River, I've never thought—"

"Save it, Jonathan. Sandra told me you moved on, but I already knew it because you had walked out on me that morning without so much as a note or a phone call. I realize you're over it. I'm working on it, but for whatever reason, I can't stop loving you."

I turned right and headed to Ben's side. When I looked over my shoulder, Jonathan was looking at me. I swear he was looking into my soul. Was that sorrow and regret I saw on his face?

As fate would have it, we were seated at adjacent tables. Every time I glanced in his direction his eyes were pinned on me. He studied me throughout our meal.

"Is that your man?" Ben asked quietly. I knew whom he meant. Was it obvious to everyone we had a connection?

"You're my man, Ben. How could you think I would cheat on you?" I teased.

"Oh, I don't know, the man doesn't take his eyes off you. He's the one you told me about, right? The one you had the connection with?" With Ben, I was always truthful and forthright. He gave me courage, so I answered him honestly.

"Yes, he was the one."

"I don't think he's done with you, and you're certainly not done with him."

"Ben, I'm not sure I'll ever be done with him."

"Is he a good man, River?" He was ignoring everyone at the table and devoting his attention to me. That was Ben.

"Yes, I believe he is. I just don't know if he's a good man for me."

"What's his name and who's he with?" I wasn't sure of his reasoning for asking the questions, but I knew if Ben wanted to know something, he would find out anyway.

"His name is Jonathan Ferris and he owns Integrity Financial Services."

A broad grin showed off Ben's forty-thousand-dollar smile. "He's a good man, River. His company has been taking care of my portfolio for the last decade."

I'd be damned if that didn't make me happy. It was nice to know I'd been right about something. Jonathan *was* a good man or at least he was a good businessman. Ben would never do business with anyone who didn't adhere to his code of ethics. Pride swelled in my chest for Jonathan.

My eyes sought him throughout the evening. He was alone. Never once did a woman approach him or sit with him. He chatted animatedly among the people at his table, but each time I took a peek in his direction, he caught me staring. Each time he was staring back at me.

Dinner was over, and it was time to mingle once again. Ben lifted my arm to help me stand. My feet hurt, but I could make it another hour or so. My shift started later tomorrow. Saturdays began at eight, which was a blessing. I'd have time to recover.

I followed Ben around like a loyal puppy. He introduced me as his project. It never offended me, as it was an honor to be considered worth his time. We walked from group to group to say our farewells. Before I could react, I was standing in front of Jonathan. That sly old devil had worked his way around the space and left this group for last.

"Jonathan Ferris, correct?" He held out his hand and Jonathan took it. "I'm Ben Daniels, and I think you are familiar with the lovely River Roberts."

Jonathan nodded his head. "River."

"River and I were recently discussing portfolios, and I told her that your company handled mine, but I had never met you and here you are. What a small world we live in."

"I hope you're happy with the services we have offered. If you ever need anything please let me know." Jonathan pulled a card from his pocket and placed it in Ben's hand.

"Actually, there is something I need. I've been asked to step out for scotch and cigars. It would be rude of me to expect River to wait idly by. If you were leaving soon, would you escort her home? I wouldn't normally ask, but I understand you two have a close relationship, and I would feel comfortable if someone she knew saw to her safety."

Jonathan looked surprised but delighted. I imagined I looked apoplectic. Earlier I had told Jonathan off *and* confessed to loving him in the same sentence. Looking at Ben I silently begged him to rescind his request, but he looked at me with a wicked smile.

"I'd be happy to see her home. It's been a while since we have seen one another, and I would love to catch up. Thank you, Mr. Daniels."

Ben turned to me and pressed a kiss to my cheek. I was still speechless. Shocked. He leaned in and whispered in my ear. "River, find out if he's your man. Time is short and life is fleeting. Waste no more minutes." He patted Jonathan on the back and walked away.

I stood in disbelief, not sure what to do. My jaw hung open from its hinge. Jonathan's index finger slipped under my chin and closed my mouth. He leaned into me and whispered, "That mouth does things to my body, River. Unless you plan to use it in a constructive way, I suggest you close it. I've got a lot to say to you. Let's go."

Stunned, I snapped my mouth closed and followed him out the door to where Howard was already waiting.

We entered the car and sat next to each other in silence. He picked up the phone and rattled off directions to Howard. I didn't pay attention, so I had no idea of his plan. My heart was pounding and the rhythm was pulsing between my legs. What was it about this man that made my heart and body sing? He had wounded me deeply, and yet I sat here wanting him more than ever.

Sex. Is that what it boiled down to with us? I had to believe there was more to our connection.

"Where are we going?" I asked.

"For a ride. Where we end up depends on the ride."

We both began to talk at once. My "why" came out at the same time as his "I". It was a muddled mess. I crossed my arms in front of my chest and silenced myself. He did tell me he had some things to say.

"I've missed you so much." His voice sounded desperate. He was parched land and I was water.

"I left you in bed that morning. I had considered leaving you a note, but what could I say? I'm so sorry, River. I had no right to claim a part of you when I wasn't willing to claim all of you. Your body belongs to you and I will never demand something you are unwilling to give freely."

"It wasn't your fault."

"Yes, it was. I did to you what I did to Claire. I made her promise me a child, and she did everything in her power to give it to me. She lost her life because she was so focused on giving me what I wanted, she didn't realize what was happening to her. By the time she did, it was too late. I made you promise me a part of you and look at what happened to you. I could have lost you as well."

"Mine and Claire's situations were totally different. She was your wife. I was your…well, we both know what I am to you."

"Do we? Do you know what you are to me? I don't think you do."

"I was your Wednesday and Saturday girl." I had spent the entire time I'd known him creating a relationship where none existed. In what world would he and I have worked? Yes, Julia Roberts got her man, but Hollywood was the only place it happened. This was New York and the streets weren't paved in gold. They were paved in the bones of those trampled so others could rise.

"You are more than that. Do you know how long it took me to fall in love with Claire?" He twisted in his seat so I could see his face. The glow of the city lights gave off enough illumination so I could clearly see his expression. He looked earnest.

"I don't have a clue." Why it mattered, I couldn't guess.

"Months. It took months. I didn't recognize the feeling of love. I'd never actually experienced it. I felt passion, I felt excitement, but I'd never felt love. Love hits you in your soul. It's attached to you like DNA. It's not something you decide on, it's something that happens to you, but I was unfamiliar with it so I didn't recognize it."

"That's a beautiful sentiment. Claire was a very lucky woman, and even though she died young she had a man who loved her completely." The words rolled easily off my tongue but painfully squeezed my heart.

How was I supposed to find a man to love me? Who in their right mind would embrace a woman with my past?

He reached for my hands and held them tight. "How long do you think it took me to fall in love with you?"

Chapter 27

Silence filled the car. Did he just say in a roundabout way he loved me?

"Why did you tell Sandra you had moved on?" I might as well have slapped him with the way his head snapped back.

"I never told her I moved on from you. I called and quit the service. I'd moved on from *it*. I'd been a member for three years, and I'd used it three times. Two times prior to you. One girl, I took to an art event. The other I took to a hotel room. I'm not proud of my actions, but until you, there was no one."

I had a very different vision of his use of Concierge Services. "I walked in the day you left, and I quit. She tried to force me to stay, but there was no way she could have enforced my contract. She made it sound like you had already selected a new girl. I was heartbroken that I could be replaced so easily since you had made me feel so special."

"You are special. I kept calling Luca and he told me you needed time to heal and you were moving forward. I assumed that meant without me. I didn't deserve you, and when I saw you across the street from my house my hope was buoyed. I thought maybe you had come to see me."

"I was walking home. My new home is not far from yours. Jade invited me to live with her. I saw you exit the car, just before the other car pulled up. I couldn't handle seeing another woman fall into your arms. I ran like a coward to protect my heart."

"That explains why you were never home. River, there was no other woman. It was Grace delivering a piece of art to my flat. It was the piece you loved at the opera. I had purchased it for you."

I wasn't sure what I felt more. Elation he loved me? Desperation and hope he still wanted me? Agony we'd wasted so much time because of the lies of one woman?

"Oh, God. All these months, and we thought the other had given up. Jonathan, I don't deserve you. I compromised my values and myself. You paid for my time when I would have given it to you freely. I wanted to give you my everything."

"No, you didn't compromise yourself, and I should have paid more. At least more attention to what was happening. You are worth so much more. I need you, River, and I believe we need each other."

I climbed into his lap and pressed my lips to his. Howard drove around the city for hours while we kissed like teenagers. We would need to drive thousands of miles before I got my fill of Jonathan.

It was near two o'clock when Jonathan walked me to my door and kissed me goodbye. It would have been so easy to invite him into my bed and my body, but I wanted this to be different. He asked me to dinner the following night and I accepted. I was on cloud nine. How could I not be? I pulled a pen from my purse and wrote my number on his palm. I should have given him my private number months ago, but that hadn't been part of our agreement. The rules had completely changed. This time we weren't working from Sandra's guidelines. We were working from our own.

He loved me. Jonathan Ferris, the man of my dreams, loved me.

———

AT TWENTY-FIVE, I should have found a better job than making coffee at the student union coffee shop. However, the hours were good and the tips were lousy. Starving students didn't have a lot to spare. The benefit was they worked around my schedule, and since I'd been a barista for years, I didn't require much training. At ten o'clock, I looked up to see the amber specks catch the light in his espresso-brown eyes. He approached the counter and ordered a black coffee.

I served him like I would any other patron except I drew a heart on his cup.

"I couldn't stay away," was all he said before he took a seat in the corner and watched me over his newspaper.

I found every reason to walk the lobby. On this particular Saturday, the tables had never been cleaner. When I was sure no one was looking, I would slide into his lap and steal a kiss. Too bad student loans had to be paid back. Too bad I couldn't simply stay in his lap and enjoy his kisses.

At noon he disappeared, and at two he returned. He slid back into his chair and watched me complete my shift. He walked me outside. Winter had hit and the air was crisp and cold. I pressed myself into his body to soak in his warmth.

"Howard is here. I didn't think you would mind the ride." I had dreaded taking the subway today. The walk to the station was bad enough, but the limited weekend schedule would have had me waiting around endlessly. He always seemed to know what I needed.

We slid into the back of the car. His hand sat on my leg, and I could feel the heat of his touch through my black jeans. I shuddered, and he probably thought I was cold. My feet were freezing, but my heart? It was warm.

"Sunshine." His use of my nickname made my heart swell. It was so full I feared it would explode. I'd missed that word rolling off his tongue. It was foreplay. That one word said in his deeply toned voice made my thighs clench and my insides shudder. "Will it ever bother you that I'm so much older than you?"

"Are you? I hadn't noticed." Of course, he was older than me. I needed that in my man. I needed him to be older and wiser. I wouldn't have been attracted to him otherwise. Luca was my age, and I didn't have the patience for his games. He was a gorgeous specimen with a child's brain, but his rod still ruled his world.

Being a gigolo was the perfect occupation for him. His friendship had sustained me over the last few months. At times I'd needed his childishness and diverting vitality. I loved him like a brother, not a lover. He could never be enough man for me.

"I bought you something." He slipped the small, blue box from his pocket. The Tiffany blue a complete giveaway to where he had shopped. He opened my palm and placed the box in the center. "You have this in the center of your palm. I'm giving it to you for all time and eternity."

Of course, he was. Jonathan never took back what he gave. I opened the tiny box and stared. A charm lay on a bed of satin. Red and beautiful, he had given me a heart—his heart. This was more than a little bauble. This was a commitment to love me.

He pulled the charm from the box and attached it next to the sunshine. Raising my hand to his lips, he kissed it gently, his eyes never leaving mine.

"I will care for your heart always, Jonathan."

"I was thinking that we might be able to negotiate an exclusive agreement."

Deciding to tease him, I bantered back. "What about Ben?"

"Ben will understand. If he doesn't, he can dine with both of us."

"So, if I understand you correctly, you want all of my days and nights?"

"Yes, I'll settle for nothing less than all of you."

"That's going to cost you."

"Sunshine, you're worth every penny."

"Take me home so we can seal the deal."

Howard drove us directly to Jonathan's. Sitting in the entry was the one picture I'd fallen in love with at the opera.

He didn't let me linger long. He pulled me into the bathroom, where he insisted I take a relaxing bath since I'd been on my feet all day. The man was going to drive me crazy. I slid into the hot bath and sank into the bubbles. I would have enjoyed it more if he had joined me, but he was up to something.

By the time I came out of the bathroom, the lights in the flat were dimmed and candles were glowing. Music played from his surround sound system, and the table was set for dinner. I was wrapped in the plush white robe he had left me.

"Jonathan," I called. I found him staring out the window.

He didn't say a word. He led me to the table, where he pulled out my chair and lifted the cloche.

On the plate was a handwritten note that said,

You are not sex...You are love.

I'd never felt like love until that moment. I'd felt *in* love, but the concept of *being* love had been foreign.

"Do you know how long it took me to fall in love with you?"

I shook my head. I had no idea.

"It took me as long as it took to see your picture. Your smile did it for me. I wanted the girl whose eyes laughed along with her body. I wanted you."

"I fell in love with you the first time you looked at me. Your eyes smiled first, and I'd never seen anything so sexy."

"I love you, River. I know our beginning was unconventional. I know we did things that we're not proud of. I also know that a life without you isn't much of a life. Your DNA speaks to mine."

My eyes glanced at the counter where silver-covered dishes awaited. He obviously had some pull with restaurants around the city. This wasn't your average take-out and delivery.

"How hungry are you, Mr. Ferris?"

"I'm starving, but not for food."

I smiled. Words weren't needed. He knew me. He knew what I needed, often before I'd known what I needed myself. My smile said, *Take me. Love me.* I exhaled audibly. *That* was the answer I was hoping for. Scooping me up beneath my knees, he carried me to his bed. On his nightstand was a silver-framed picture of me. It was the one he had taken when I'd lain naked in my bed. Like Sandra said it would, it *had* shown up somewhere.

I looked up at him, and he shrugged. He was making no excuses, and I wasn't asking for any. I'd been the last face he had seen before he'd fallen asleep every night.

He pulled the tie of the robe aside and let the plush fabric fall to the bed. I watched his chest rise and lower as his eyes scanned my body slowly. It had been months since I'd been naked in front of a man—in front of him. I had my IUD removed because it gave me heavy periods and unbearable cramps. He wouldn't be happy, but we had to use condoms.

My pubic hair had happily grown back. That might have been the best thing about quitting my job. I would never be subjected to that torture again. It shocked me how people paid good money for that treatment.

"My memory of you was already perfect, and yet here you are, more than my mind could have ever conjured." He stripped off his clothes and lay next to me. His fingers traced my collarbone. The bumps rose from my skin like they were reaching for his touch. Minutes were spent caressing and exploring one another.

"I love this." His fingers ran through my neatly groomed thatch of hair. I was so glad.

"I love that you love it because waxing is a hard limit for me." Those were the last coherent words that left my mouth. Breathless panting, throaty moans, and tremulous screams were what came next.

He slipped between my legs and ran his tongue along my wetness. Hot, slick passion dripped from my center. When he slid one finger in me, I came off the bed. It had been way too long since I'd been touched, not only on my body but also in my heart.

With slow precision, he took me to the edge and brought me down. He never let me soar, but he didn't let me fall. He kept me in that beautiful place in the center, where I floated on a cloud of his love.

He treated my body like a treasure chest full of priceless jewels. My breasts, my bottom, my sex were erogenous zones, gems he plucked from the treasure chest and buffed with his hands and lips until they sparkled under his care.

He settled between my legs and pulled in the treasure he found nestled between my slick folds. This time intent on making me fly. He rolled his soft lips over the hardened bud and sucked it into the heat of his mouth. When I thought he was pulling away, I grabbed his hair and held him in place. I loved the place he kept me, but I craved the place I knew he would take me.

He gently sucked and pulled until I trembled uncontrollably against his lips. He pulled every shudder from my body before he took his place above mine.

"Condom," was all I could say. My brain was scrambled, but I wanted to be responsible. He looked disappointed, but he didn't question my request. He pulled the foil packet from his drawer and sheathed himself.

The heavens sang when he sank himself deeply into my body. I was so moved, I cried. This was where I was meant to be—with him in every way possible. How did I think I could ever be without him? He was not someone you got over. He was not someone you moved on from. He was not someone you could replace. He was someone who changed lives by his mere presence. And, *he* was mine.

We rocked together until I was on the edge and he was diving off the cliff. Seeing the intensity in his eyes as he let himself go was beautiful. When he uttered the words *I love you* toward the end of his release, I flew. We were connected by something bigger than our sexual attraction. We were tethered by our souls. We were one.

Chapter 28

"Do you have any idea what time it is?" Jade stood in the hallway with her belly jutting out and her hands on her hips. She was already trying out her mothering skills. "I haven't seen you since your last dinner with Ben. Do you have any idea how worried I've been? I left you two messages today."

I lowered my head like a repentant teen, but inside I was filled with joy. We had promised to never cause the other undue concern, and I'd been MIA all day. I owed her an apology.

Over her shoulder, I saw the duo raise their eyes as she began her interrogation. Initially, I had no idea how she handled them both. Now, I wondered how they handled her. I was starting to question who was the sub and who was the Dom, as my Jade was a force to be reckoned with. It would take two men to keep her under control.

"I'm sorry, my phone was dead." I raised my phone to show her the blank screen. My charm bracelet dangled in front of her. She saw the red heart, and her face relaxed. The tension drained away.

"Time to talk." She pulled me from the hallway and into my room. She piled the pillows against my headboard and made herself comfortable.

"I was with Jonathan. He was at the fundraiser, and Ben asked him to take care of me."

"I'm liking that old geezer more all the time. He was the only highlight in your week besides me." She gave me the coy look that made strong men like Eric and Todd weak in their knees.

"I took a drive with Jonathan last night, and we cleared the air. You were right. Sandra had been a bitch and had lied. She told me he had moved on, when in reality he had quit the service."

"I'm not defending her, but did she actually lie?" She pulled a pillow from behind her back and tucked it under her knees. She had been complaining about lower back pain lately.

"No, he had moved on from the service, but she had said she felt he was talking about me. That was a lie. She made me believe he wanted nothing to do with me."

"You had his phone number all along. Why didn't you call him? I kept trying to get you to do just that."

I sat on the end of the bed Indian style and answered.

"I couldn't take the rejection. For the first time in my life, I'd felt loved by someone other than you. How sad is that? I can't even say I ever felt love from my parents. The saddest thing is I have no gauge on how to measure feeling and emotions. I just knew that what I felt with Jonathan was different from anything I'd ever felt. Whatever that was, I wanted more of it, and it was gone."

"I know. I've watched you struggle to breathe since you showed up on my doorstep. I've also watched you grow in spite of the devastation you felt. I'm proud of you and the progress you've made. Tell me what's happening. I see someone got a new Tiffany's charm. Tell me about it."

I told her how he had spent his morning watching me at the coffee shop. How he'd disappeared for a few hours, and how he'd returned with the little blue box.

"The man is symbolic in his gestures. That's so romantic."

"Yeah, it is, isn't it?"

"When am I going to meet this guy? I've seen his flesh, but I want to see him in the flesh." I regretted ever showing her his picture. I was fine showing her what I had, but I didn't want to share any of what I now had.

"He's picking me up for breakfast tomorrow morning. I can have him come up to meet you and your men."

"Fabulous." She clapped her hands and bounced on the bed until her little one complained with a kick.

DRESSED in faded blue jeans and a white polo shirt, Jonathan looked classically casual. No one would ever mistake him for an average man. There was nothing average about him. He was incredibly wealthy but humble. Unbelievably handsome, yet unaffected by his looks. He was a genius in his business dealings and a sweetheart when it came to relationships.

He walked the gauntlet of the entryway and introduced himself to Eric, Todd, and Jade. They insisted we stay for a cup of coffee, but Jonathan told them we had so much time to make up for. He would be happy to chat another day, but today he had something special planned.

Howard was nowhere in sight when we walked from the building. Jonathan bundled me up next to him as we walked toward his home.

He undressed me and placed me in bed. "I don't want to wake up another day without you. I owe you so many coffees in bed, so many kisses goodnight. We have to work out some kind of arrangement, Sunshine. I need you." He disappeared from the bedroom while I snuggled into the bedding that smelled like him.

Several minutes later, he arrived with the perfect latte. I had no idea how he had procured it, and I didn't ask. Jonathan had a way to get whatever he pleased. He stripped and climbed into bed next to me. He didn't dive right into lovemaking. He dove into conversation. I sipped my coffee and listened to him tell me about how he had sold his house on Center Island.

"That must have been hard for you. So many memories."

"It was time to let it go."

I was sure it was hard to let go of that part of his past, but I was equally glad Claire's ghost wouldn't be haunting us forever. He asked me to decide where I wanted to hang my picture. The question confused me. Did he want to hang the painting here, or wherever I landed next? Jade's wasn't a permanent solution.

He reached into the drawer and pulled out two more boxes. One was a familiar blue box, and the other was white and nondescript.

I opened the blue first, and inside was a new charm. A key. I had no idea what it meant, but I clipped it next to the heart and jingled the bracelet around. The white box was opened to reveal a Rubik's cube keychain with a key. Could this be what I'd hoped for? Was he offering me everything?

"My place is your place. I want you with me always. I want to be your distraction."

"I don't know...you or the Rubik's cube? So many choices."

"I'll give you choices." He snuggled into my side, nibbling at my neck. "You get two. Me...or me."

"I'll take you."

We tossed everything aside and made love slowly. When it came time for the condom, I promised I would solve the issue of birth control soon. We both wanted nothing to come between us.

A crash from the kitchen startled me. I jumped up from the bed. "Who's here besides us?"

"Don't worry. We've missed so much, and I'm making sure we catch up. There is a team of chefs preparing our Thanksgiving dinner. I don't know how yours was, but mine was spent eating day-old pizza and watching black and white movies alone. Today is Thanksgiving in the Ferris/Roberts house."

The Ferris/Roberts house? He wanted me here. In his home. Where he would love me and cherish me. *How could I not love him?*

Three hours later we sat down to a gourmet turkey dinner. Above my plate was another blue box. The turkey charm inside was clipped next to my key. My life with him was showcased on my wrist. My heart was filling up as quickly as my charm bracelet, and I couldn't have been more content.

The following week was our Christmas do-over. I don't know how he did it, but when I arrived on Sunday, there was a six-foot spruce sitting in front of the window. We spent the afternoon hanging ornaments and listening to Christmas music.

He persuaded me to take a bath, and when I returned to the living room the underside of the tree was stacked with packages. I could only give him myself. Of course, there was a charm, a beautiful bedazzled Christmas tree that he clipped next to the turkey.

We sat in front of the lit Christmas tree with the room lights off and the music playing softly in the background.

"I have opera tickets for next weekend. Care to join me? I have a private box."

"Ooh, I love the opera. By the way, I have a private box, too."

"You are a very bad girl." He tugged at my pants and covered himself with the condom he loathed. I really did need to get on the birth control issue, but with school, work, and Jonathan, I had no time for anything else.

I straddled his body and let him slide into *my* private box. All was forgotten but our bodies as they rocked together in unison.

Chapter 29

Jonathan had decided the opera would be our New Year's. The last time we were in his private box, the Earth had shattered and the ground had fallen out from beneath my feet. Tonight's show was The Magic Flute. Much like last time, I couldn't have cared less about what was going on below us. All I wanted was to play with the magic flute in front of me.

"I knew that dress would be stunning on you." He patted his lap, and I crawled onto it. The slit of the blue gown fell open, revealing everything. Jonathan knew his dresses, as this was reminiscent of the silver dress. He slid his hand up to the space between my legs. I didn't have a thing on underneath. My arousal was apparent by the ease in which his fingers slipped inside me. He stalled when he came into contact with the soft sponge inside me.

"Contraceptive sponge," I said. I'd never used one before, but I was tired of not being as close to him as I could be.

"Genius." The music played below while we created our own opera together. He pulled our chairs back from the rail and into the shadows. I covered his mouth as I slid myself over his shaft. His groan was too loud to not have been noticed.

He pulled me down and buried himself deep inside me. "Oh God, I've missed this. Why haven't we used these before?"

"They have a high failure rate. We are taking a risk. Pull out if it terrifies you. I have a condom in my purse."

"Baby, knocking you up would be the highlight of my year." How did I respond to that? He wanted to give me his child, but was *I* ready for that? I would have to give it some thought. I'd always assumed I would be married and finished with school before I had a child.

"You're letting your very happy part talk. Tell me the same thing when you're not buried balls deep inside me." I shifted my hips and stroked him until his eyes rolled back and his groan rose with the music. He always had perfect pitch.

That night he clipped on a musical note to my bracelet. I thought a golden penis would have been more appropriate, but the note touched me. Several weeks later, he took me to Per Se. It was the perfect place for a Valentine's Day repeat. We talked over nine courses as he fondled me under my dress. He had a thing against underwear, both his and mine.

Who was I to complain?

I learned how to discreetly fondle him, and we both found our pleasure before dessert was served.

When the waiter brought the tray of assorted chocolates, the familiar blue box sat in the center. I couldn't wait until I opened it to see what charm lay inside. Shock overwhelmed me as I tossed the lid aside and glanced in the box. It was a charm shaped like a ring with a note that said *Debt-Free*. I stared at both for minutes. When I looked up, Jonathan had taken a knee beside me. In his hand was the real deal. Tears streamed down his cheek as he presented me with an enormous yellow diamond. It was the color of the sun.

"River Jordan Roberts. I have squeezed an entire year's worth of holidays into the months we've been together. I have loved you for longer than the time I've known you. You were put on this Earth for me, I for you. I'm not perfect, but I'm perfect for you. I know in my heart we were made for each other. Spend your life with me, and I will do my best to never disappoint you again." He held out the box and looked pleadingly into my eyes.

I hadn't said a word. I was too stunned to speak. Had he really just asked me to marry him?

He pulled the ring from its satin pillow and slipped it on my finger. It felt perfect. I nodded my head and pulled him to my lips. How could I ever say no? This man had given me everything. He saw me, knew me, valued me, and loved me. With him, I could be me, and that would always be enough.

***

"We have to go *now*," I yelled as I flew from the bed and pulled on some clothes. I would slap Jade for interrupting what was turning out to be an amazing orgasm. Her call came just as I was flying into the abyss.

Jonathan ran through the flat, grabbing his keys and jacket. "I'm coming." The child was not his, and yet he was frantic.

"We can't miss the birth of our godchild. What would that say about us as godparents?"

"We are going to be amazing godparents," he said as he called for the elevator. Thankfully, Howard was close by and would meet us downstairs. I just hoped we would make it to the hospital before Jade pushed out her child.

I fidgeted in the back of the car as we made our way there. Jade would do fine. Eric and Todd were with her. In fact, they had stopped their travels weeks ago, allowing me to stay permanently with Jonathan, giving us the chance to see how perfect our lives would weave together.

I was eager to see whom the baby would look like. It didn't matter in the end because I had never seen three people more committed to one another. That kid would be one of the lucky ones. Loved forever by people who surrounded her.

We paced the hallway for hours. Seven hours later I heard the scream of a woman and the wail of a child. Tears streamed down my face when the door opened, and Jonathan and I were invited in. Gabrielle Elise Mendelsohn had entered the world. Her initials spelled out the gem she would always be.

After she was cleaned, weighed, and checked, she was passed around her family—the family I belonged to. I watched Jonathan hold the little bundle in his arms. He looked at her with wonder.

"River, I think you're up next. I hear these things are contagious." Eric looked from Jonathan to me, and back to Jade. She was dozing in her bed, and there was a look of serenity on her face. Todd sat on the edge of her bed and brushed the sweaty hair from her forehead. He kept telling her how beautiful she was, and how beautiful their daughter was, and how proud she had made him.

In all honesty, I couldn't tell who had fathered Gabrielle. She looked exactly like Jade.

We left the threesome to enjoy their moment. Jonathan and I traveled home in silence. He kept pulling my left hand into his and tracing the ring he had given me. I knew he was wondering when we would make the commitment legal. I was wondering the same.

I told him to take a shower when we got home. He looked like *he* had just given birth. I needed to slip downstairs to the drugstore. He didn't question my motives. I'm sure he assumed I was getting contraceptive sponges.

I found him wrapped in his robe, sitting in his favorite chair in front of the window. The newspaper was spread out around his feet. He patted his lap, and I climbed into the spot that had become mine.

"Did you get what I think you got?" His eyes sparkled with delight. He loved that we had done away with the barrier between us. The benefit had been worth the risk.

"No, I got something different." I pulled out a little white box from my pocket. It was similar to one I'd given him before. Confused, he opened the box and saw a keychain with the stork attached.

It had been eight weeks since our night at the opera, and

Jonathan *had* used his magic flute well. In thirty-two weeks, I would give him the ultimate gift. I would give him a child. Ours.

He stared at the keychain and wept.

"I'll be expecting the perfect charm," I teased. I wiped the tears from his eyes and pulled his hands to my stomach. Inside grew our future. Inside grew our love.

Our journey had been unorthodox. Our relationship had started with a list, The Dean's List.

By its very definition, it was special. To the general public, The Dean's List was a category of overachieving students. High grades, honor, and consistency were generally synonymous with its members.

In reality, my experience with The Dean's List had been slightly different. I hated what it had done to me, but loved what it had given me. I'd used it. It had used me. I'd discarded it, and it had spat me out like a sour grape.

If I had the chance to rewind time, would I join again? You bet. I'd gained independence, confidence, and self-esteem. Without it, I'd still be a victim. I'd let go of my past and moved on to my future. A future that wouldn't have been possible if not for God's grace.

Ironically, my parents had used grace as a weapon against me. They'd used the gift it was meant to be, as a yardstick for my inevitable failure. I hadn't heard from them since that phone call. I'd become whole without their demeaning influence and censure. I now knew love.

For all its faults, thank God for The Dean's List.

Sneak Peek into Honor Roll

When I stepped off the bus on 6th Avenue, I felt tired. I'd been selling myself by the inch all week, and my twenty-six-year-old body couldn't keep up. With thirty minutes to class, I hit the student union to get caffeinated. The funky little cafe had been the landing place for Jade, River, and me when we started work at Concierge Services. Our weekly meetings were what kept us sane.

The coffee was hot, and as it cooled, I looked around campus and watched the couples walking hand in hand. Happy. Content. In love. They flirted and giggled while I stared in envy. I'd never had that. Hell-bent on getting my degree, I'd given up relationships. When I started escorting, it wasn't possible. River became my friend and a surrogate girlfriend until she fell in love with one of her clients. Jade was pregnant with her second child and still living with her two men. Then River married Jonathan and had a little boy.

And here I was, still single and whipping my dick out for dollars. The bitterness of the coffee tamed the bitterness of my mood. Twelve more weeks and I'd never have to sell myself again.

The weight of my emotions, or maybe my backpack, slowed my pace to a crawl across campus. Professor Thieland was my favorite instructor and my graduate advisor. Twice a week I attended his commodities class. The Monday and Friday classes were the highlights of my week, but even the prospect of attending one of his lectures couldn't diminish the cloud hanging over my head.

The auditorium hummed with the quiet voices of at least fifty students. At the podium, a ZZ Top look-alike tapped at the microphone.

In the fourth row, I sat in my Hugo Boss suit and waited. Did we have a guest speaker? The screech of audio feedback silenced the room.

"Good morning." The high-pitched voice of the man at the mike didn't mesh with the man in the Grateful Dead T-shirt and ratty jeans. "I'm Professor Saunders, and you've got me for the rest of the semester." Groans echoed through the lecture hall. "Jack Thieland had a family emergency and will be taking a sabbatical until next year. Keep him in your thoughts. This is Commodities in the Twenty-First Century, and I'll be using the synopsis and following the same curriculum of the class."

What else could go wrong? The last thing I needed at the eleventh hour was change. I pulled a paper out of my notebook and wrote 'screw me' over and over again. I wanted to scream it, but writing it in big bold letters with exclamation points seemed my best option. I crumbled the paper up and set the balled up page in the cup holder beside me.

A slim and sexy little brunette stood beside Professor Saunders. She was good-looking, curved in all the right places with long, shiny dark hair and eyes the color of sapphires. She handed him a few notes and stepped away. I watched her walk off the stage and take a seat at a makeshift desk set up to his right. She puckered her lips and blew at the hair that had fallen across her face. She appeared as happy as I felt.

"Twelve of you are graduate students and owe me a graduate project. Be patient as we try to squeeze you into my schedule. My assistant, Mim, will be here after class to talk to those of you who have already scheduled their presentations." He picked up a remote control and turned on the overhead projector for his lecture. "This is not an ideal situation for any of us, but like the stock market, there are highs and lows, and those who fare the best know how to ride the wave."

The rest of class slipped by in a haze. I was preoccupied with thoughts of work and mesmerized by Mim. Something about her drew me in. I didn't know if it was the way her hair flowed over her shoulders and curled on top of her breasts, or if it was the way the light bounced off her blue eyes. I'd been a point A to point B guy for so long, I'd never noticed anything else along the journey, but Mim could not be overlooked.

Class dismissed, I made my way to the table.

"Name?" she asked without looking up.

"Hi." One word was all I spoke. I wanted her to look up at me so I could lose myself in her eyes.

"Name?" she said again, with more than a hint of impatience.

"Hi," I repeated. "I know you're busy, but there's no need for bad manners. Mim, is it?"

She lifted her eyes from the paper and placed her pen to the side. "I'm sorry. This…" she spread her hands on the table, "was not what I had planned today. Yes, it's Mim, like Mom with an I." She let out a sigh.

Her English accent took me by surprise. "Well, Mom with an I, life has a way of throwing you curve balls at the least opportune times. I'm Luca Gregorio by the way."

I held out my hand, and she gently placed the tips of her fingers in my palm. I should have shaken her hand and dropped it, but being the suave Italian I was, I lifted her fingers to my lips and hovered over her knuckles. The roll of her eyes wasn't what I expected, nor was the snap of her hand like I'd burned her with my touch.

"Does that work for other girls?" She picked up her pen and scrolled down the names on her list. "Are You Getting What You Pay For? Commodities in the twenty-first century?" She recited my project title like it was an offering on the menu of a low-end diner.

"Yep, it generally works, and yep, that's me." I squatted down so we were at the same level. Eye level. When our gaze connected, I would have sworn I saw a glimmer of something other than impatience. Mim was a tough sell but hey this was my field of study.

"May ninth at two o'clock." Her voice was direct leaving no room for negotiation.

"What? No. That's three weeks earlier than I planned." Holy hell, how was I supposed to meet that deadline?

"You heard the professor. Those who do the best are those who learn how to ride the wave."

"This isn't a wave. It's a damn tsunami."

She wrote the date and time on a sticky note and handed it to me. With a tilt of her head and a smile on her face, she said, "There's no need to be rude." She looked past me to the woman standing behind me. "Next."

Speechless, I stormed out of the auditorium and went directly to the gym. The only work I'd put into my project was picking out the title. Unless I dropped everything, getting it done was a long shot. I rolled my shoulders, but the tension wouldn't ease. The only way to get rid of my stress was to sweat it out. I had three hours until my next appointment. Two would be spent working myself into a state of exhaustion.

The Athletic Club was a perk of working for Concierge Services I'd lose soon. Jack, my trainer, was by the weights when I arrived.

"Luca, what are we doing today?" He was always in high spirits, and I wondered if he got off torturing people. I worked out all the time. It was the only way to maintain the body my clients expected, and the added benefit was stress relief.

"Work me hard," I told him. "I've had a shit day." I changed into shorts and a cotton tee and met Jack at the weights. Bench-pressing my max for three sets would help right things in my twisted world for the moment.

One-press

Two-press

Three-press …

After three sets, I rose from the bench and bent over to hold my knees. I was pumped to continue once I caught my breath.

"Give me thirty minutes on the elliptical. I want it set to cardio, raise the resistance and the incline." Jack pushed me toward the machines and walked away.

The only machine available sat between a female with a sweet ass, and a fat dude with a visible plumbers crack. I climbed aboard and began. A glance to my left, and I nearly fell off.

"Not so smooth now, are you?" Mim pulled the handles and pressed the pedals like a pro.

What could I say? My swag factor had hit a low. "I'll get it together, don't worry about me."

"I'm hardly worried, Luca."

She remembered my name. That had to be good, right? Not wanting to be outdone. I upped my speed, resistance, and incline to match hers. Game on. "Odd that we would meet here. There have to be hundreds of gyms in the city." I huffed out the words. Cardio wasn't my thing. I did it to gain endurance, but now that I was at the end of my tenure with Concierge Services, I'd be able to cut back.

"It's the best, and I like quality." Her eyes ran the length of my body.

"Like what you see?" I tightened my hands on the grips so every muscle in my arms would bulge with definition.

"I love muscle. It's a damn shame most of yours seems trapped in your head. Inflated ego much?" She stopped her machine and hopped off.

"Hey, you've got me all wrong." I stepped off and followed her closely.

"Prove me wrong, Luca. Buy me a drink. I'll be at the coffee bar in ten minutes." She disappeared into the women's locker room before I could reply.

Shit. I had the time, but what was the point? *The point was, I wanted a distraction from my life, and she was hotter than hell.* I raced to the locker room and showered. I ran in the direction of the coffee bar with my tie in my hand. Nine minutes had passed, and I didn't want to miss the opportunity to get to know the brown-haired girl who had gemstones for eyes.

Dressed in an off-the-shoulder white tunic and black yoga pants —*God, I loved yoga pants*—she sat at the counter and watched me cross the floor toward her. I slid onto the stool beside her.

"What can I get you?" I waved the barista over and waited while Mim decided what she wanted.

"Chai tea with honey, please." She was all sweetness and sun-shine to the tired-looking barista.

She was vinegar and hot sauce to me, but I liked flavor in my life. Mim intrigued me. "Double shot latte, please." I pulled my tie over my head and proceeded to finish dressing.

"That much caffeine will keep you up all night."

"Would seem that I'll need it. I have a project to finish three weeks early." I pulled a napkin from the dispenser and folded it in half.

Her smile didn't reach her eyes, but her lips twisted in a satisfied grin. "That's a shame."

The barista placed our drinks on the counter in front of us.

"Definitely."

"Will that cut into your social life?" She pulled the cup to her mouth and blew on the steaming liquid. I could smell the spice in her tea waft through the air.

"Are you asking out of interest?" *What was her game?* I was so out of the dating scene. I had no idea how women my age behaved.

"Possibly."

"I thought my ego offended you." I wasn't used to people casting me aside and pulling me back. She was playing me well.

"Your ego arouses my curiosity. I'd love to see what holds that up."

'Arouse' was an interesting word to use when talking about my self-esteem. "I'm told it's my incredible traps." I flexed my muscles to make a point.

She tried to suppress her laugh but ended up bursting out loud.

"No wonder you work out. It must take a lot of muscles to hold up your head."

"Now you're just being mean, but I'll forgive you if you have dinner with me." *What the hell was I doing?*

She pulled my folded napkin from under my cup, took a pen from her backpack and wrote her address on it. "I'm free next Thursday. Seven works for me. I like Italian." She checked me out again before she rose from her seat and walked away.

I sat there, dumbfounded. I had a Thursday date with a frustrating woman who apparently liked Italian. That was one area in which I could deliver. A slow smile spread across my face.

The Saturday night crazies were swarming Times Square by the time the cab dropped me off at the hotel. I was never late to an appointment, although I'd come close yesterday when an accident in the subway delayed me by an hour. Today, I'd started out early. I picked up the key to Claire's hotel room with plenty of time to spare.

I'd let myself into the room decorated in various shades of white. The purity of the color contrasted with the darkness of my soul. Life had become blurred. The only difference between a porn star and me was a porn star got paid to get laid on camera. I got paid to satisfy women. I didn't allow cameras. Voyeurism wasn't my thing.

After a glance around the suite, I knew Claire would want to be had on every surface in this room. The bed, the sofa, the tub, and the damn granite counter of the bar. My dick would be on fire before the evening was over.

The windows beckoned with the bright light of Times Square flashing before me. I yanked the curtains closed, shutting out the real world around me while I produced one client's fantasy.

After a call to room service, I set about earning my pay. Claire had specifics she liked ready when she arrived. The tub had to be filled with hot water and bubbles. The champagne chilled in a silver bucket by the bed. I started the bath, lit the candles, and prepared the items she'd had delivered. When I took the lid off the box left behind, I wanted to scream. I hated this stupid fetish of hers. There were cuffs and a flogger, a handful of hundreds, and a brand new package of condoms.

I knew how this would play out. I'd answer the door in my thousand-dollar suit, and she'd pretend she was the escort. She'd show up in a trench coat with little or nothing beneath it. I'd sweet talk her into taking a bath where she would make me watch her masturbate. Priming herself was what she called it, but all it did was make the second orgasm much harder for her to reach. It lengthened the game I wanted to shorten.

I'd pretend to pay her, and she would tie me up and have her way. In any other setting it could be considered rape, but in this setting it was prostitution. I would sell myself once again to reach my goals: success, financial freedom, and respect.

When the knock came, I checked myself in the mirror. I ran my fingers through my hair, giving it what Claire would call a mussed up, sexy look. Making her wait was part of the game, so I straightened my tie and picked lint off my collar until the second knock sounded. It would annoy her to have to wait, but she got off on pent-up frustration. I rubbed the exhaustion from my eyes and prepped for the long night ahead. I tucked my self-loathing away and put on my Ken doll smile. *Showtime.*

I opened the door in a coat and dagger fashion, a sliver at a time. It added to her excitement. "Are you the girl?" I deepened my voice because she loved it. A baritone voice would earn me a sizable tip.

"Yes, I'm what you wanted," her words breathy and soft. So unlike the powerhouse of a woman I knew her to be. She was a CEO at Evictus Financial Group, a large firm specializing in penny stocks. I always gave Claire what she wanted because she had what I needed— money and a foot in the door at her company.

"You are indeed what I ordered." I ran my hand down her cheek.

"Stunning." I pulled her into the room and peeked out the door as if someone could be watching. I had to play my part to perfection.

I'd been screwing my way into the door of Evictus for eighteen months now. A year and a half was a long time to be with the same client. She was one of my first, and we had this date every Saturday night like clockwork. Different hotel. Same situation. I'd pound her flesh so she'd be sore until our next date. She'd pay me and often press a generous tip in my pocket. In turn, I'd pay my rent, buy my groceries, and chip at my student loans. It was a living, but hardly a life.

For a second, I thought of Mim and locked the thought away behind my smile. She wasn't part of this world, and I wouldn't dirty her by thinking about her while I was on the job.

"Don't forget," said Claire. "I get paid up front." Yep, she always did, and she'd turn around later and hand over the cash for a night well spent.

I pulled out the bills I'd put in my wallet. Two circular divots marred the inside pocket. One came from the MBA coin my favorite professor gave me when I was struggling to pass my classes. "Keep your eye on the prize," he told me, and I've kept the talisman in my pocket ever since. The second circle used to contain my Saint Christopher, but now the space was empty. I had taken it out and put it in my drawer. I didn't need a daily reminder of how far I'd fallen.

I fanned the bills in front of her. "This should take care of it." I folded the wad of bills and placed them in her coat pocket. *Let the games begin.* With a firm tug, I pulled the belt of the coat loose and let it fall open. Hmm, black lingerie tonight. She must have had a terrible week. Anxiety slithered up my spine, wrapped around my neck and threatened to choke me. If her mood was dark, she'd want it rough and hard, which meant she'd give my body no mercy.

"What should I call you?"

"Call me Claire." The use of her real name was a surprise. She dropped the coat on the floor and pushed her body against me. For a woman in her forties, she had a rockin' body, but I was pretty sure it was because she devoured lesser men for sport.

"Well, Claire, I've prepared a bath for you. Climb in while I get you a drink." She turned toward the bathroom and walked away, exaggerating the sway of her hips. I knew she'd turn around and expect me to be watching her. I stayed and stared, and she looked over her shoulder and smiled. She was pleased, and that would earn me another bonus.

When I entered the bathroom, she was tucked neck deep in the water with her hair pulled up in a clip. The light of the candles flickered across the bubbles, creating a kaleidoscope of colors.

"Champagne?" I offered her a filled flute.

"No, you drink the bubbly. Tonight, I need something stronger. I'd prefer scotch." Her jade green eyes had turned the color of beached seaweed. Something was up. She was a creature of habit, and this wasn't our usual routine. "Get me a real drink."

What the hell was going on?

If I asked her, the fantasy would be ruined. I couldn't afford for that to happen. I needed tonight's gig for my rent, so I buried my questions and did as I was asked.

When I returned to the bathroom, she had her knees pulled up to her chest and was crying. "Tears?" The scotch sloshed back and forth from my unsteady hand. "What can I do?" I wasn't prepped for this. I was hardwired to avoid emotion since the day I began this job.

"Take off your clothes and get in the bath." Her voice cracked ever so slightly. Whatever was happening, she was clutching the ledge with her fingers, causing the tips to turn white.

Moisture had affected her mascara, making the black gel run into the fine lines on her face. Typically so put together, Claire seemed a bit worn tonight, and that made her look vulnerable and soft—a side I'd never seen from this woman. We didn't share love or affection, but we had a mutual respect for one another.

I wanted to reach out and comfort her, and that scared me. "I don't think so, I hired you." It was important for me to get back on script. "I want you bathed, naked, and in bed in ten minutes." Pivoting on my heels, I exited the bathroom.

Her scream followed me into the bedroom. "Forget the script! I need to be held and comforted. Earn your money, Luca, and get your ass in here."

Rage surged through me. When I sold my body, it came with a bit of my soul attached. I felt thin, stretched out, and so very cold. My teeth ground until my jaw hurt. It was the only way to hold in the anger.

Since the Dom Perignon was mine alone, I pulled it from the bucket and guzzled straight from the bottle. Something told me things were about to change, and I'd need the 12.5% alcohol by volume to survive the night. Hell, I might need Claire's scotch to make it through the next hour.

I walked back into the bathroom, tugging at the tie Claire had given me last month. The Windsor knot of the blue silk tie nearly choked me. Whoever said fake it until you make it must have worked on Wall Street. Every day I showed up to work, I prayed it would be my last, but the reality was, I knew I'd keep doing this until my goals were met.

Claire's eyes dimmed, and I suppressed the panic that inched up my throat to gag me.

"Get in the tub, Luca." She tipped the scotch glass back and emptied the tumbler. "Refill first." The crystal glass screeched as she pushed it across the marble surround of the tub.

This was my life. She called, and I came. She demanded, and I delivered. She paid, and I performed. Rather than pour two fingers of scotch, I poured four to avoid another trip to the decanter. Despite wanting to drown myself in alcohol, I abstained. One of us had to be in control.

I transferred the glass to her hand hand began the slow process of removing my suit. She needed comfort, and I needed money. With sixty thousand dollars remaining on my student loan, I couldn't take my eye off the goal.

I slid into the hot bubbles and situated myself across from her. I left the foil condom wrapper in clear view so there was no doubt where me, naked, and in the bathtub, would lead. She cupped the amber liquid with both hands and watched me over the rim.

Like a cat being stalked by a mouse, my internal protection mechanisms screamed for me to escape and evade, but I planted my ass and held my ground. For enough money, I'd ignore the warnings.

"Do you want to talk?"

My relationship with her was unique. She never shared personal information, which was probably why this arrangement had lasted so long. We weren't friends. Once all the bells and whistles were removed, I was simply a dick for hire, and she was a checkbook and a reference letter. For fourteen hundred dollars a night, I'd suffer through it.

"No." She stretched her foot out and rubbed her toes between my legs.

Habit required I make a sound of satisfaction. "Mmm," came from my mouth without thought or feeling. It was amazing how much a body could do on autopilot.

"Feel good?"

"It always feels good."

Slow, steady breaths helped me get my head in the game. I was like Pavlov's dog. In the zone, I could perform without thinking. When thrown off my game, it took a lot of coaxing. Tonight, I was out of my element.

Below the bubbles, I massaged her foot with one hand and my dick with the other. Once hard, I pulled her body toward me and set her between my thighs.

"What do you want, Claire?" The question was asked out of courtesy. This woman was a whip-wielding rough rider. She was a take-no-prisoners client. I imagined she operated much the same way in the boardroom as she did in the bedroom.

"I want to feel wanted." Her usually demanding voice diminished with each word. "I want to feel valued." Her shoulders rolled forward. "I want you to take charge."

Whoa. "What the hell is going on here? If you want to change the dynamics of our relationship, I need to know the new rules." This dicking around was driving me crazy.

"I was fired today."

Her body shook, and sobs escaped.

"What the hell?"

The air was sucked from my lungs. Although I was head and shoulders above the bubbles, I was drowning under the weight of what her statement meant. All my eggs were in her basket. I'd nourished this relationship, made it a priority because making her happy gave me what I needed. Now, after eighteen months of letting her use me and control me, I was no closer to getting what I wanted. Eighteen damn months of whips and cuffs for nothing. Despair made me go limp. I threw my head back and stared at the ceiling.

"I don't want to talk about it. I want to forget about it."

She turned around and straddled me. She squeezed and pulled at my flesh, but there was no way my flaccid penis would rise to the occasion. My libido had sunk as low as my hope.

After several minutes, she gave up and collapsed back into the water.

Other Books by Kelly Collins

An Aspen Cove Romance Series

One Hundred Reasons

One Hundred Heartbeats

One Hundred Wishes

One Hundred Promises

One Hundred Excuses

One Hundred Christmas Kisses

One Hundred Lifetimes

One Hundred Ways

One Hundred Goodbyes

One Hundred Secrets

One Hundred Regrets

One Hundred Choices

One Hundred Decisions

One Hundred Glances

One Hundred Lessons

One Hundred Mistakes

One Hundred Nights

Cross Creek Novels

Broken Hart

Fearless Hart

Guarded Hart

Reckless Hart

Recipes for Love

A Tablespoon of Temptation

A Pinch of Passion

A Dash of Desire

A Cup of Compassion

A Dollop of Delight

The Second Chance Series

Set Free

Set Aside

Set in Stone

Set Up

Set on You

The Second Chance Series Box Set

Holiday Novels

The Trouble with Tinsel

Wrapped around My Heart

Cole for Christmas

Christmas Inn Love

Mistletoe and Millionaires

Up to Snow Good

Wilde Love Series

Betting On Him

Betting On Her

Betting On Us

A Wilde Love Collection

The Boys of Fury Series

Redeeming Ryker

Saving Silas

Delivering Decker

The Boys of Fury Boxset

A Beloved Duet

Still the One

Always the One

Beloved Duet

Small Town Big Love

What If

Imagine That

No Regrets

Small Town Big Love Boxset

Frazier Falls

Rescue Me

Shelter Me

Defend Me

The Frazier Falls Collection

Stand Alone Billionaire Novels (Steamy)

Dream Maker

Making the Grade Series

The Learning Curve

The Dean's List

Honor Roll

Making the Grade Box Set

A Pure Decadence Series

Yours to Have

Yours to Conquer

Yours to Protect

A Pure Decadence Collection

Get a free book.

Go to www.authorkellycollins.com

About the Author

International bestselling author of more than thirty novels, Kelly Collins writes with the intention of keeping love alive. Always a romantic, she blends real-life events with her vivid imagination to create characters and stories that lovers of contemporary romance, new adult, and romantic suspense will return to again and again.

For More Information
www.authorkellycollins.com
kelly@authorkellycollins.com

Acknowledgments

This book was inspired by an article written in a popular newspaper. When I decided to write the story the following authors gave me the encouragement I needed to write a love story based on a controversial topic.

No book gets written without a village of people. I'd like to give a shout out to my village. Sharon, Anne, Leeann W., Heidi K., Heidi B., LeAnn F., Zam, Melinda, Connie, Margie, Janice, Joyce, Terry, and Cynthia Collins.

Whew! I couldn't have done it without you.